Praise for the novels of
New York Times bestselling author
Heather Graham

"Heather Graham delivers a harrowing journey as she always does: perfectly.... Intelligent, fast-paced and frightening at all times, and the team of characters still keep the reader's attention to the very end."
—*Suspense Magazine* on *The Final Deception*

"Immediately entertaining and engrossing... Graham provides plenty of face time and intimate connection, all lightened with humor, to reassure and satisfy romance readers. Though part of a series, this installment stands well alone." —*Publishers Weekly* on *A Dangerous Game*

"Taut, complex, and leavened with humor, this riveting thriller has...a shade more suspense than romance, [and] it will appeal to fans of both genres."
—*Library Journal* on *A Dangerous Game*

"Intense... A wild, mindboggling thriller from start to finish." —*The Reading Cafe* on *The Forbidden*

"An enthralling read with a totally unexpected twist at the end." —*Fresh Fiction* on *Deadly Touch*

"Graham strikes a fine balance between romantic suspense and a gothic ghost story in her latest Krewe of Hunters tale." —*_____ ____ning*

D0395257

Look for Heather Graham's next novel,
available soon from MIRA.

* * * * *

For additional books by Heather Graham,
visit theoriginalheathergraham.com.

HEATHER GRAHAM

CURSED AT DAWN

mira

mira™

Recycling programs
for this product may
not exist in your area.

ISBN-13: 978-0-7783-3426-2

Cursed at Dawn

For questions and comments about the quality of this book, please contact us at CustomerService@Harlequin.com.

Mira
22 Adelaide St. West, 41st Floor
Toronto, Ontario M5H 4E3, Canada
www.Harlequin.com

Printed in U.S.A.

Dedicated in loving memory to E.D. "Dan" Graham, my amazing father, strong enough to be gentle, wise, and wonderful, and to have given me the best of life's lessons, so many of his words still guiding me today.
Also, to my grandfather, John,
"The Old Scot," and to the Graham clan, Stirling, Scotland.

CAST OF CHARACTERS

The Krewe of Hunters—
a specialized FBI unit that uses its members "unique abilities"
to bring justice to strange or unorthodox cases

Adam Harrison—
philanthropist founder of the Krewe of Hunters

Jackson Crow—
Supervisory Field Agent, Adam's chosen leader for the team

Angela Hawkins Crow—
original Krewe member, exceptional in the field and on research

The Euro Special Assistance Team or "Blackbird"—
a newly formed group created to extend the Krewe's reach into
Europe to assist with crimes abroad

Della Hamilton—
late twenties, five-eight, light brown hair, green eyes,
with the Krewe almost a year

Mason Carter—
six-five, dark hair, blue eyes, FBI for six years, has been
working solo since the death of his partner in the line of duty

Jon Wilhelm—
early fifties, experienced law enforcement
with Norway's National Police Directorate, speaks English
with an American accent because he studied at Yale

Edmund Taylor—
early forties, London's Metropolitan Police Detective
Chief Inspector

Jeanne Lapierre—
fifties, tall and solid, long-time Parisian detective,
excellent at his work

François Bisset—
forty-five, light blue eyes, friendly and professional manner,
their Interpol liaison

Stephan Dante/the King of the Vampires—
organized serial killer, globe-trotting to bring his "kingship"
from country to country, newly escaped from prison

Lachlan Mackenzie—
midthirties, tall, dark hair, blue eyes, Detective Inspector,
Police Scotland, Edinburgh Division

Brianna Adair—
soft blond hair, born in Ireland, technical analyst,
working for Police Scotland, Edinburgh Division

Boyd Breck—
fought alongside William Wallace and later with
Robert the Bruce, died circa 1312

Margaret and Hamish Douglas—
helped feed those "closed" in during the plague of 1645,
died of it themselves

Prologue

Yes, he was bleeding.

No, he didn't care.

He'd replace the blood soon enough. Because for now…

They were rushing to make sure that the bleeding was stopped. He lay with his eyes closed, waiting. The right moment would come. They checked his heart, they monitored his breathing…

The medical profession offered people who were rather pathetic. They took their Hippocratic oath, and then they were bound to save every man. Of course, many of them tended to think that they were gods, that they had the power of life and death. Arrogant gods, but gods could fall. Like Dr. Henson. But all around him, people were rushing to save the life of the prisoner who had been plugged with a shiv in the dining room.

Rather foolish! That prisoner might well get the death penalty from either the federal government or the state of Louisiana, not to mention the other places he faced charges.

But, of course, his intent was to live.

And he had faked the riot in the cafeteria, with a little help from his friends.

He was good at making friends. He was such a nice guy.

"Steady," the nurse said, issuing a sigh of relief. "His blood pressure was so low...but it's climbing. One-ten over seventy. I think we've got the bleeding stopped."

"I guess whoever hates this guy hasn't got the best aim in the world," the doctor said, shrugging. "Well, I guess he'll make trial. Or trials. I understand that the charges against him are massive and that a lot of people want a piece of him. We have provided the whole so they can all have their pieces. Sometimes... Yeah, well, we're here to save lives, right? Even if they don't deserve to be saved. Yep. We save lives. I'm going to get the guards to get back in here—we'll keep him in the infirmary, but I want him cuffed to the bed."

"He may not make it yet, Doctor!" the nurse murmured. "I saw the floor where he was lying when they dug out the pile of prisoners. He's lost so much blood—I hope that the transfusions are enough—"

"I want him cuffed. Hold tight."

It was going just the way that he wanted—the way the axe murderer, Justin Miles, had said that it would. So much for high security! Guards outside? But then he'd been a dying man, and they'd worried so to save his life; it wasn't good for prisoners to die in the penal system!

The doctor went out. And it was a piece of cake.

A stab of the needle into the nurse, who was so shocked she never let out a peep. Then a very brief wait for the doctor. He hid behind the door, seizing the man in a neck lock the minute he walked back in, cutting off his breath…

Cutting off any chance of him screaming.

High security, right. Men running around, armed, all ready to keep prisoners under control!

When the first two guards walked in, they naturally assumed that he was the doctor and then…well, then they were easily dispatched—dead or dying, he wasn't sure. He arranged the room so that the bodies couldn't be found quickly and the stage was set. The nurse was out of the way in the closet. The doctor was on the table in prison garb, ready for a transfusion because of the massive amount of blood found with Dante's fallen body.

Except, of course, there was no chance that any amount of blood would help the man.

With the doctor's wallet, keys and clothing, the rest was easy.

Accused of so many horrendous murders! Expected to receive the death penalty.

And there he was, smiling and waving as he walked out into the sunshine. And freedom.

He could already envision his next…transformation. A beauty, of course, sleeping in eternal peace, immortal in beauty.

He could almost see it.

He could almost *taste* it.

He truly was king.

One

"I still don't see how it was possible," Della said. They had worked so hard, taken such risks, to arrest and incarcerate Stephan Dante, the self-proclaimed "king of the vampires," that it was unimaginable that he had managed to escape while awaiting trial.

They were headed back to the United States, ready to meet with the horrified warden of the jail where Dante had been awaiting trial. They were both exhausted but wired, as they hadn't slept since they'd heard the news that the man was back on.

Just days after they'd finally caught up with one of his protégés—who had shed the concept of competing in the vampire field to become "king of the Rippers"—they had learned that Stephan Dante had somehow managed a miraculous escape. He had killed the doctor who had assumed he was desperately trying to save his life, sent the nurse to intensive care, where she remained, and had killed one guard and seriously wounded another on his way out. He'd walked easily into the sunlight, having taken the doctor's clothing, identification and keys—and therefore, he had simply driven away. The most bizarre thing seemed to be that it was on tape, though Dante had managed—through a tech friend he'd met while incarcerated, Della believed—to create false images of the infirmary while he had carried out his attacks with a scalpel.

They hadn't been "vampire" assaults and kills.

They had just been murders and attacks that had been expedient. He had his way of killing that he considered unique and special. But he was also a cold-blooded killer who would rid himself of anyone who got in his way by any means necessary.

"Dante continues to carry out the impossible." Mason Carter, seated at her side in the FBI's Blackbird plane that was rushing them back to the States, shook his head, staring straight ahead as he spoke. "He manages to befriend every criminal who can do something he wants done or provide something he needs. I've never seen a criminal as capable of accruing funds and forged documents in the way that he has managed." He let out a sigh. "I've been conflicted on the death penalty all my life. You execute the wrong man—or woman—and you can't fix it if you're later proved wrong. You let a man like Dante live and…others have already paid the price."

"He never made it to trial, Mason," Della reminded him. "Mason, this is horrible, but it isn't on us. And we will—"

"Get him again," Mason said.

He was still staring straight ahead. She wasn't worried about Mason as her partner—no inner conflict would interfere with his abilities as an investigator—or as a man to have at her back. He was adept at numerous martial arts, with a knife, and was also a crack shot who could move with incredible dexterity, speed and quiet when necessary. He had blue eyes that could appear as dark as the deep blue sea—or as piercing and cold as shafts of ice. It didn't hurt that he was a dark-haired man who stood at a good six foot five, but as they all knew, a bullet or an explosive could kill, no matter your size or expertise.

He had told her once that a good agent's mind was the greatest weapon they could carry.

She just worried about whatever torture he might be putting himself through. He'd been military before the FBI, been responsible for the apprehension of some of the country's most heinous killers and seen his last partner gunned down before him. He had grown weary of killing and he'd been working solo until he and Della had met on a case in a Louisiana bayou, taking down a serial killer there before becoming the first chosen agents for Blackbird, a unique unit created to help when the very specialized assistance the Krewe of Hunters could give was needed in Europe.

They had worked with local law enforcement from Norway, Scotland, Ireland and France. Their liaison from Interpol, François Bisset, as well as French Detective Jeanne Lapierre, English Detective Inspector Edmund Taylor and Norseman Jon Wilhelm, would be joining them the next day.

Their sixsome had followed Dante, in one way or another, through France, Britain and Norway, then back to the States.

They'd all expected to be here; Adam and Jackson had set up a meeting for the group of them at Quantico, one to debrief and the other for a chance to discuss the future of their new unit—within the Krewe of Hunters.

Della wondered if Jackson and Adam knew things about their team that they didn't know themselves. They had discovered that Edmund, a striking and formidable-looking man in his thirties, could converse with the dead. As always, very few among the spirit world chose to communicate with the living for their own reasons. But she didn't know about Wilhelm, François or Jeanne. Law enforcement might often speak about protocol, especially within different countries, but in meeting people one seldom just asked bluntly if their fellows could see the dead.

They were back in the States. But with Stephan Dante on the loose, they could be heading anywhere in the world in the days to come.

"Mason, we can't second-guess anything," she said quietly. "We take oaths. And you and I both believe in standing up and honoring our oaths. We follow the law," she reminded him.

He smiled and turned to her. "Of course. I just…I just thought that we were done worrying about him. And seriously? It was nice being tourists in London. For what? All of three days."

She grinned back at him. "They were good days, though, right? They had to end because we were due back here anyway. And I talked to Jackson earlier. When we get Dante locked up again, we get a month, he promised."

"Right. Unless something else happens," Mason said.

She shook her head. "I know Jackson and Adam.

They're busy building up Blackbird and in time, we won't be the only American representatives."

He nodded, pulling up his tablet. "Not sure if all this is the order in which it occurred, but this is still just... I don't see how... All right, according to the reports, Dante was bleeding out so badly that it was assumed he wouldn't make it. He wasn't shackled to the bed because everyone thought he was all but dead. He caught hold of the scalpel when the doctor and the nurse were urging quick care, ordering blood for transfusions. People ran out of the infirmary, he downed the nurse and then the doctor and stole the doctor's clothing, wallet and keys. Two guards walked in and he took care of them. He had apparently already gotten someone to somehow get him a fake MD's identification and all the right certifications to slip into the doctor's wallet. How the hell did he go from bleeding to death to slashing others and escaping in the blink of an eye?"

"Well, he isn't a vampire," Della said flatly. "The problem with Dante is that he doesn't use force as much as he uses charm and wiles. He is extremely clever, an intelligent man. I believe that he's one of those people who constantly studies online. And, of course, as we've known, he's great at making friends among the killer elite."

"Killers, forgers, bank robbers... I doubt if he bothers to befriend those who can't do anything for him, but to others... I don't understand. Then again, I still don't understand how Jim Jones got nearly a thousand people to drink poisoned Kool-Aid. The power of the mind is incredible."

"Beyond a doubt. We've said it before—people believe because they want to believe. They grasp on to concepts and ideas that work for them because they're down and out, because they're bitter or because they're in pain. Some are too smart to be swayed, but I believe that our Mr. Dante recognizes those he can control and those he can't—and he wastes no time on those who aren't going to fulfill any of his needs.

"The power of the mind!" Della murmured, continuing. "I spoke with our friend and colleague Special Agent—Dr.—Patrick Law. He warned everyone that Dante might well pull something. They believed that they had him in control, that they had so much security that he couldn't possibly escape."

"They tried to save his life," Mason murmured.

"They're bound by their oaths, too, Mason. For those in law enforcement, oaths similar to those we took. And for a doctor…"

"I know. I know. The Hippocratic oath," Mason said.

"No choice," she reminded him.

"So, of course, we know that he's out. We will learn more on the particulars of how he did it. But he *is* out—so his escape isn't the question."

Della nodded and looked out the window. They would be landing soon. She rested her head back against the comfort of her chair, wishing they'd managed to sleep.

Smiling grimly, she turned to Mason.

"He has escaped. He escaped in Louisiana and we know that he does love the bayou country, and who doesn't love New Orleans? So he escaped here, but the main question remains," she said quietly. "Just where will he strike next?"

* * *

When a man managed to escape when he was known as high risk, he had to have had help, Mason believed.

While Della headed to the intensive care unit at the hospital to interview the nurse who had a slim chance of surviving the assault, he worked with the warden, a man named Roger Sewell, still in disbelief that such a thing could have happened.

"I'm sure you have already heard the particulars, but I'll go over them again," Sewell told him as they walked along the aisle where prisoners spent short incarcerations or awaited trial.

"It started in the cafeteria with the riot. Ridiculous thing, of course. No matter how hard anyone tries, there's always a pecking order in a facility like this—you wind up with rival gangs within the walls themselves. Someone hit someone else in the face with a spoonful of grits. Then all hell broke out with food flying back and forth, crowd insanity followed, several guards were injured and Stephan Dante was found on the bottom of a pile of men with a blood pool the size of Texas under him. Naturally, we rushed him straight to the infirmary, calling the doctor, warning that the prisoner might exsanguinate within minutes."

"You found him in a pool of blood," Mason said. He imagined the scene—and why guards and a smart man might be fooled.

"With a toothbrush shank still in him."

Warden Sewell was a serious man, known for having handled the facility in his charge with diligence, running a tight ship while recognizing human rights as known in the country and the state. His guards respected him; there had never been such a serious incident before during his tenure. He continued disgustedly with, "Food fights happen. Gang members gang up on a target and break his nose. But this food fight...ridiculous food fight...escalated into disaster."

"It wasn't a ridiculous food fight," Mason told him, pausing along with the warden at the cell where Dante had so recently resided. "It was planned. And that pool of blood didn't belong to Dante—some of the blood, sure. But you're going to find that you have one or more other inmates who lost *pools* of blood in that fight."

"Wait, you're trying to tell me that Dante planned a food fight to escape? But he didn't attack any of the guards, he didn't—"

"He planned to get to the infirmary," Mason told him. "Just as he found someone—someone here on a more minor charge—to rig it so that Dante's assaults on the staff weren't seen on the cameras. One of your prisoners is a damned good tech guy who breached the system."

"No. That's not possible—"

"Warden, I'm not throwing any stones here, trust me. This man has taken all of us in one way or another. But I doubt your guards were all asleep at the wheel. And when the police ran the security tapes, they saw nothing but a nurse moving back and forth across the infirmary. We know that Dante assaulted his caretakers. And the guards who then tried to stop him. And then—caught on camera—he used the dead doctor's identity and clothing to escape. Oh, yes, Dante was shanked. But he's a man who made sure that he drew blood without hitting any vital organs—"

"You think that he shanked himself?"

"I do. Or he had a friend hit him in just the right place in just the right way."

"But the blood—"

"The 'pool the size of Texas' belonged to one or more other men. And a forensic crew would find DNA so mixed that it would be worthless. But, trust me, the entire escape was planned from the time the first spoonful of grits went flying," Mason told him grimly.

"What do you need from me now?" Sewell asked him. "What the hell can I do now to help?"

"Interviews. I need to speak with anyone who was close to or friendly with Dante in any way."

Sewell suggested, "Start with his cellmate?"

Mason nodded. "Have him brought to an interview room. I'll observe him a few minutes before going in. What's the man's name and what is he in for?"

"Terry Donavan. His third DUI in a month involved a vehicular manslaughter charge."

"Sounds like an alcoholic and not a cold-blooded killer. Interesting that he was in with Dante."

"Overcrowding in the system, I'm afraid. Special Agent Patrick Law had suggested that we keep Dante in solitary and we were planning on moving Dante to follow the suggestion." Sewell paused, wincing and shaking his head. "We were planning to do the right thing—just waiting on the move. We have some hardened folks here, awaiting their days in court. One man is accused of killing his entire family—for the life insurance payouts. Another in here is presumed guilty of five robbery/invasion homicides. Sometimes it's hard as hell to see the forest for the trees."

"Gotcha," Mason assured him.

"Observation here," Sewell said, stopping by a door. "Entry to the interrogation room just down a few steps."

"All right. Tell the guards not to shackle the man. I'm going to have to build up some trust—get past whatever blind faith he might have in believing whatever lies Dante might have told him."

"You think Terry Donavan might be involved? He's… In my mind, the man is a pathetic waste of what he might have been. In here, he's polite, agreeable and, so it appears, truly remorseful for what happened. Went through hell when he first came in—in fact, the doctor Dante killed helped get Terry through the worst of withdrawal when he came in here. If the kid—"

"Kid?"

"Sorry. He's just twenty-three," Sewell said.

"Right. If he'd had help and embraced it, he wouldn't be where he is," Mason said.

Sewell nodded. "Step on in. I'll get Terry in there," he said, pointing to the stark interrogation room.

"Would you mind seeing if you can arrange coffee and water for us both? Sounds like he's the type who just might help if I can reach him."

Sewell nodded. Mason stepped into the observation room and looked through the glass at the room with its simple table—equipped with attachments for shackles when necessary—and gray walls and flooring. That was it. The table, the walls, the floor. Planned for focus.

A minute later, he saw a guard bringing Terry Donavan in to sit. The man sat. But he wasn't shackled and after he'd been left a few minutes, he began to pace the floor.

He did look like a kid. Short hair still showing something of a rakish and shaggy appearance, movements nervous, eyes caught in a concerned face as he walked the few feet within the room.

The guard returned with two cups of water and two cups of coffee. That seemed to perplex the young man even further.

Mason waited another few minutes. Then Terry Donavan sat again, looking suspiciously at his cup of coffee before sipping at it, then letting out a sigh as he apparently decided that it hadn't been laced with any kind of poison.

Mason stepped out of the observation room, nodded to the guard and thanked him, and headed on in, taking the seat across from Terry Donavan.

Donavan looked at him nervously.

"Who are you? Why are you here?"

"My name is Mason Carter," Mason told him. "Special Agent Mason Carter. And I need your help."

"You need help—from me?" Donavan asked nervously. He looked around the room as if afraid that someone might be watching him, might see him.

Guards were watching. But Donavan wasn't afraid of the guards. He was afraid of the possibility that another prisoner might hear him.

Or maybe even Stephan Dante himself.

Mason nodded, leaning toward him, deciding to first use what he knew. "You know that your doctor is dead, right?" he asked quietly.

He saw the young man look down quickly and wince. The doctor had meant something to him. He had helped him.

"That had to be…an accident. I mean—"

"Terry, I know that you were in a cell with Stephan

Dante. I know how mesmerizing and hypnotic the man is capable of being."

"He never hypnotized me!" Donavan protested.

"Dante doesn't sit you down in a chair and tell you to count backward while concentrating on a point," Mason told him. "He charms you—the same way a dad might charm his child while telling a bedtime story. He talks and creates a new world. And it's all right—trust me. Plenty of men and women have fallen for his stories, so well told. And you fell for him, too. If you help me, I can talk to the district attorney. It will help."

"I never meant to hurt anyone—"

"I believe you. Addiction is a terrible disease. And the doctor who has now given up his life is the man who helped you through the agony and suffering of withdrawal."

Terry looked down again, not wanting to face him.

"Why?" Mason asked very softly. "Did Dante promise that no one was going to be killed as he planned his escape?"

"If someone died, it was an accident—"

"It's not an *if.* People died. And it wasn't by accident, Terry. Stephan Dante killed the doctor and took his clothing and his wallet and his car to escape. Hard to do that if—"

"He was just going to knock him out. You know. Drugs. It's an infirmary. They sedate people all the time—I mean, seriously, our infirmary is like a hospital setting!"

"You don't sedate a man with a scalpel," Mason said quietly.

Donavan looked down for a long moment, his thumbs

moving nervously as his hands lay on the table. He shook his head.

"Terry!" Mason said. "Hey, I can tell. You are not a bad guy. You didn't want to hurt anyone. Alcoholism is a disease, and it can take a hell of a lot to cure it. The doctor who finally led you on a path to relief—"

"Hey, I'm locked up awaiting trial where they'll want to put me away forever," Donavan said bleakly. "Had to get cured in here."

"But it could have been a cruel cure. In fact, if withdrawal isn't handled correctly at the level you were drinking, you could have been left to rot and die. But they did things here by the law—even using compassion where it fit. Dante killed the man who offered you every kindness and every ounce of compassion. How the hell can you still stand up for him?"

"I—I—I never thought the doctor would die! The doctor or anyone else. And you don't understand," Donavan told Mason, shaking his head. "And you must be blind. Don't you see it? Stephan Dante tells the truth. He said that he'd be out. He said that it was easy to play the authorities when we all played together. He did it. And he's coming back for me."

"He's coming back for you?" Mason asked.

"Yes! He will regain his power, all that was taken from him, and when he does have his power again, he'll come back. And he'll find us, wherever we are. He'll come in glory and he'll sweep us away to his place where his believers become immortal—"

"Oh, good God, Terry! You've had trouble, yes, but you don't seem to be a stupid man. Seriously, you believe that?"

"He has already done what he said that he'd do!" Donavan reminded Mason.

Mason shook his head. "I just don't understand you falling for a ridiculous theory. Do you believe that the Heaven's Gate suicides jumped on spaceships to travel to a heavenly astral plane? You do believe that the earth is round, right?"

"Of course!"

"Terry, do you want to believe in something solid and real? I'm solid and real and right here and the FBI does have sway with the Justice Department. Let me show you something else that's real." He pulled out his phone and flipped to pictures of Dante's victims. "They look beautiful, right? But I don't believe that you meant to hurt anyone. And when Dante steals all their blood, Terry, they die. They are the beautiful dead who—as all living creatures—will now rot and decay. They are not buying anyone a ticket to vampire immortality. I can help you, Terry. Trust me. Stephan Dante has gotten what he wants from you. Oh, well, first he's not going to turn into an immortal and he knows it. By the way, he trained Jesse Miller, who is no longer with us—having been tutored by Dante, but deciding the heck with vampires, he'd just become Jack the Ripper. An honest thing at least—he just liked the power of stealing life from others. That's not you, Terry. Accept this—Dante is not coming back for you. He not only can't help you, but if he could, he wouldn't. You don't offer him anything more than he needs. I know that you're not a cold-blooded killer. So does he. You've no history of forging, and to the best of my knowledge,

you're not sitting on a multimillion-dollar haul anywhere. Help me—and I will help you."

Terry stared at him a long time and then hung his
head. "I… He didn't say that I had to kill anyone. He
said that my work here would be enough for me to gain
my place with him."

"He lied. He gave you a bold, all-out lie, Terry. And
somewhere inside you, you know it. You wanted to believe in him. You wanted it so badly because it was better than the prospect of twenty years to life behind bars.
Anything was better than that. You know, sometimes
it starts with someone promising all good things. A
truly equal society. That's pretty much what Jim Jones
promised his followers. Social justice. But what turned
him on, what kept him moving forward at all times,
was a desire for power. Dante doesn't believe in the
least that he's going to be immortal. What he loves,
what he craves, is power. He also loves the act of playing God—he loves killing. Terry, this is your chance
to help me out."

"Yes!" Donavan said, suddenly looking up at him.
The man had tears in his eyes. "Yes, I will help you.
I am so sorry. I—I was a wretched alcoholic. I didn't
want to kill anyone, but when I didn't drink the shaking and the headaches got so bad, all until I was in
here…all until the doctor… I…" He stopped speaking
and looked Mason in the eye. "I will help you. I don't
know everything, but I will help you."

"Libby Larson has two small children," Alexandra—
Alex—Beaufort told Della. "Her poor husband—he's
beside himself. I don't think that Libby will be returning

to work with prisoners, not after this! In this crazy day and age, the woman has a beautiful home life, people who truly love her, and now this…"

"She's still touch and go?" Della asked.

"The doctors believe that she will make it. We were just fighting different situations. He hit her with a needle filled with sedation, stabbed her in the side— luckily missing major organs—and knocked her on the head with something…no one was even sure what he grabbed. But we've been giving her constant transfusions and, of course, done everything possible to clean out her system from the overdose of morphine. Such a good person!"

Della smiled and nodded at the young nurse speaking with her. "Did you know her before she came in after the attack?"

"I did. We went to nursing school together. She believed that everyone deserved a second chance. That human beings were basically good, and that…"

Her words trailed.

"I still believe, just like Libby, that most people are good," Della told her ruefully. "It's like anything—we hear the most about the bad. And sometimes we're unfortunate enough to see it. But I've been at this awhile and I can tell you that most people are good and want to help when help is needed. We know about the bad— which I believe is the fringe—because the bad is always loud and makes us question all else. Anyway, sorry, I understand her—and understand if she doesn't go back to work at the facility. I didn't come to cause further problems—I don't want to upset her any more but if possible, I would like to talk to her."

"She wants to see you," Alex said. "She heard the FBI had brought him in and she wants to help catch him again. Still…for her safety and well-being, five minutes?" Alex asked.

"Five minutes," Della promised.

Libby Larson was in a private room. An IV ran fluids into her arm, while a tube in her nostrils provided oxygen.

Even in a hospital bed with tubes and wires all around her, Libby was a beautiful young woman. Her eyes were closed when Della entered the room, and she couldn't help but wonder if Dante had been furious that he couldn't tend to her as he did his victims—dressing her up to lie in "sleep" like a fairy-tale princess just waiting for true love's kiss.

Her hair was dark black and swept across the whiteness of the hospital sheets. When she opened her eyes, they were an incredible deep brown.

"FBI?" she whispered.

Della nodded, smiling, drawing up a chair. "And so grateful to see you alive and on your way to recovery."

"I knew who he was. And still…we thought he was going to die. The doctor… Oh, God, we were even discussing the fact that we were compelled to do everything we could to save life. He should have been dead! I was one of the medical personnel who rushed into the cafeteria when the guards had it under control and I saw the blood… He shouldn't be alive! But he is, and Dr. Henson is dead and others and… I'm so sorry!"

"What happened?" Della asked. "Do you remember anything at all?"

"Yes. When Dante came in, naturally he wasn't

cuffed. I don't remember exactly, but one of us figured he needed to be cuffed and the doctor went out to see the guards. Then I felt a stab, a little prick, and I was bleeding and then I think something hit me on the head but I barely even felt it…he was so fast. I—I don't remember more!"

"Did he say anything at all?" Della asked. "We're trying to ascertain where he might be heading."

"No. Not a word. But…"

"But?"

"I'd seen him before," she said softly. "Prisoners get vaccines, checkups. He was always so polite, friendly to those around him. And prisoners…talk. When they don't think that others can hear them. He made friends with everyone in here—the worst of the worst." She paused, wincing. "The only hard-core people he seemed to ignore were pedophiles—he had no interest in them."

"To the best of my knowledge, he doesn't kill children," Della said.

"How can a man appear to be so decent, polite, even charming and be such a monster? And I can't help but feel that it's partially my fault—"

"Never think that. Never. Saving lives is a beautiful thing. Trust me. Stephan Dante has fooled just about everyone he's ever met. Don't let him succeed. Don't let him change you," Della said softly.

"He whistled sometimes."

"What did he whistle?"

"I can't quite put my finger on the tune, but…"

"Yes?"

"It seemed as if he was taunting people with it. A lot of what I'm saying is hearsay. I only saw him a few times while he was incarcerated. I just…" Tears stung her eyes. "The doctor is dead. A guard… That man is a monster!"

"Thank you," Della told her. "Thank you. And get better! Rest, get better."

"I will. I have children and the dearest husband in the world. Do you have children?"

"No, I don't. But I've heard yours are wonderful."

"Little boy, little girl. And my husband! Are you married?"

"No."

"I'm sorry. That was rude—"

"No, it's okay. There are people in my life who make it very precious, too."

"Hold them close. Because we never know. We just never know." She smiled weakly. "Ah, no children, but there is someone you love. I mean, besides your family!"

"Yes," Della said, smiling in return. "There is someone very important in my life."

"Make sure he knows! There were moments when I was semiconscious when I thought I might die, and I wondered what the last words were that I had said to my husband. And I was so glad… We'd been on the phone. He'd told me he could pick up the kids and I thanked him and I told him that I loved him. I was so glad to realize that! Well, happier that they think I'm going to be okay, but…tell people that you love them. Because none of us knows what our last words to anyone will be!"

"I will. I will remember your words. And thank you. Thank you again. I'm going to leave my card on your bedside table. If you think of anything else that might be helpful, will you have someone call me for you?"

"Of course, yes. And I'm going to work on my memory—and my whistle."

As Della rose to leave, Libby Larson indeed began trying to whistle. Trying to replicate what she had heard.

Despite her condition, she found a tune.

And as she walked out, Della went still. At first, the whisper of a whistle just teased at her memory as well.

Then she thought that she recognized the tune—and that yes, it had been meant to tease and taunt.

And knowing Dante, she thought bitterly, it was almost an invitation. He wanted them to run around trying to follow him.

He didn't want them missing any of his handiwork.

Two

Terry Donavan had spoken and then gone silent, his head low.

Mason didn't push him. He waited. And when he spoke again, he spoke in a mumble that Mason couldn't understand. But then he looked up and said, "It was me."

"What was you?" Mason asked. "Did you toss that first spoonful of grits?"

Donavan shook his head. "No...not sure who he got to do that. Was the riot planned? Yes, but you knew that without me agreeing. I... Well, it was a shame that genetics and my own lack of willpower threw me here, where I am today. I could have been a computer genius. I'm the one who fixed the cameras. I didn't know I'd be trying to conceal assault and murder, I swear it. He was going to sedate the medical personnel working on him and slide out disguised as the doctor. You may not believe me, but...I wouldn't have done it if I'd known he was going to kill someone."

He frowned and new tears stung his eyes. "Now...

Oh, God. Now they're also going to charge me with conspiracy to commit murder."

Mason shook his head. "No. I believe that you didn't know that he was going to kill at the infirmary. And you are cooperating. You will do time—you understand that you killed someone, though you didn't intend to."

He lowered his head, sobbing.

And Mason believed that his tears were real. This man just wasn't a killer.

"She was… She died on impact. She was a grandma with six grandchildren. I know that much. And I understand that her family must hate me and… I am so sorry."

"And there is a lot to be said for that. How did you hack the system?"

"Library time."

"And no one caught on?"

"You'd be amazed by what good hacking can do."

"Probably. That was your contribution to the escape?"

Donavan nodded. "That was it. And…"

"And?"

"May I stand?"

"Yes."

He stood and lifted his prison shirt. There was a long gash along his stomach.

"I…supplied some of the blood at the riot."

"And I assume others did as well."

Donavan nodded. "I don't know who all was involved in that. Blood promise. I think…"

"Yes?" Mason prodded the man gently. Donavan was telling him what he knew. He would have Patrick Law interview the young man, too, but he'd stick to his own promises—Adam Harrison had great sway when it came to cops, other agents, DAs and judges. He didn't intend for Donavan to get off for manslaughter, but he'd do his best to see that he received fair treatment.

But the man suddenly looked as if he might hyperventilate.

"What is it?" Mason asked.

Donavan shook his head. "If he ever knew... If Dante ever knew...and..."

Mason willed himself to patience. "Please," he said quietly. Leaning forward, he added, "I can have you in protective custody if you feel it's necessary."

Donavan's shaking slowly subsided. "Lawrence. Charles Lawrence. He...well, he—he killed at least seven people in banks. Didn't blink an eye. They didn't listen or they were in his way. He was the one who came close to Dante, and while Dante was in with me, he knew...he knew never to touch me. But if he ever finds out—"

"Curious. Did he provide a lot of blood for the 'pool'?"

Donavan nodded and said flatly, "He'll kill me."

"No, he won't. You're going to be moved," Mason assured him. "I just need one more thing from you. I need to know where Dante was going."

"That is something that I don't know. He told me that the world was his oyster."

Great, Mason thought. And yet it wasn't a surprise.

"Think, please. Did he say anything at all about an intended destination?"

Donavan frowned, thinking. "Oh. I think he intended to head back to Europe. He wanted to go to a country with no death penalty. A 'life' sentence didn't matter.

A man could always escape. I guess he proved that to be true."

And so he had.

"Did he give you any indication at all about a country?"

Again, Donavan sat frowning, thoughtful. "He tended to be supremely confident. But…there were times, just a few, in the planning of his escape, when it felt he was warning me not to mess up. He said the exact same thing many times, but… Well, it wasn't a place or anything like that."

"What was it that he said?" Mason asked.

"I think…no, I know. He said it often enough. I knew it was a warning for me, but I knew that I was okay, I'd…oh, God, well, I'd played with the system a few times before."

"Donavan, for the love of God, what did he say?"

"'Better to keep the devil at the door than to have to turn him out of the house.' He was the devil, of course. And by carrying through with my part, I was keeping the powerful god within him on my side—because, of course, we all know that Lucifer was an angel first," Donavan said.

"Thank you. I'll see that you are kept in safety, transferred—and not charged for conspiracy to commit murder," Mason said.

Rising, he saw that Donavan still looked like a deer caught in the headlights. He looked at Mason. "I believed him," he whispered.

"That's his talent," Mason said.

"I will be afraid the rest of my life."

"No, you won't. Because we will get him again.

You'll still have to go to trial for tampering with the cameras, but my boss will write a letter to the DA and my superiors will verify that you helped us. You will be kept in protective custody, no matter what or where your sentence is."

"Thank you!" Donavan whispered.

Mason left the room, thanking the guard again. He found the warden in the observation room, shaking his head.

"Our cameras were breached that easily," he murmured.

"Pity. He may be a computer genius," Mason said. "Warden, I need to keep my word with him. That's the only way we get help when we need it."

"I'll see to it," the warden promised.

"And I'll speak with my superiors so they can work on the legal side to get him a transfer in case a few of Dante's more cold-blooded friends here decide Donavan should be taken out."

"I don't think that will happen," the warden said.

"Oh?"

"Another inmate just died. Apparently, he was the one to provide most of the materials for the 'pool' of blood beneath Dante. Most of his brainwashed flock will see the world in a new way."

"Still, I think Donavan needs out of here."

"That will be fine."

Mason left the facility and put a call through to Angela at headquarters.

"'Better to keep the devil at the door than to have to turn him out of the house,'" he quoted.

"I know that saying without looking it up," Angela said.

"Okay?" he pressed slowly.

"He's heading to Scotland," she said flatly.

"All right then, I'll get Della and…"

"Are you two all right to head back so quickly?"

He laughed. "This time, I think we will sleep on the plane. But then again, thanks to Adam, it's a darned comfortable plane on which to sleep."

They might have just arrived in the States, but they'd be leaving immediately.

He had barely ended his call with Angela when he saw that his phone was ringing again. Della was calling from the hospital where the nurse assaulted by Dante had been taken.

"Mason, I know where he's going," she said quickly. "The nurse heard Dante whistling somewhere along the line and I know the tune. I believe that he's going to—"

"Scotland," Mason said.

"What? You know?"

"'Better keep the devil at the door than to have to turn him out of the house.'"

"And he was heard whistling 'Scotland the Brave,'" Della said.

"He wants us to follow him. He managed an impossible escape. His confidence is soaring and he really wants to rub our noses in his genius. We can only hope it will be his undoing. We're going to have to oblige him. Meet me back at the airport."

"Headed there now. I'll let the others know—"

"I've spoken with Angela. She's already on it and warning authorities in Great Britain again. It's rather a good thing that the others hadn't headed to the States yet."

"Hey, we are lucky. We have an amazing plane at our disposal."

"Yes, we do. And nice, since…"

"We are headed right back. See? It was important that we split up—we were able to interview two people quickly and—"

"You shouldn't be on this case."

"Don't start."

"Okay, okay. See you at the airport."

They ended the call as Mason reached his car.

Stephan Dante was going to Scotland.

And so was Blackbird.

"We really do need to sleep," Della told Mason, taking his hand and smiling.

He was frowning, staring at messages on his tablet. She had practically spoken into his ear; he didn't appear to have heard her at all.

"Mason?"

He glanced at her at last.

"We've just gotten a message from Edmund. I take it you're not online."

"No, I was thinking that—for real—we're eventually going to suffer some jet leg and we really need to be at our best—"

"Yes, we do. We've been reading his clues—or his invitations—correctly. Stephan Dante is back in Britain. This time, a paper in Edinburgh received a note—standard print. It first congratulated them on being the chosen speaker for the king of the vampires, and then assured them that the king lived and he'd be active again. They should watch for beauty."

"No prints, no—"

"Somehow, it was hand delivered and yet wound up in a pile of other mail on the editor's desk. He called the police—the police grilled his people. Edmund got there and talked to the staff, too. He doesn't believe that any of them are involved, which again, creates a mystery regarding the chameleon-like abilities of our vampire king."

"He's almost ethereal, if not a vampire, that's for sure," Della said dryly.

"He's not a vampire," Mason said flatly.

"No, he's the worst kind of killer—intelligent and charming, a man who has cultivated friends among the criminals who can aid and abet him in all that he needs—forgery, finances, information, tech support and more," Della said. "But, Mason, we knew that he was out, and it's good that we realized he was in Scotland. Edmund, François and Jeanne are already there, waiting for us, and Jon Wilhelm is on his way—we'll be our formidable team of six again with whatever other law enforcement is on this, and…we got him once, Mason. We'll get him again."

"His note went on," Mason said dully, leaning back and closing his eyes.

"And?" Della pressed.

"'The king will seek the company of many while he awaits the arrival of his true bride.'"

"Right. He just likes to kill," Della said.

Mason shook his head and turned to look at her. "Della, he means you."

"If he does, all the more reason I should be investigating every second of the day, Mason. You know that."

She paused. Krewe members tended to be drawn together as couples when they worked together; sharing their ability to speak with the dead along with a passion for law enforcement wasn't something that always worked with outside relationships. Adam Harrison and Jackson Crow had a unique ability to observe agents in the field—and out—and determine who just might be right for the Krewe. They also had an uncanny ability to put people together who seemed to have a natural chemistry. Of course, when they had first started together, she reminded herself, she'd felt an edge knowing that his last partner had been killed in the line of duty and he had been working solo for many months and had a great deal that he kept to himself.

He'd also been brand-new to the Krewe of Hunters. She, at least, had been there just under a year and been lucky to get to know many of the players at their headquarters.

And when Jackson had first approached her about the new Euro division, she'd been surprised. He had many seasoned agents. But she hadn't been opposed to the concept. She'd always loved traveling, loved the world. She would be in on something brand-new.

And so would Mason Carter. The man who had been something of an enigma but was now far more than her partner. They shared more than their abilities with the dead, and far more than simple chemistry. There was a strange blending of their minds and souls, she thought.

Blackbird had "taken flight" with barely conceivable speed. None of which had changed her mind on travel. The world was incredible; places, peoples and cultures were wonderful and fascinating and she had felt herself lucky. As a child her parents had traveled so frequently, her mom an artist and her father an extraordinary marketer and salesman. It made fitting into the concept of Blackbird a smooth transition for her. She loved all of it.

Maybe hopping across "the pond" twice in as many days wasn't easy, but she could still look back and value—as she did now—the wonder of the world.

Including Norway, where their Blackbird division had begun their first case, and now Scotland, where her mother had loved to draw and paint.

And yet again, they were looking for Stephan Dante. They'd gotten him. And now they had to get him again.

She knew why Mason was so grim. He worried about her. It was natural for a partner to worry. But they were more than partners. Mason was an open individual; he respected everyone and cared for any victim, no matter their ethnicity or anything else about them.

He worked well with women. If he felt any superiority as a male, he didn't let it show. They were naturally concerned for one another, something that kept other couples from working together in many veins of law enforcement. But when you had to discuss the fact that you were getting information from the dead, it was good to be on the same page.

Mason respected her and her abilities.

But somewhere in him there was a little core of instinctive masculinity—maybe something biological, maybe something that had been cultural for so long it was hard to break. He was protective of her, but under most circumstances, he trusted in her abilities as much as he would a man's.

She knew that it bothered him that Dante knew her,

and besides his desire to kill women by draining them of blood, he had a special determination to see her at his mercy—she had been so instrumental in his capture. He relished throwing out taunts. It had already become a game or challenge, it seemed, between him and his followers, since one of those followers—determined to be the Ripper king—had wanted to make her his crowning achievement, his Mary Kelly.

"The best defense is a good offense," she said, staring straight ahead. "Mason—"

"I know. And I hope I act accordingly. I can't help how I feel."

"And you know that I can't help but worry about you equally," she said softly.

"Right. Got that. But Stephan Dante creates his tableaux by killing women, not men. Yes, I know. A doctor is dead and a guard is dead. But they were in his way."

She arched a brow to him. "You don't think that he finds you to be an enormous annoyance in his way?"

"If he needed to, he'd kill me. But he's longing to kill you."

"I understand that. And I don't intend to be anywhere alone, Mason. But I can't sit back under some kind of protection and wait for him to find me. He was watched—they knew he was dangerous. He got out. We have to be proactive. All of us."

He nodded, slipped his arm around her and pulled her close. "I know. I will be the perfect platonic partner, I promise."

She smiled. "Um, not that perfect, okay?"

"Are you suggesting something? Here, on the plane?"

She laughed. "The only thing I'm suggesting on the plane is sleep!"

"Darn!"

Grinning, she used his shoulders to rise and walked back to one of the comfortable cots in the back, lying down.

"Hey!" she yelled. "Sleep!"

"Yeah, yeah."

He rose, taking the cot across from hers.

"We are so lucky with this plane!" she said.

"Luckier if the cots were a king bed and we were behind a door that closed."

"Behave!" she laughed. "Remember, you need sleep for all kinds of energy."

"Amazing how you can find certain forms of energy when other forms elude you!" he teased. But then he rolled on his side and said, "Seriously. I will go to sleep. And so will you. We'll land soon enough."

Della nodded and closed her eyes. And while her mind raced at first—as she knew his did—exhaustion and comfort won out.

She didn't wake until the pilot's voice came over the intercom, warning them that they were about to land in Edinburgh.

Rising, Mason helped her up so that they could both buckle back into their seats.

Edmund was going to meet them at the airport. It was still dark, but the sun was about to rise, Della thought, though she'd lost all track of time, flying back and forth. The sun was just beginning to hint at its arrival in the sky.

But she knew that something was wrong when they deplaned and she saw Edmund's face.

"He's struck already. *Already?*" Della asked.

"He's on a real mission," Edmund said.

"What's happened?" Mason asked him. "Dante is here and he's struck again. But where? When?"

"The crime scene hasn't been touched. Local police and the ME knew you'd be here—you were on the way—and thought you should see just what was done. He's brought his displays to a new form of horrendous showmanship. François Bisset and Jeanne Lapierre are setting up a headquarters for us—Jon Wilhelm will be arriving shortly. We're heading to the crime scene."

"*Where* did he strike?" Mason asked, glancing at Della as he repeated his question. Edmund was distracted, deep in thought.

"Sorry," Edmund murmured. "A secondary school—what you would call a high school."

"A school?" Della said with horror.

"A play," Edmund told them. "During a theatrical production they were putting on. Oh, it's theater, all right. Come on. Let's get to the car and then—then you can see for yourselves."

Edinburgh was one of the most historic and beautiful cities Mason had seen. He had loved seeing the grandeur of Edinburgh Castle as he'd walked up the hill when staying in the area—the beauty and the strength. The Royal Mile offered everything from history to trendy restaurants and more. At one end, the castle. At the other end, Holyrood Palace. There was Old Town, with the oldest parts of the castle and St. Margaret's Chapel, which dated back to the twelfth century. In the years since, building had continued until it was both residence and fortification, the massive stone structure on its high volcanic rock truly a landmark that might be recognized around the world.

"Bobby," Della murmured.

"What?" Edmund asked. He'd been quiet most of the drive, explaining that Dante had outdone himself, but that they needed to see the crime scene themselves, with fresh eyes, lest he say something—though he wasn't sure what he could say—that might color their opinions.

Della, Mason thought, was determined to break through, to make their English counterpart realize that they were gathered again.

That whatever horror they faced, they would do it as a team. And get through it.

"I always loved the story about Greyfriars Bobby," Della said. She was seated next to Edmund in the front and twisted to look back at Mason. "When I first came as a child, I begged my parents to get me a dog just like him. The little guy sat at his owner's grave every day for fourteen years, or so they say. He had belonged to a fellow named John Gray—no relation to the church or kirk—who was a night watchman with the Edinburgh police. The story goes—"

"Actually, there are many stories," Edmund said. "But the standard is the best."

"The story goes," Della said firmly, "that neighboring families and businesses looked after him, fed him scraps and all, as he stood guard all those years. He lived to be about sixteen, from 1855 to 1872, and was buried just outside Greyfriars Kirkyard, not far from the grave of the master he had guarded all those years. Later, a statue was created of Bobby above a fountain—"

"Because an English philanthropist, Lady Burdett-Coutts, was so taken and charmed by the idea that a beloved dog had cared so much for his master. And he is remembered to this day!" Mason said, grinning as he interrupted.

"Hey, there are some great stories about good things in Edinburgh," Edmund said. "The world has a lot about caring in it, even if Edinburgh also offers...well, you know, stories about many wars, the horror that took place in many of the closes or—"

"Alleyways," Della provided, smiling.

Mason leaned forward to speak, his elbows on their headrests. "I know the story about Bobby, and of course, I had a wonderful tour of the closes with an incredible guide known as Davey the Ghost—not a ghost, just a wonderful historian who can tell the tales in a great way. He talks about what really happened and then what is said to have happened. Anyway, I know the stories, sounds like Edmund knows the stories, but what I want to know is this—did you get your dog?"

Della laughed softly. "Yes, I got my dog. Not a pure-bred. My parents always believed that too many pets needed homes to select a specific breed so we went to our local humane society and I found a darling mutt who resembled Bobby and I named him—"

"Bobby!" Edmund said.

"Yep," Della said. "And he was a grateful little furry thing, my best friend. I got him when I was five and he made it all the way through to about my junior year in high school—my mom was so heartbroken we soon got another, her dog when I went away to college."

"Aww!" Edmund said. "Cool story, Della. A true one?"

She laughed. "Yes, true. Why would I lie about my dog? Hey, dogs are great. Patrick Law, one of our agents, and his sisters—one of them also an agent—all have great dogs who have helped on many cases. Dogs are good."

"I'm a cat man," Edmund said. "Little bastards are independent and come with attitude."

"Cats are good, too," Della said.

"Pets are great—but hard when you're jumping from country to country," Mason noted. "From what I understand, the Law family dogs are amazing and work perfectly. But the Law triplets also stay in the US. Unless they're traveling for vacation. Which they probably never get."

"In other words, you don't want a dog," Della said.

"Not right now. We never know where we're going to be. But—" he lifted his shoulders at her in a shrug "—who knows. I am fond of our furry friends. I'm thinking we might be needing a few well-trained canines here. And I know the Edinburgh police will have what we need. What I'm wondering right now is this—why Edinburgh?"

"Why did he come here?" Edmund asked.

"Right. He escaped in New Orleans. New Orleans offers 'vampire' tours. The city was where the beloved American author Anne Rice set *Interview with the Vampire* and several more novels featuring vampires,"

Mason said. "Other authors have built on the legends there."

"Ah, well, if we're looking at legends…trust me. There are many legends that aren't nearly as sweet as the story of dear Bobby," Edmund said. "Legends, of course. Sometimes with that grain of truth that got the stories started—and sometimes with lots of truth within. *Baobhan sith*, by the way, are the oldest form of Scottish vampires, I believe."

"Baobhan sith," Mason repeated. "So…"

"Scotland has hosted all kinds of legends, seriously, from ghosts to poltergeists, witches…a great history with that, of course… And let's see—vampire legends throughout the centuries. One comes to mind—a place called Croglin, near the English border, nineteenth century. A woman was attacked by a bloodsucking creature repeatedly in her bedroom. Her brother came to watch over her—shot the thing in the leg when it returned. Followed it to a grave, dug up the grave and found mummified remains. But! Those remains showed a fresh gunshot in the leg. There are more. Of course, we have the not-so-bad vampire legends, too. Those are about beautiful women seducing young men and drinking their blood. But they don't kill—they just go back for more. The theory is that those vampires are in truth old hags—getting back their youth and beauty by drinking the blood of the young men. I could go on and on."

"It's a beautiful land of legend and lore," Della murmured.

"And it is," Edmund agreed. "Scotland has had such a rich and mixed history, kinship and bloodshed. And, of course, the line of succession that brought the Stuart line to the crowns that stretched across the British Isles. Heroes like William Wallace and Robert the Bruce—horror like the execution of Wallace when the English got their hands on him—and tales of witchcraft embraced by James VI of Scotland and James I of England. The man was quite fond of fire—burning and torture. But back to vampires, it isn't surprising that in a land of some of the best storytellers, vampire legends should run rampant."

"It's not just Scotland. It's just humanity seeking to find something beyond what we are as mortal creatures. If you believe in good, you also know there's evil. If there's a god, it's likely there's a devil. Once you have that…it's easy to have fairies, good ones, bad ones, angels, demons—vampires. We have an American vampire story, too, one that is now quite explainable," Mason said. "Mercy Brown, aged nineteen, died in Rhode Island in 1892. Tuberculosis, known as consumption back then, was ravaging the area. In one family, the mother died, oldest daughter died…and the general concept at the time was that when several family members died, it meant that one was the undead. It gets really creepy—her father was convinced to exhume Mercy's body after she died because her little brother was suffering from the disease. Other family members were exhumed, but only Mercy's body showed little sign of decomposition. Anyway…according to thoughts at the time, her heart and liver were burned and they were made into a tonic and her brother was forced to drink it."

"Did it save him?" Edmund asked.

"No. He died a few months later. Tragic story—but Mercy Brown's grave is constantly visited since she's known as America's first vampire. There might be more, of course—that's just a story I happen to know. Poor kid. Sick as a dog—and drinking his sister's burned heart and liver."

"Time does amazing things," Della said. "Now we recognize diseases—and new diseases arise all the time, but we've come further with science."

"But trust me on this," Mason said. "Stephan Dante is loving the fact that many people will believe that he is a vampire, the way he can slip in, the way he can slip out… I'm assuming we'll get to a press conference soon. We need to make sure that we emphasize that the man is a brutal killer, a human monster—and not a vampire."

"Agreed," Edmund murmured.

"Fear creates panic, panic allows a killer like Dante greater control," Della said. She looked back at Mason. "Trust me on this, Mason. I will not let this man control me. I will respect the fact that I know he's intelligent, conniving and can twist just about anyone into anything—and because of that, I will not let him twist fear into me. We must move forward. We must beat the man at his own game. We know that Stephan Dante isn't a vampire. Of course, the problem remains that there is always the truth—and then there's the perception of truth."

"And we see it every day," Mason said, shaking his head. "News stations are skewed, anyone can write anything online and those who choose to believe—will." He looked at Della. "Too bad Stephan Dante didn't put his resources toward curing disease or ending world hunger. Because he's good, so good that we have to be better."

"The school is right ahead," Edmund said. "And it's

good that we've remembered a great story about love and loyalty because... Well, you'll see. We're in Old Town and the medical examiner and forensic team is already on-site, along with the detective inspector in charge here, Police Scotland, Edinburgh Division, CID, Lachlan Mackenzie. We'll park a bit out."

"We don't mind walking a few blocks," Della assured him.

"There's room for emergency vehicles, of course, it's just that—"

"We can walk," Mason said flatly.

"Sad, truly sad," Della murmured. "There really is little as spectacular as the castle on the hill, and the Royal Mile leading to Holyrood Palace and the park... and..."

"It's an international school full of bright, promising students. Brutally sad," Edmund said. "And I love Edinburgh myself. My mom hailed from just north a ways, up in Stirling. Not that bad things don't happen here—they do. And God knows, there isn't a place on earth where you don't get bad things happening—now, and throughout history."

"That's why it's good to think about cute little dogs sometimes," Della murmured.

"True, so true," Edmund assured her with a smile. "And we have good days because we get to stop some of it."

"An international school," Mason said. "Security cameras, right?"

"Security cameras everywhere—just like a prison," Edmund said. "They went out an hour or so before the show started. Dante got in sometime after those cameras went—"

"Dante made the cameras go out," Mason said.

"How? How the bloody hell did he get in to fix the cameras?" Edmund said. "He did, of course, you're right, but..."

"Friends," Della said quietly. "He got to someone in the school. What amazes me is that he can only be a day ahead of us, if that. He escaped—he found someone close to the facility who owed him, got his hands on another fake ID and headed out within hours—then he found someone here involved with the school or in the school who knew how to hack into the system."

"Then we have a hacker on our hands, most probably," Edmund said grimly.

"We'll find him. You went into lockdown, right?" Mason asked him.

"Edmund, before we get there, tell me, please. He didn't kill a child?" Della asked softly.

"No, a beloved teacher, Mrs. Elizabeth Grey," Edmund informed them. "The students...they're quite distraught. Anyway, we are here. Let's go."

He hesitated, pausing before opening his car door to exit. Then he added quietly, "Be prepared—Dante truly went for the dramatic."

Three

The school had been closed. Officers guarded the entry but Edmund quickly produced his badge, though it was probably unnecessary as it seemed the officers standing guard recognized him. They nodded grimly as Edmund assured them that he knew the way to the auditorium.

Entering the auditorium, Mason quickly ascertained that it held about five hundred students.

And the stage had been set.

"The play was a student production of a Grimms' fairy tale, 'Snow White,'" Edmund told them. "And there's where Dante displayed his victim."

They walked down the long central aisle, veered to take the steps up to stage left and paused a distance from the corpse.

And there they discovered Stephan Dante's latest handiwork.

She truly lay in beauty and Mason thought that Dante must be living on an adrenaline high—what he'd managed here was eerie and certainly, in his mind, spectacular.

Mrs. Elizabeth Grey had not been dressed in a costume—the appropriate costume would have been on the actress and not even he could supernaturally switch clothing on those awake and aware and oblivious to his presence. Rather she was in the pretty dress she had chosen to wear to attend her students' play, a soft white long-sleeved knit. And still, in the glass casket, hands folded sweetly over her rib cage, dark hair lying gently on the pillow beneath her head, it was almost as if they gazed upon the storybook version of Snow White herself. The glass coffin in the woods was a prop, of course, but she had been set to lie there when the teenage actress, Mary Malloy, had headed to her mark after the intermission, ready to begin the final act of their play. The glass "coffin" was surrounded by fabricated trees and flowers—there were even fake birds in the trees—and the scene was truly set, for it was as if she really lay in a forest, as if she were really the fabled fairy-tale princess.

The stage, other than the glass coffin and the beauty within, was empty. Edmund explained that Lachlan Mackenzie had seen to it that the students had quickly been ushered away to the cafeteria and that no one but the medical examiner and the forensic team had been allowed up there. But as they stood, studying the scene, Detective Inspector Lachlan Mackenzie came walking to greet them from the wings.

He didn't introduce himself immediately; he went right to the situation.

"I heard about the escape in the States of the serial killer Stephan Dante, and when we received the call to come here, I expected the team that caught him originally to be back on the case—changed-up protocol, since we know who we are looking for—especially after the messages received by the paper. I have several hundred parents and students in the cafeteria—I let no one go. Of course, we couldn't stop from leaving those who managed to get out before the school security and the police stepped in. We brought in one of our police techs—he's getting the cameras brought back up. I didn't know if you wanted to speak to everyone as a group. I have the immediate players back in the dressing rooms, both the actors and the crew."

Lachlan Mackenzie was a wiry man, tall and dark-haired, blue eyed, perhaps thirty-five or so. As he finished speaking, he shook his head, and apologized, offering his hand. "I'm Lachlan Mackenzie and—"

"Della Hamilton," Della said, moving a foot closer to shake his hand.

"Mason Carter," Mason said, extending his own hand once Della was done.

"This is…like nothing I've ever seen!" Mackenzie assured them. "This place functions well. School security was right on it—we were called in almost immediately. And how a killer managed this… She was exsanguinated! Bled just about dry, according to Dr. Douglas. This should have been impossible. But the actors and stage crew were in the wings and whatever was happening onstage, the audience wouldn't know—they would think that any noise was just the crew changing sets. And the timing! I don't know how, but the school security cameras went down just a bit before showtime. The victim was seen in the wings by cast and crew members as the previous act ended—the intermission was only about twenty minutes."

"Who discovered her?" Mason asked.

"The young man playing the prince, Alistair Clark, and our Snow White, Mary Malloy," Mackenzie told them. "After the break, they both enter from the wings stage right—Alistair is center stage when the curtain opens, having come through the forest, and Mary quickly takes her place in the coffin. Both, seeing the body in the coffin, went dead still in shock—then screamed bloody murder as the curtain opened. Both are backstage—we've had them wait there in their dressing rooms. I've spoken with them and naturally, they were incoherent at first, so I've tried to give them some time to settle down. Edmund told us that you would be here in a matter of hours, so..."

"Thank you," Mason said.

"You did apprehend this monster before," Mackenzie said.

Mason nodded grimly.

"And then he got away and came here. To kill," Mackenzie continued.

"We were stunned as well. He's a clever man who has befriended every kind of criminal for help when he's in the system, and outside of it. Trust me—"

"No, sorry. I'm not attacking anyone. We've had our share of bad things in the United Kingdom—some killers... Well, anyway. And, of course," he said wryly, "we are here, in the haunted land of Burke and Hare and others. I just hope that you catch him quickly. I have no desire for jurisdictional superiority—I just want to get this bastard, and since you know him, you should take the lead."

Mackenzie's tone rolled with his accent, sincere, angry and determined.

"That's what we all want," Della said quietly. Her eyes remained on the corpse in the glass "stage" coffin, upon the victim.

Elizabeth Grey had been in her late twenties, perhaps, a beautiful young woman. She did appear to be sleeping in peace, just awaiting true love's kiss to awaken.

But this Snow White would not awaken.

"Detective Inspector," Della said, "I'd like to speak with Mary Malloy—"

"She's terrified, thinking that she was meant to be the victim," Mackenzie said.

"Of course, but he prefers adults—he studied the situation. The teacher was perfect for him, a beauty who was of age. In his career, to the best of our knowledge, while he kills young women, his victims have all been out of school. And perhaps, in the meantime, Mason can interview Alistair Clark."

"Certainly. I don't think you'll get anything helpful. The killer came, took out Elizabeth and disappeared, all within half an hour."

"Oh, I doubt that he disappeared that quickly," Mason said.

"The parents and audience are all in the cafeteria, so—" Mackenzie began.

"He's not in the auditorium now," Della said. "And I sincerely doubt he'd let himself be caught in the school after the body was discovered. But…" She paused, glancing at Mason.

"This—this was just too good for him. A coffin, a

woman…an audience. This man is something of an illusionist and a chameleon, Detective Inspector," Mason explained. "I believe that my partner is right—he probably pretended to be a parent, needing to see a crew member or actor backstage. He quickly found and subdued the teacher—he's great with drugs and he's also experienced with needles and drawing blood. He carried it all out in that twenty-minute period, laid out his victim and rejoined the audience. He would have wanted to see the shock and the horror as his victim was discovered—then chaos reigning as the audience as well as the actors realized that there really was a dead woman onstage. Then there must have been mass confusion. Someone thought to call security, security called the police—and then control was reinstated by you and your officers. In all the confusion before your arrival, our killer, who we are sure *is* Stephan Dante, managed to depart the premises. He's off somewhere now, reliving and relishing every second in his mind."

"He's made his kill. Does that mean that he'll leave Scotland? I understand that he's come through the country before, that he trained more killers wherever he went," Mackenzie said grimly.

"I'm afraid what you know is true. And…I don't think that he's done with Edinburgh yet. He's had too much of a thrill tonight," Della told him.

Mackenzie was frowning, deep in thought.

"Curious. He killed the teacher, and not our Snow White," he said at last.

"Curiously enough, some monsters have their own set of rules. Dante doesn't kill children," Edmund told him.

"But he does kill young women, some little more than children," Della murmured.

"I'm going to suggest a news conference, showing the populace many of the ways our sketch artist has shown us he might appear, though, of course, that won't be all of them," Mason said. "But young women need to be on guard, and young men can't assume that they aren't in any danger. He drinks anyone's blood and kills anyone who might get in his way."

"Right on it," Mackenzie assured him. He glanced down at his phone. "Your mates are down at my head-quarters—Bisset, Wilhelm and Lapierre. Do you want them here, or—"

"Get François on a press conference with you. Edmund will talk to Jeanne and Jon Wilhelm—they can start trolling the Royal Mile. Our 'vampire king' is going to be celebrating his achievement somewhere close. He loves to taunt law enforcement," Mason said. "And for now…"

"Off to trolling," Edmund said dryly.

"Wait, Edmund, will you go and speak with the people in the cafeteria? People saw him, but I'm sure many of these people were strangers to each other. Speak with anyone who wants to offer anything. But we need to find out who was backstage during the night."

"Will do," Edmund said. He looked at Mackenzie, who quickly gave him directions to the cafeteria.

"He's a great investigator and great with people," Mason assured Mackenzie.

"Right. The killer would have talked to someone back here. He would have found a way to make sure that he knew the layout—and who was where when,"

Mackenzie said. He sighed. "I figured a stage manager would have to know. But Elizabeth Grey directed the show and then worked as her own stage manager on this production."

"A stage manager would have helped. What about the crew?"

"Music was run from the pit. Lights were run from the board—stage left. There was no change of set or even props because the last act ended with the dwarves leaving our Snow White in her coffin in the forest and walking away sobbing.

"Come this way," Mackenzie said to Mason and Della. "Actors are in their dressing rooms."

They followed Mackenzie backstage. It was eerily silent, one officer standing guard by the dressing rooms as they entered.

Mackenzie pointed to the two doors with names on them.

"It's an international school, privately funded, but it's still a school and performing arts are just a part of it. Only two private dressing rooms back here," Mackenzie said. "First, Miss Mary Malloy, second to our prince, the lad Alistair Clark. I'll be here when you're done."

Mason nodded to Della and headed on to the door marked Alistair Clark—the name handwritten in elaborate cursive on a paper and slipped into the glass slot where a new name could be placed when a new actor was cast in a lead role.

He tapped and despite the door, he could hear the jump of the person inside.

"Eh?" came a nervous voice.

"Alistair, my name is Mason Carter and I'm with a

special task force to bring down the man who did this. May I come in and speak with you?"

The boy was quickly at the door, opening it to look at Mason anxiously. He'd obviously been crying. He was a handsome young man, cast to fit the role of a prince well, Mason thought. He was about six feet tall with sandy hair, green eyes set in a face with strong, classic bone structure. Despite his look of strength, he was obviously shaken to the core.

"I need your story," Mason told him. "From the time you arrived tonight, until now."

"She's dead!" he said. "Our theater teacher…she's dead!"

"I know that," Mason said gently. "And we intend to catch the man who did that to her. We need your help."

"It's true," the boy said, shaking his head. "I always thought my aunt Tilly was crazy as a loon, but I think she's right. From the beginning…from pagan times, from the druids. There's something here, something that…well, you know! King James VI of Scotland— and I of England—was hell on witches, witchcraft, in any way. And he might have been right! I mean…well, everyone knows we had Burke and Hare, grave robbers turned murderers, and then there was Half-hangit Maggie, sir! A tart, so they said, who killed her newborn, and they hung her, kept her up twitching in agony for a half hour, she went still, she was dead, but after being placed in a coffin she beat at the wood and she was alive! I think 1774, somewhere around then, but she came back to life! The devil's work? And now a vampire! A damned vampire— Sorry, sir, sorry, but—"

"He's not a vampire. He's a man."

"She was whiter than a sheet! He sucked out all her blood! He's real, I'm so afraid—and she was good! Mrs. Grey, she taught us to write, to understand. Actors did lights, they did props, we all needed to know what others were doing and—"

"Alistair, I understand, and we're so sorry for your loss, but this is a man, and we need to arrest him and as quickly as possible. Anything you can tell me may help. Calm down, please, because the best thing you can do for her now is help us catch her killer," Mason said gently.

Alistair nodded and swallowed painfully. He half sat and half collapsed into the chair at his dressing table. There was also a stool in the little dressing room and Mason drew it up to sit before the boy.

"Please, Alistair. This man, your teacher's killer, was here. You saw him before he carried out the deed."

"There were hundreds of people here. It was opening night. Our parents…friends, people from the papers…"

"Right. So tell me who saw you, who talked to you," Mason said.

"My parents brought me here about seven, yes, just about seven, eight-o'clock curtain," Alistair said. "I saw my friends in the cast and Mrs. Grey…she was so wonderful!"

"I'm so sorry," Mason said, knowing he had to be patient. Alistair might physically be growing into a man, but he was still just seventeen.

Alistair nodded. "Our cast…the stepsisters were funny in this presentation. Elly, Shauna and Melissa. The evil stepmother was Clarissa and she was funny, too—she accidentally poisons the apple in our version. And the dwarves… It was a good show, a really good show. We all liked each other, we were excited about it and Donald—Donald Foxworthy, who wrote the show—hoped that he could publish it, that the play would go on, and now…"

"According to some, there is no such thing as bad publicity," Mason said.

Alistair shook his head. "It will never mean anything to me except for the loss of Mrs. Grey."

"Of course. You saw your friends, the students in the play and who else? Was anyone else backstage before the show?" Mason asked.

"Ona—from our school paper, another student," he said thoughtfully. "Oh! Yeah, and three others, two men and a woman. She was from an Edinburgh paper… I don't remember names. We were all in the wings but then it was time to get dressed. The one man said that he was London and the other…he had a strange accent. Maybe English, but I know English accents. He wasn't a Scot, I don't think. Maybe South African or… He said that he worked for a paper in Glasgow."

"Interesting. Do reporters from faraway places often do reviews on shows done at a school in Edinburgh?"

Alistair shook his head thoughtfully. "Sometimes they come from Glasgow or other Scottish cities. London, maybe once before? We all thought it was cool and great for the possibility that the show might be produced other places, that it might be sold."

"Describe the man who said he was from London."

"Tall, an inch or two taller than me," Alistair said. "Red hair, red beard, red mustache…very thick, heavy hair. And he was wearing a tartan—Royal Stuart. And a navy jacket, white shirt."

"But his accent was not Scottish."

Alistair leaned forward. "Mrs. Grey was one of the finest drama teachers any lad could ever hope to have. We spent hours learning about languages, especially the English language, Scottish, Irish, South African… Canadian, Bahamian, you name it—the language as it is spoken around the world, even regionally," Alistair said. "She taught us that many of us might wind up working other places—where it might matter." He said the last with an accent that would pass as a deep Southern American accent with anyone in the world. "He might have been trying to sound Scottish, but not to me!"

For the last, he switched to a manner of speech that would have done the most hardened New Yorker proud.

"Did you wonder why?" Mason asked him.

Alistair shrugged. "Maybe he didn't want people to know that he wasn't a Scot if he was working for a Glasgow paper."

"I think you met our man," Mason said, rising. "And you're right. He's not Scottish. I'm sorry to say that if I'm right, he's an American."

"Oh, trust me, we all know that 'evil' comes in every nationality! I didn't mean to—"

"Offend me? You didn't," Mason assured him with a smile. "I've been known to say it myself—evil comes in all nationalities. So does good. Thank you. I'll see that you're escorted home."

He hurried out of the dressing room in time to crash into Della.

"I think he's out on the street. I think he waited to see

his handiwork when the curtain opened, and that he—" she said.

"Is out somewhere now on the Royal Mile, celebrating his brilliance," Mason continued. "Your Snow White? He talked to her, too?"

Della nodded. "Poor girl. She's traumatized—she'd lain in that coffin through dress rehearsals and she should have been in it tonight. But, yes, she said that she was surprised—flattered, of course—that a journalist from Glasgow wanted to talk to her. And she's feeling horribly guilty because he asked her who directed the play and she proudly said that their teacher was their director. Anyway, alarm bells went off in my mind but I tried to assure her that he certainly knew who had directed the play and he knew, too, who the drama teacher was. Still… Anyway, I believe, as you do, that the supposed journalist from Glasgow was Stephan Dante. And we need to go after him."

"Except that he will have shed that disguise by now," Mason said. "Come on, we've got to get Edmund, have him get a posse out on the street and find our teammates and start looking ourselves. Stephan Dante is going to be on an unbelievable high right now. Ready to taunt us some more. Mackenzie was going to set up a press conference with François and we need a warning out there—fast!"

"Right. I'm sure Edmund has managed the crowd in the cafeteria."

As she spoke, Lachlan Mackenzie came striding toward them, a brow arched.

"I think we have something. Or, I believe—"

She paused because Edmund was hurrying toward them as well.

"I've spoken to the people waiting in the cafeteria and I went table by table, staring at people. Stephan Dante isn't in the cafeteria. School security has gone classroom to classroom, they've checked out the toilets and the utility rooms...you name it. He's not here." Edmund paused for breath and glanced over at his Scottish counterpart. "We both talked—and I believe that they're clueless as to what happened as well. I do guarantee you this—Stephan Dante is not in the school."

"No," Mason said. "He's long gone. He waited long enough to see the horror on the faces of the cast as Snow White failed to crawl into her glass coffin and the two kids were staring in horror as the curtain went up—then he took off."

"We let the folks in the cafeteria go," Makenzie said quietly.

"You had to let them go. They were in there for hours," Mason assured him. "But there is something we need to do now immediately. Cameras were out. I don't know if the security cameras would have reached the stage area with the curtain down, and that's where our killer went to work. But they would have caught him backstage and could have alerted security to the fact that something was wrong. We need to find out how the cameras went down."

Mackenzie smiled. "We have great techs on our team here in Edinburgh. I've already got two of them in the security room, getting into the computers and cameras."

"May I see them?" Della asked.

"Of course," Mackenzie said. "If all of you—"

"Edmund and I are going to head out and do a lot of walking," Mason said. "Della, we'll catch up. Hopefully, we can get a name on whoever Dante so quickly connived into fixing the cameras."

"You're certain that Dante managed that? He couldn't have been in Edinburgh that long. How could he have befriended and coerced someone so quickly?"

"We know that he had a 'friend' fix the cameras when he escaped prison. He's learned it's a great way to get things done. Trust me. Dante is talented using his charm—and when that doesn't work, he manages coercion, threats…whatever is needed," Mason assured him. "Edmund, I'd like to start getting a good focus on the Royal Mile."

"He'll stay on the Royal Mile?" Edmund asked. "The city is much more—"

"But the Royal Mile is best known," Mason said.

Mackenzie nodded. "Right, if you need to know the lay of the land, I'll head out with you and leave my second-in-charge here. No one know this city as I do," he assured them. "Della, if I may escort you?"

He offered her his arm politely. She shrugged, smiled and accepted, glancing back at Mason and promising, "I'll be on the phone, and I'll catch up."

He nodded and watched and waited as they moved away from the backstage area and out of the auditorium.

Mason looked at Edmund and shrugged. "Might as well head on out," Mason said.

Edmund nodded. "How strange," he murmured.

"What's that?"

"I find myself thinking more like you all the time. Stephan Dante is surely considering his next strike. And

I agree. He turned a fairy tale into a murder. He's not going to go back to displaying his beauties on a river-bank. He's going to go for something equal to or more dramatic than what he's already accomplished. And the Royal Mile…"

"At one end, a palace. At the other end, a castle." Mason nodded. "He will play upon history—and royalty. After all, the man calls himself a king."

"Yes, the king of the vampires," Edmund agreed. "What better for the 'king' than the 'royal' mile? Mason, there has to be a way to outwit this monster, before he 'royally' kills again."

Four

Lachlan Mackenzie glanced at Della as they made their way through the hallways, heading for the security room.

She glanced up at him. "I'm sorry. Do you resent our being here?" she asked.

"Resent?" he asked, shaking his head. "Ah, lass, trust me, no! A usual case, far more than all the forensic photography, our fellows dusting for prints, seeking whatever they can find that might lead to a suspect. This is…different, to say the least. We know who the killer is. We don't know how to find the bloody bastard. I've read up on your group—the Krewe in the States, and in Europe. I know that you've already worked in Scotland, in the Orkneys. I am grateful for any help. Jurisdiction doesn't matter to me—never did. Stopping monsters is what counts, and your fellow may want to be the best vampire ever but I will give him this. He is a monster. And to rid my land of this monster, I am more than happy to have any assistance possible."

"Thank you," she murmured, smiling. "He is a monster. And, trust me, we desperately need your help. This is your home. You know it as we cannot."

"That I do. And as a lad, I loved our history and our whimsy and the many tales my gram loved to tell at night. But then, of course, the monsters were things that hid in a closet or under the bed, and there was a hero to come save the day. But now… Honestly, maybe that's why I wanted to be with the police, except that I have no mystical powers."

"But you must be an excellent investigator—else you wouldn't be on this case," she said.

"I do my best with a passion for it," he said quietly. "And now… I suppose I should be grateful that he didn't kill a child, but Elizabeth was not much older and…"

"Speaking with her family fell to you?"

He nodded grimly. "Everyone is someone's child," he murmured.

"I am so sorry."

"Her husband will be in to speak with us later. He had been on business on the Continent when we reached him. He thought he might be a person of interest at first, since he hadn't seen much news and didn't know what had happened here—we managed to keep the media from any pictures of our sleeping beauty—and between sobs he assured me that there were many people who could attest to him having been in Milan through the night. I told him that we did have a suspect. But I do want to speak with him—perhaps Elizabeth came across our killer at an earlier time—even years ago or when Dante was globe-trotting on his earlier killing spree. I doubt he can be of any help, but…"

"There is no avenue we should not pursue," Della assured him. She liked Mackenzie. He was almost as tall as Mason, imbued with straight posture, steady eyes and a manner of speaking that held authority without being obnoxious or overly aggressive. She enjoyed listening to him, too—he had a pleasant burr in his voice that clearly defined him as a Scotsman, and he was equally clear and easy with colloquialisms that seemed to be universal in the English language.

"And here we are," he said, opening a door.

The security room did appear to be state-of-the-art; screens were now up that displayed a dozen different classrooms, the auditorium, the cafeteria and the offices. There were five chairs in front of the computers that sat below the screens, but there were only three chairs that were filled. When they entered, the man and the two women who had been staring at the screens turned quickly, rising when they saw Lachlan Mackenzie.

"Back up!" the one woman said. She was tiny, just five-one or five-two, with graying hair and serious dark eyes. The other woman was younger, late twenties or early thirties, with a soft blond mane of hair that curled gently around her shoulders. The man was medium in height, sandy-haired and leanly fit.

"We got it! Well, Brianna got it—" the man began.

"Team effort!" the blonde said. She had been proud of their achievement, but her smile quickly faded. "Too late, I'm afraid," she said softly. "And...?"

Her voice faded as she looked from Della to Lachlan.

"This is Special Agent Della Hamilton with the Euro team," Lachlan said, frowning and smiling at once as he said, "Blackbird? I understand. Anyway, Della, please meet Jane Porter, vice president of the school and head of security here, and Brianna Adair and Matthew MacLeod, both of whom work for the tech department with me."

"Pleasure," Brianna said quickly. "How may we help?"

"Thank you, and of course," Della murmured. The young woman's accent was different, Irish rather than Scottish, she thought.

"Our cameras are up," Matthew added earnestly.

"We're horrified. There was no reason for what happened," the tiny Jane Porter said.

"Well, there is, though—a cunning man-made reason, I believe," Della said. "We would appreciate your help to find that reason. We know that the killer is Stephan Dante, and he's not a technical genius himself, he's simply capable of finding the technical geniuses around him."

"Yes, indeed, mum," Matthew said. "How?"

"I need the footage that would encompass any computers that might find a way into the system. I realize the students are all walking around with computers, but—"

"The library!" Jane Porter said, looking at the others. "The library. No one breached this room, and the only other possible way…not really possible but if we're talking about a computer genius, that would be where one could try!"

"Bringing it up…from…" Matthew turned to look at Lachlan. "From thirty minutes or so before the cameras went down?" he asked.

Lachlan looked at Della.

"Maybe just twenty," she said.

"As you wish," Matthew said.

The central screen switched images in a split second, showing the school library.

A librarian sat behind her desk. Another librarian or a student worked at reshelving books. Students read and chatted softly at chairs scattered around the room.

And six people sat at a bank of computers, apparently working diligently.

Those were the people Della wanted to study.

"Is it possible to zone in on their faces?" Della asked.

"Aye! Ask and ye shall receive," Matthew assured her.

He went through the first three computer users facing the camera angle that was up: a girl appeared to be no more than sixteen, another boy looked even younger and the third also appeared to belong to a young student.

"Switching angles," Matthew said.

And there, Della thought, was their culprit.

He was dressed in the blue shirt that seemed to be part of the customary school uniform along with khaki pants, she thought.

But he was no student.

While his hair appeared to be as wild as a school might allow and his face appeared to be fresh and maybe clean-shaven by the removal of adolescent fuzz, Della just didn't believe that he was a student. Something told her that he was a great deal older.

"Do you know him?" she asked Jane, the tiny woman who must have been a small package of power to manage the school security team.

Jane shook her head. "I do not. I'll call Miriam, our librarian." She was doing so even as she spoke, pulling her cell phone from her pocket. Her conversation was quick, and she ended the call abruptly.

"He was, according to the card he gave her, a student at the school. She remembers him because he was a new student and our librarians come to know those who frequent the library. She had not seen him before, but he was pleasant and she was impressed, thinking that we had gained another child eager to learn. She was, in fact, dismayed when the computers and cameras went down because of him—he appeared to be so disappointed that he couldn't finish his work."

Della turned to Lachlan, grimacing. "I believe that's him. We need to get his picture out there... Find him, and we might find Dante."

"And at the least, he's guilty of accessory to murder," Lachlan said quietly. He frowned, looking over at Brianna.

"What is it?" he asked.

She shook her head, appearing bitter. "I saw him. I saw him when we arrived. He was walking away from the school, toward the castle. He wasn't wearing the uniform shirt anymore and something was different about his face, I'm not sure what, but..."

"Dante would have taught him about professional putty—he probably changed the appearance of his nose or cheeks, maybe even his chin," Della said. Looking at Lachlan she added, "Just as the kids in the play were interviewed by a journalist from Glasgow with red hair and a shaggy red beard who will no longer have red hair or a beard."

"I'd recognize him!" Brianna said.

"Then you need to come with us now," Lachlan told her.

She frowned. "Where?"

"Down the Royal Mile," Della told her. "We're going to wander about."

"Don't you think they'll both be hiding?" Brianna asked.

Della smiled. "Dante takes great pleasure in taunting the police. He will be sailing high as a kite right now on what he sees as a fabulous victory. He may be out there. At the least, he may have left someone somewhere with something that resembles a lead."

"Shall we…? And thank you!" Lachlan said to the three techs.

"We will continue to do anything we can!" Jane swore, and Matthew nodded.

"You two—get some sleep, you've been up all night," Lachlan told Matthew and Jane. "And, dear Brianna, we will get you home shortly, I promise."

"I'm fine," she assured him.

"We join your mates?" Lachlan asked Della.

She nodded, quickly putting a call through to Mason. He listened to what they had discovered and sounded tense as he assured her that he and Edmund were waiting at the entry to the school.

They hurried to meet them.

Edmund was telling Mason what he knew about popular pubs along the Royal Mile. Lachlan was quick to introduce Brianna to the two men, explaining that she might recognize the "student" who had knocked out the computers and the security system.

"Irish?" Mason asked Brianna.

"Born in Dublin, theater school in Edinburgh, and then I discovered that my real talent lay with computers and that…" She paused and shrugged. "I like thinking that I help?"

"And you surely do," Mason told her.

Lachlan's phone was ringing. He answered it quickly, frowning and wincing. They all watched him as he finished his call.

"We have to stop this man as quickly as possible," Lachlan told them. "That was Deputy Chief Constable Lyndsey. The paper has received another missive from our killer, gloating." He looked down at his phone, saying, "He sent me the monster's poetry.

"Evil witches may not be real,
But vampires are the truest deal,
Rest in beauty, rest in grace,
The vampire king will win the race,
Taking those he cherishes in life,
All will be a wife,
Yet one will be a queen.
The curtain has risen, the play is set,
Just wait my lovelies, soon, if we haven't met."

He finished reading and looked up. "The constable spoke with your teammate, François, and he'll run a press conference with the constable at his side. Whether this man changes like the wind or not, the warning must go out."

"Aye," Brianna said softly.

"They'll speak to the news stations in front of the local station. They are gathering the press," Lachlan told them. "Mason, Della, if you feel you should speak—"

"No," Della said quickly. "He knows us—better that he sees others."

Lachlan studied her for a minute. "You're not afraid of him? I must admit, I've wondered, hearing his poems…"

"If he's after me specifically?" Della asked. "Maybe. But I feel much better going after him than worrying about whatever devious method he might use—or who else might die—if I sit biding my time and hoping that he gives himself away."

"Bait," Brianna said worriedly.

"As you've seen, he can manage the most impossible feats. I feel much safer on the offensive with people I trust," Della said.

"And I will be keeping a close eye on her," Mason said pleasantly.

"All right, so we're headed off together," Lachlan said. "But! Should we wind up separated at any point, I've sent maps to your phones. The Royal Mile is easy enough to cover but there are dozens upon dozens of closes and wynds along the way, both what you would think of as alleys or small streets—"

"Mason and I have both been here before, thank you!" She grinned. "As young people, as tourists. We don't know it as you do, but we'll be fine," Della assured him. "And Edmund has family not far from here—"

"And I do love the city!" Edmund said.

Mason's phone was ringing now. He glanced at it and then at the others.

"Jackson Crow, our field supervisor," Mason explained to the others.

He listened to the call, grimacing at the others as

he explained that the Scottish police were right on it—
they were receiving news within seconds of events and
though they weren't sure what they might find, they
were seeking the man who had sabotaged the school
cameras and cruising the Royal Mile in case Dante
was going to be arrogant enough to celebrate in plain
sight. Then he was listening again and when he ended
the call, he glanced at Edmund.

"Jon Wilhelm has arrived. He's with François and
Jeanne, but Jackson suggested, since you do know the
city, that you meet with him and Jeanne and start from
the castle end while we begin here, at the palace end,
and meet in the middle. In all honesty, I believe we're
going to need clues to find Dante, but there is a chance
that the man he charged to bring down the school system might be out here, blithely unaware that anyone
has a clue regarding his identity."

"I am happy to join Wilhelm and our French friend,"
Edmund said. "However, I don't know what to look for
in this man—"

"Oh, but you will!" Brianna offered. "My coworker
Matthew has seen to it that an image has been sent to
me and Lachlan and we will get it going on a group
communication. He changed a bit when I saw him on
the street, remember. No blue shirt, face a bit different
in sculpture…nose smaller, chin not as pronounced. I
will know him, but I believe that you will, too. What
he did was not that drastic, or perhaps not quite drastic enough."

"That's great, Brianna, thank you," Mason said. "We
should, however, get it to François, too. He might be as
dangerous as Stephan Dante. It might make our search

harder or useless, but I feel that it's most important that people be warned."

"Agreed," Lachlan said.

"So…"

"Pubs are open now, are they?" Della asked.

Lachlan laughed softly. "Aye, you landed at the crack of dawn! But time flies when you're seeking to hunt a beast. It's well past the midday. Pubs will indeed be open."

Edmund had his phone out and he smiled, looking from Lachlan to Brianna. "I've received the photo. We're all connected?"

"Matthew went through the deputy chief constable, I believe," Brianna said. "He had all the numbers necessary to set you together. Communication to all and from all should be easy for you now."

"What about you?" Edmund asked her.

She smiled. "I am not police— Well, I am, but not an officer or an agent or trained in any way! I'm tech," she told him.

"Ah, well, a pleasure then, and deepest thanks," Edmund said. He waved a hand in the air. "'Til we meet in the middle!"

"'Til we meet in the middle," Della repeated. She turned to Lachlan. "Where to?" she asked.

"Monroe's?" Brianna suggested, looking at Lachlan.

"Monroe's," he agreed. Looking at Della and Mason, he said, "About a city block and a half up across the street. Lovely outside seating at this time of the year. Wonderful people-watching."

"And I just realized something else," Della said.

"What's that?" Brianna asked her.

"I'm quite starving!" Della said.

"Indeed," Mason agreed.

"Ah, well…from what I understand, you've been in a most ritzy private plane through the night—well, what was night to us—while my fellows and I have stayed up endless hours—"

"Excuse me! I've been hacking away in a tiny room!" Brianna teased.

"The plane is great. The food surely not as good as something delicious in Scotland, especially Edinburgh," Mason teased in turn.

"Onward then, and we are quite lucky. An investigation that chimes in most perfectly with a deeply desired meal!" Lachlan said.

"Onward!" Della agreed, and Brianna echoed the word as well.

They were good companions—coworkers, Della thought. And glancing at Mason, she knew that he felt the same. Their work could be horrifying, frustrating, tedious…more.

And it was good to appreciate moments, and people.

Like people, no matter where in the world they might be.

As they walked, they chatted. But they were all people watching as well. They arrived at the pub Brianna had suggested and Della thought that it was perfect. Tables were on the walkway, but the front was open and they could easily see those walking along the Royal Mile as well as those within the pub.

A friendly waitress offered them menus and Della and Mason studied theirs.

"If you're looking, they do indeed serve haggis,"

Lachlan told Della and Mason as they looked over their menus. "Special very Scottish dish. Offal of sheep or calves, mixed with suet, oatmeal and seasoning, usually created within the animal's stomach," he added cheerfully.

Brianna groaned. "And are you having haggis?" she asked him.

Lachlan grinned. "Haggis, like shepherd's pie, true Italian pizza and many other dishes, are what they are because the ingredients were what was left. The best cuts of meat were usually sold, and so... Anyway, my father told me that he worked hard for a living and earned a good cut of meat. If I kept a good job all my life, I, too, could buy a good cut of meat. No, I'm not having the haggis. They make a lovely roast beef sandwich."

Della glanced at Brianna. "I take it you're not having the haggis?"

Brianna laughed. "I'm a vegetarian. I'm having their very excellent salad, filled with delicious nuts and cranberries. Quite wonderful!"

Mason's phone rang and he answered quickly, murmuring, "Sandwich, like Lachlan," so that they could get an order in.

The waiter returned as Mason stepped aside for his phone call and they put in their order for the meal.

Mason quickly returned to tell them, "Edmund met up with Jeanne and Jon Wilhelm—and Jon Wilhelm, he told me, is more determined than ever to be on the case to see that Stephan Dante is locked up again. Truthfully, he wants him brought down, and I don't think he cares how," Mason said. He shook his head, looking at the others. "I think we're all conflicted. The moral fight. If one of us had just shot him in the first place—"

"Let's not go there," Della said quietly. "It doesn't help. We have to do what we do under the oaths we're sworn to uphold."

"I know, I know, and we've been through it before—"

"Call me crass, if you wish. Only certain officers in the UK carry firearms. I am one of them. But I believe I understand my new Norse friend. If you have to shoot the bastard, you have to shoot him," Lachlan said flatly. "Pardon me, ladies."

"Been heard before," Della assured him.

"Said before," Brianna agreed.

"All right. So, lunch. And the press conference...?"

"Will be in the next hour," Lachlan said.

"And after, both Dante and his new lackey will know that we are aware of the man who fixed the cameras for him," Della said. "So after we eat, should we split up?"

"Hell no," Mason said.

Della gave the others a quick grimace and faced him. "Mason, I may have to be the bait here! We've been through this and he knows that we're partners and—"

"He can recognize both of us easily," Mason said. "Alone, together. He'll be in a new disguise, of course. But something easy—he'll have doffed the red wig and mustache and beard, and—"

"Could he have doffed a kilt so easily?" Della asked.

"It's Dante. He will have planned. He'll be watching for us, but we'll have police out on the streets as well—"

"Who don't understand how thoroughly he can change his appearance."

"Um, pardon me!" Lachlan said. "My officers are very good."

"I don't doubt that," Mason assured him. "And, Della, François will explain in the press conference that both men may be like chameleons. Della, please, humor me. Let's stay together. We could be wrong, you know. He could expect us to be out on the streets—and in his great Dante way, know that we assume he'll celebrate, and therefore he'll head to his hidey-hole, wherever that may be."

"Close to the Royal Mile," Della said.

"Probably," Mason agreed. He looked at her and stood, taking her hand. "Excuse us, just a second!" he said, leading Della back out to the Royal Mile.

"We need to find a dead person," she said.

Mason winced and Della realized how her words had sounded.

"No, no, not another victim. Sorry, a friendly spirit. And, please! This is Edinburgh. Through the centuries, there have been hundreds of deaths that might lead to a spirit seeking to be helpful."

He smiled and nodded. "Let's start with a different kind of spirit."

She arched a brow.

Mason glanced at his watch and told her, "Almost three. Amazing how much time can pass while you're at a crime scene interviewing possible witnesses."

"All right, you and I stay together—"

"We stick to the plan. We meet up with Jon Wilhelm, Jeanne and Edmund in the middle of the mile. For now…"

"Starving."

"Right."

"And I shall have a good Scotch!"

They returned to the table, where it seemed that Lachlan and Brianna had been in on their own private conversation as well.

"My most sincere apologies," Mason said.

"Not at all," Lachlan assured them. "I've taken the liberty of ordering something that you must taste while in Scotland—a good Scotch. Just one, neat."

"Sounds lovely. Two and I could fall asleep at the table," Della said.

"A good spirit!" Mason agreed.

"Spirits about. Legends," Brianna murmured.

"I was just talking to Brianna about coming from Dublin to Edinburgh," Lachlan said. "She jumped along the rocks, I believe."

"The rocks… Northern Ireland?" Della asked.

"Indeed! The story of the giant's causeway!" Lachlan Mackenzie said.

"Different, when it's told from the Scottish side," Brianna said, grinning at Lachlan. "The true side is the Irish side! I will explain. The great giant Fionn Mac-Comhaill—"

"Or Finn MacCool, whichever you like," Lachlan supplied.

"He was the strongest, best of the Irish giants, living in what is now Northern Ireland. There was a massive giant—said to be the largest giant ever—living just across the water in Scotland. According to the way I heard it, the Scottish giant—"

"Benandonner," Lachlan said. "Even she says biggest and best!"

"I said biggest," Brianna corrected. "Anyway…the Scottish giant heard about Finn MacCool and he sent over a challenge. Well, Finn MacCool was angry and ready to accept a challenge from any other giant! But to reach Scotland, he decided he had to create a path from himself. So he started ripping out chunks of the coastline and throwing them. He got to Scotland—and found Benandonner sleeping—but he saw the size of him! Bigger than ten giants—there would be no way to beat such a huge creature. So he hurried home and told his wife. She, being the cleverest of the group—"

"Not the way I heard it!" Lachlan said, rolling his eyes.

"She dressed Finn MacCool in baby clothes and they created a huge cradle. So when Benandonner came over the causeway—having heard that Finn MacCool had been in Scotland—he looked for Finn everywhere! Couldn't find him, but he found the biggest baby he'd ever seen. And, of course, the father of such a baby must be…well, more gigantic than any giant! Benandonner hightailed it back to Scotland—"

"Not the way I heard it!" Lachlan teased.

"And Finn MacCool ripped up most of the stones to keep Benandonner from ever returning. The end!"

Della laughed. "I have to admit, I had heard that it was over a girl, that Finn MacCool coveted the love of Benandonner's life and threw the stones to come over and seduce her and MacCool was sent back to County Antrim, where he furiously ripped up most of the stones so that none would ever travel again from the wretched land across the water."

"Most legends have several versions," Mason supplied diplomatically.

"Oh, of course, I know several more twists on this one," Brianna assured them.

"And, of course, the 'stones' were really formed by volcanic activity, now thankfully dormant," Lachlan said. "Then the great hill that the castle sits on today and much of the terrain surrounding it is thanks to an ancient volcano—even more thankfully now dormant. Geography—"

"Can be incredibly strange. The rocks, hills, craigs…" Brianna murmured. "There are so many places that a monster might hide just outside of the city. There has been so much bizarre that has happened in history and… Well, geography can help."

"I just don't believe that Dante is going to leave Edinburgh," Della said, looking at Mason.

"I think he'll be near. But…"

"But what?"

"I like the story of the giants. And I know there are many more legends. I'm going to hone up on them tonight. Because—as you've seen—Dante likes the dramatic. I just don't believe that he's going to hide," Mason said.

Brianna suddenly went dead still.

"What is it?" Della asked her softly.

Brianna looked at her. "I don't know about Dante, but…the man who hacked the security system just walked by. He's in the street right now!"

Five

Mason leaped to his feet, seeing the man Brianna was pointing to as he casually walked down the street. Now his brown hair was neatly combed back and he was wearing a blue denim jacket, jeans and ankle boots. Mason could only see the back of his head, but he pointed as well and Brianna nodded.

Of course, Lachlan and Della were up as well.

"He isn't going to run—he isn't tough. He just thinks he's in the clear," Della said.

Mason glanced at her and nodded, knowing what she was thinking. Doubtful, but Dante could be around. Brianna was a tech, not a trained officer or agent, and she was unarmed.

"I'm here," Della said flatly.

He nodded and looked at Lachlan.

"I'll take left and front."

"Right and back," Lachlan agreed.

Mason headed straight out of the café, walking to the other side of the Royal Mile, moving quickly. He knew that he was keeping pace with Lachlan and he needed to move ahead by about twenty feet. He did so, aware that Lachlan was right where he was supposed to be.

He gained the movement that he needed, noting a tour group that had paused as their guide explained about the history of St. Giles' Cathedral, begun in the fourteenth century. The guide had a loud and booming voice, pleasant and burred with rolling *r*'s—but loud. Necessary, of course, but his very prowess with speech was causing a jam-up where he spoke and others—not on the tour—paused to listen.

Mason disentangled himself from the group and hurried forward, glancing across the road at Lachlan.

Lachlan was grinning—glad he had taken right when Mason had gone left.

But he passed Lachlan's position to head twenty feet in front of their suspect before circling around the front.

The man smiled at him, thinking they had just walked into one another.

"Tourist, eh?" he asked Mason, grinning.

But despite his grin and easy manner, he appeared to be miserable.

Miserable—rather than frightened.

"I'm sorry, sir. But this isn't happenstance. My mate—the fellow now standing behind you—is here to arrest you for hacking and tampering with computers."

"What? There's—there's no proof I did any such thing!" he protested.

"I'm afraid there is. Before the cameras went out, we saw video footage of you at a library computer hacking into the systems. Please come along without protest. The charges—"

"May include accessory to murder," Lachlan said,

coming up from behind and penning the man between himself and Mason.

Della had been right—this was no cold-blooded killer, just a pleasant-looking nerd who had been talked into an evil deed.

Lachlan didn't need to threaten again. Tears stung the man's eyes and he stretched his arms forward, waiting for cuffs.

"I didn't… I swear, I didn't know that anyone would be killed. He said it was for a lark, all for a lark, that he was going to slip a blow-up doll into the coffin and see how the cast managed it. He paid me five hundred pounds—"

"Someone paid you five hundred pounds to hack a system, and you didn't think that something might be very wrong?" Mason asked.

"That school…many of the children are from very rich families. That would be pocket change to many a mum or dad at that place!" their culprit told them.

This wasn't the place to question him. Passersby were looking at them curiously. Some were stopping. He looked at Lachlan.

"We'll get him to location," he said.

Mason wasn't sure what "location" meant, but he nodded.

"The Euro house. Your supervising director, Crow, set it up with the Scottish police. We have our own headquarters."

Apparently, Lachlan felt as he did, that the man was no threat. He didn't cuff him; he took him by the arm and told Mason, "My car is at the school. Let the others know we'll take him to the Euro house, talk to him there, decide on charges."

"I swear I knew nothing about a murder!" the man cried. "I wouldn't have… I didn't know… I saw it on the telly at the pub, and… I'm sick, sirs, I swear it! I am guilty of hacking, and I will serve my time, but I swear on my immortal soul, I'd never kill!"

Lachlan didn't answer him; Mason called Della to tell her where they were going—except, of course, he didn't really know himself.

"That's all right," Della told him. "Brianna knows where—she set up the security for our stay there. It's just down a block in what they call New Town, an old mansion from the 1700s—I'm guessing that's in contrast to the twelfth and thirteenth centuries. Anyway, go—we'll meet you there and I'll let Edmund know since you obviously are walking and it may be difficult to do a group text!"

"Be careful," he told her.

"Always," she said.

When he ended the call, they were off the alley, or wynd, that fronted the school. Edmund's car filled one of the few spaces in the narrow drive before the guarded entry.

An entry that meant that those without proper ID shouldn't have been able to get into the school. But then again Dante was a master at acquiring ID.

Apparently, he had managed to accrue friends who were forgers in countries around the world.

Edmund was rough but controlled as he set a hand atop their hacker's head to guide him into the rear of the car. Mason chose to take the seat next to him; he might appear to be a sobbing nerd, but it wasn't a time to take chances, especially since he remained uncuffed.

A short drive brought them the rest of the way down the hill from the Royal Mile—and yet to a street within easy walking distance of the Holyrood area start of the "mile" in Old Town.

"What—what…am I under arrest?" the man asked.

"Charges pending," Edmund said briefly.

"We need to know things," Mason told him. "Let's start with your name. Your real name."

"Sam Hastings," the man said. "I swear, that's my real name. Samuel Hastings."

"All right," Mason said. "Now what we need to know is just how you met—and how to now find—the man who paid you to cut the cameras and computers and allow him to murder Elizabeth Grey."

"Thank you for staying with me," Brianna told Della. "I mean… I guess you wanted to rush off with them—because that's what agents do—and you stayed with me. And I must admit, I love tech, and I love what we can figure out with computers and science—but I'm not brave and I don't want to do any fieldwork!"

Della smiled. "I'm amazed at what you do. We have a great team at headquarters, too, and they're wonderful giving us what we need to find criminals through fingerprints, shoe prints, DNA and so much more. And we work as partners and as a team—Lachlan is great, by the way. I haven't come up against a lot of the jurisdictional troubles that I've heard can exist, but I find Lachlan to be exceptional. This is his territory, his case, and…"

Brianna smiled. "He is terrific. And quite the handsome lad. We have a great time, bickering constantly over who tells it and has it better—the Scottish or the Irish. In our line of work, well…levity is sometimes necessary!"

The food arrived as they spoke and Brianna arched a brow to Della. "Um?"

"May we have this all packed to go?" Della asked the waitress, adding, "I'm so sorry."

"Not a problem, luv," the young woman said.

She hurried away to pack up their food.

"I don't have a car nearby," Brianna said. "It's not much of a walk, but if—"

"I'm all into a walk," Della assured her.

As they sat, Della noticed a man standing not far from them, watching them from the entrance. He wasn't dressed in a tartan, but rather wore tight-fitting breeches, mail, a strange-looking cap and an overtunic with a symbol—she couldn't quite determine if it was a lion or a dragon.

He was staring at her, aware that she was staring at him.

And he might be of help. But she was there with Brianna and…

"Brianna, I need to step out and make a phone call. I will keep you in my sight. Would you give me just a minute?" she asked.

"Of course. I'll wave when she returns with the food," Brianna told her.

"Thanks!"

Della pulled her phone out, thankful that the world was filled with cell phones and it was easy to speak with the dead without passersby calling the nearest mental facility.

"Sir?" she said, approaching the figure, her phone in hand.

"American?" he asked, his voice bearing the heaviest accent she had heard as yet in just one word.

"Yes, sir. But here for a very good reason, of course, beyond the fact that—"

"Scotland is beautiful. Kin ye understand me, lass?" he asked.

She smiled. "Yes."

"English be me second language. Grew up with Gaelic, fighting the English, though, I assure you, no man is more grateful for peace than me! I fought with William at Stirling Bridge, I cried great tears when the good fellow was captured and so brutally executed! But I went on to fight with Robert, to see him reign for years and years and… Well, to the point. You are here for that bloody murderer who does not fight for country, for defense of the innocent and weak. The monster who kills for pleasure."

"Yes, sir, that is why I'm here. How did you know?"

"I saw the wretch leave the school—I heard about his deed. I had heard other things… May I know your name, dear lass?"

"Della, sir. Della Hamilton."

"And I am Boid Breac, better known today as Boyd Breck. I have watched the horrors of the centuries, the cruelty of the witchcraft years, wars on end, peaceful unity…and now I guard this great city from the likes of the monster you seek!"

"And did you see him, sir?" she asked.

"I did. I tried to follow him. He disappeared into one of the closes off Canongate, one that leads deeply downward where they ushered plague victims once upon a time. I followed with all the power that I now am privy to and... I fear that I lost him!"

"Hello."

Della was startled by the word spoken so softly beside her. She turned to see that Brianna was next to her, carrying their to-go food—and looking at her ghost.

The ghost didn't seem as surprised. He nodded to her. "Lass, Boyd Breck here."

"Brianna Adair," she said.

Della didn't mean to stare at her in surprise, but she must have done so.

"Irish," she said with a shrug.

"And Irish automatically see—" Della began to ask skeptically.

"Oh, no, not at all. I just happen to be one of the— weird."

"Gifted," the ghost of Boyd Breck told her. "And you, too, lass, are a freedom fighter."

"I fight with the power of computers," Brianna told him. "Oh, that's technology—"

"I've not stayed about these many centuries not to know what comes into our world each year, my dear," the ghost assured her. "But you—"

"Field agent," Della told him. "We had your monster once, but—"

"Ye had the man, and ye let him escape?" the ghost demanded indignantly.

"Sir, you know about technology—you know about

the law," Della reminded him. "I did not let him escape. He killed and wounded others to do so."

"Well, then, there are things to be said for me day!" the ghost told her. "Be what it may—I will look for your man."

"We're staying not far in New Town, at a place they call Euro-house," Della said.

"I know it—the police have used it before," their ghost said. "When I know something, fear not, I will find you." He frowned. "Are you with people who…?"

"Might see you?" Brianna asked, looking at Della with amusement. "Lachlan, certainly."

"Oh," Della murmured.

"And?" Brianna asked.

"Mason and Edmund—I'm not sure about the others."

"Easy enough. So…"

"Irish!" the ghost said, smiling at Brianna. "The wife of my good King Robert was an Irish lass, ye know."

Brianna nodded. "History," she said. She looked at Della. "Okay, not as big here as in the States. Your mum might have come from Seattle and your dad from Atlanta. We've a lot of that. One parent Welsh or English, another Scottish or Irish…a wee bit like one from St. Augustine and one from Los Angeles and one from New York City."

Della smiled. "I am simply grateful for all and any help!" she said. "And, sir—"

"Ah, call me by me given name, Boyd," he told her. "As I refer to you—as I am quite dead, I will do as I see fit!"

"My given name is just fine," Della assured him. "And thank you."

"Thank you. When you get him this time—"

"We will keep him," Della assured him.

"If he makes out alive," Brianna whispered.

Their ghost waved and disappeared into the crowd.

"You didn't tell me, or even hint, that you might—" Della began to Brianna.

"You didn't tell me! Or so much as hint!" Brianna said.

Della smiled. "Fair enough. And it is very good to know."

"I so agree!" Brianna told her. She smiled. "Imagine how we might surprise the others! No, never mind. Not in this situation," she added in a whisper.

"No, we need to tell them," Della agreed. "And tell them what our friend Boyd Breck has told us! What do you know about the closes? What he's talking about."

She sighed. "Closes, wynds—as you know, small streets or alleys and some lead beneath ground, and… some are on ghost tours as a given."

"Right. I've been on a tour that included many of the closes—during the plague in the 1600s, hundreds of people were forcefully herded into certain ones and left to die, the way at the time to control the pandemic, or so they thought."

"Plagues were bad. But the past in these isles was often brutal," Brianna said. "Archeological digs at a little village on a potato farm prove that people were in Scotland at least seven thousand years ago. Then, in Skara Brae, Orkney—proof of a village with all kinds of buildings. Still, while the Egyptians were building great monuments and the Phoenicians were creating an alphabet, tribe after tribe moved into the British Isles and tribal warfare led to great families seeking power—the early Scots were made of many peoples. Let's see, the Romans arrived to take a look at Britain as early as about 50 BC but didn't start conquering until the middle of the next century. It wasn't until 79 AD that the Roman governor started mapping Scotland— there was gold here, and there were other resources that would have been nice to have as well. The Caledonian tribes in the north knew that they had one hell of a battle on their hands. If you ask Lachlan, he'll tell you that the northern warriors were too strong for the Roman soldiers so they built Hadrian's Wall. If you ask an Englishman, he'll tell you that the barbarian painted tribes in the north weren't worth bothering about and so the wall was built. Then Antoine's Wall was built and then—a true moment of power from what is now Scotland—tribes got together, a Barbarian Conspiracy, Caledonians, Picts or 'Picti,' Scoti moving over from Ireland, and more. The Romans left—"

"The year 367 AD," Della said, glad of the history that remained in her mind.

"Right, I'm impressed!" Brianna said. "But a few hundred years later the Vikings came and there was more slaughter. Our ancient history is very confusing, though I guess most ancient history is confusing. Anyway…moving forward, you have William Wallace, truly immortal for his victory at Stirling Bridge, and, sadly, of course, for the fact that he was drawn and quartered and disemboweled. Robert the Bruce— despite popular belief, it's most likely he and Wallace never met and it's true that there were times during Wallace's fight for Scotland that Robert the Bruce was aligned with Edward I of England. But not long after

Wallace was killed, Robert the Bruce was king, Edward I died and Edward II didn't fare so well against the Bruce, and those wars ended."

"Wait!" Della told her. "I know this! And there are several ways of looking at what happened. Historically, Robert the Bruce—and/or his men—killed his closest rival, John Comyn. Some say that Comyn was going to betray Bruce when he planned to go up against Edward I, and some say that Robert the Bruce just wanted Comyn out of the way for his shot at the crown, which he did get, and he did lead his men to beat overwhelming forces at Loudoun Hill in 1307."

"That's true. Was Robert a cold-blooded murderer who just wanted the crown, or did John Comyn betray him to Edward!" Brianna said. "Bruce did get the crown. And then, of course, time went by. The Stuart line came into being and what is truly a sad and bizarre period came in with James VI of Scotland and I of England—witchcraft stories so bizarre it's amazing that even back then… Oh, well, wait, what am I saying? People will still believe what they choose to believe."

"No surprise there," Della murmured.

"But," Brianna said, "the Acts of Union, 1707, came about not because of war, but because the same monarchs had been sitting on the thrones of both countries for a hundred years or so. And—you can see the great buildings that were created for the new parliament— there hadn't been a Scottish parliament since the Acts of Union, but in 1999, our new parliament came into existence. But all peacefully—well, for all that anyone can call politics peaceful. Again, people will believe just about anything."

"And so they will," Della agreed. "Back to history that might help us. And, of course, I am American, but I do read. The thing, though, was that back in the witch frenzy days, you still had rites that survived the druids and pagan days and you had healers. Certain people seem to have a touch to this day—they make the best nurses! But there are those, too, who knew herbs, healing and things learned and passed down. Somewhere in there, witchcraft became a crime. One of the most outrageous stories might well have had to do with dementia—a woman named Agnes Sampson was accused of being a witch, along with others, and in the accusations, she was supposedly plotting with the devil to kill James VI. The devil came to witches, of course. By the time she was tortured long enough—fingers crushed, nails pulled out, metal bridle, etcetera, etcetera, she confessed, named her fellows and whispered—supposedly—to the king words that he had said in the privacy of his bedchamber to his new bride. She was Margaret of Denmark, and the plot was supposedly that the witches had performed a rite to create a storm and drown James and his bride on their way home from Denmark. A storm did rise, a ship was sunk—but not the one that carried the king. Anyway, the brutality of the witchcraft trials and executions in Scotland are rivaled by few. After all, if the king believed in witches, they must exist, right? Over the years, I've met a few spirits who had been caught up in that terror, many watching to see that history does not repeat itself."

"They say that Agnes—interrogated and tortured at Holyrood—still roams the halls. If you read up on the tortures they practiced, if it had been me, I'd have confessed to being a flying monkey! Anyway, again, there are several versions of the story, but under James VI, witchcraft trials ran rampant," Brianna said.

"But he'd also seen the trials previously in Copenhagen, right?" Della asked.

Brianna nodded. "So…well, the Scots could be brutal. But good point—the Germans and others on the Continent hung, garroted and burned thousands as witches and even in your colonies, some were hung. It's a brutal world, right?"

"Yes, a brutal world, but I like to believe we've come a long way," Della told her. "Some in power will always seek more power, wars will go on. But as far as people, I still like to believe that most people are good—"

"And so you chase the monsters who slip in," Brianna said.

"As do you."

Brianna grinned and said, "There—right around that corner. Our Euro-house. I think you'll be pleased. The house is 1700s, Georgian architecture, updated, set with plenty of security, and always stocked with tea, coffee and plenty of shortbread!"

"Shortbread works, as do tea and coffee!"

The house was built of stone, like many in both Old Town and New Town. It was also fronted by a stone wall with a keypad for entry. Brianna keyed in a set of numbers. She glanced at Della and said, "We're home. Let's see what they've discovered from our hacker."

"We need you to think, to think of anything at all that might help us. We need to know more about this man," Mason said, leaning on the table to confront Sam

Hastings. He wasn't sure just what they could discover from him because he believed that the young man had simply believed that he could make some good money by helping with a simple prank.

"I—I thought that he was telling me true!" Hastings said. "I... Oh, dear God, but I am sorry, so deeply sorry!"

They had set him in the room and left him to pace nervously for several minutes before heading in to speak with him.

What he had done was illegal. Tampering with the computers and cameras was beyond a doubt illegal in most any country, Mason was certain.

But the young man wasn't a murderer. His distress was real.

"We believe you," Lachlan said. He was leaning against the wall and Mason knew exactly why Lachlan had chosen to come straight here—Euro-house had been set up as something like a private precinct. The upstairs offered bedrooms while the downstairs offered an entry, a parlor, a conference room equipped with screens and computers, and an interrogation room that even featured a small observation room.

Lachlan took one of the chairs facing Hastings. "We believe you," he repeated. "But this man who conned you has a name—a real name in contrast to whatever he may have told you. He is Stephan Dante, responsible for murders in Europe and North America and maybe other places as well."

Hastings winced and nodded, looking down. "I—I saw the news. I know that... Oh, God! I know that."

"Please, think of anything," Mason said.

Biting his lip and looking down in distress, Hastings was thoughtful for a minute. "He—he said that he was going to watch the fun and that he wouldn't see me again, that I should probably take off. He told me that he had a date after the show."

"He had a date. With whom—and where?" Mason asked.

"He didn't say except—except…"

Hastings paused and looked up excitedly. "The Royal Mile. He said that he'd be busy on the Royal Mile, that he loved it, that—that he loved the wynds and closes. Many of the closes are private, you know, they're like alleyways that lead to dead ends and belong to the various property owners at the end. But it sounded to me as if he wanted to take a young lady somewhere nice and private and off the beaten track…somewhere he might seduce a lass and get—get lucky!"

Lachlan looked over at Mason. "He didn't care if we caught Sam or not—and if we did, he wanted us to know that he intended another kill. Tonight. But there are dozens upon dozens of closes and wynds—"

A tap on the one-way observation window caused Lachlan to cut off.

"Della and Brianna are here," Mason said. "Excuse us," he told Sam.

Mason followed Lachlan out a side door that led to the small room that attached to the interrogation room.

"We can help!" Brianna said excitedly.

"You found something?" Mason asked.

"Della found a ghost who is determined to help!" Brianna said.

Mason was dead still, staring at Della. She shrugged and said, "She's Irish."

"What?" he asked, glancing at Lachlan.

"Oh, don't worry, Mason. He speaks with the dead, too," Della said.

"You're...cursed as well?" Lachlan asked Mason.

"Gifted, gifted!" Brianna protested. "Okay, get over the fact that we're all weird. We can use all the help we can get."

"And we're grateful for it. Our fellow—old, experienced ghost, fought with Wallace and then when Bruce finally stood up against Edward II, he fought with him. The point is, he knows about Stephan Dante. He followed him to a close off Canongate. He lost him there— but it's a great place for us to start searching for him. And quickly," Della said.

"I'll call Edmund," Mason said, pulling out his phone.

Lachlan set a hand on his arm. "What about your mates, Mason?"

Mason shrugged. "Edmund, yes. Jeanne and François, I'm not sure. But we all need to get out there and start searching and alert the local police as well. Let's pray he doesn't get another victim so quickly...another victim at all!"

Lachlan nodded as Mason put through his call. They'd meet at the crossroads for the mile and Canongate and divide to take all directions possible.

"What about our friend Sam here?" Della asked.

Lachlan grimaced. "We can't just let him go. What he did... I don't want him charged with accessory to murder, but..."

"I'll stay here, Lachlan," Brianna said. "This fellow

is not going to get violent, but have a patrolman outside, just in case."

"Aye," Lachlan murmured, reaching for his phone as well.

"May I make the fellow tea?" Brianna asked.

"Fine," Lachlan said. "He will do time, but…aye, give him some tea."

"Shall we?" Mason asked.

"We shall. Walking—one can walk the entire distance from Holyrood to the castle in thirty minutes or less with a bit of sprinting, so…"

"A sprint will be lovely," Della said. "Let's do it!"

They headed out of Euro-house, walking fast to head the few blocks back into Old Town and then uphill toward the castle. At the appointed intersection they met with Edmund, Jeanne, François and Jon Wilhelm, and after introductions for Jon and Lachlan, they learned that the press conference had gone off—the populace was now warned.

"We showed every conceivable image that your Krewe artist, Maisie, created and warned as well that he might appear as anything, but no one, no one, should go anywhere with someone they don't know," François said.

"I'm afraid that he found someone before the press conference," Mason told them. "So we the police are out, but let's follow every wynd and close around here and search for…"

"A victim," Lachlan said.

"North," François said.

"François, you're our Interpol liaison," Della reminded him. "You don't need to—"

"I'll team with Jeanne, Edmund can team with Jon, and you, Della and Lachlan can create a third search party—Lachlan will know the area best," he said.

"Southeast," Lachlan said. "Go."

They split and Mason knew that François had done his division making sure that Della didn't have just one partner, but two.

Because they all knew that Stephan Dante wanted her as a victim. He knew his "immortality" as the vampire king was bull.

He wanted revenge.

And, of course, he would kill anyone in his way if he deemed it necessary—and he could. Mason was determined that he would not.

"Not all the closes are dead ends, though many are," Lachlan said, walking quickly and twisting down a narrow alleyway. They passed old stone buildings, many of them homes, and only one a coffee shop.

The close he had chosen was narrow and headed downhill, down steps to an underground alley. There were even twists and turns off the main alley.

"This is a favorite on ghost tours," Lachlan said. "Supposedly a coven of witches once met here and performed their rites—before being arrested and accused of having murdered several victims here, and… Well, you know."

"Have you seen a ghost down here?" Della asked him.

"No. And I don't believe that so-called witches killed anyone here, but…"

He paused and Mason saw that Della was staring at a crevice in the stone that lined the alleyway.

"Here!" she murmured.

Before Mason could stop her, she was crawling through the crevice. He followed quickly, with Lachlan right behind him.

The crevice opened into an overgrown yard. Strange, broken headstones littered the area.

"Historically protected," Lachlan murmured. "We're in the ruins of a seventh-century church, gated from the street above, no entry, not considered safe..."

"Ambulance!" Della shouted.

Mason raced off after her as she sprinted across the yard, hopping over a broken and crooked stone. She reached an area of debris and skirted around it.

And Mason saw what she had seen.

A young woman, lying at the foot of what had been a headstone. Della was down on the ground in two seconds by the young woman's side.

This was different.

Her hands were not folded on her chest, as was usual with Dante's sleeping victims.

"She's alive! Barely, weak pulse! We need an ambulance!" Della said.

"Lachlan, we can't drag her back through the crevice," Mason said. "Get someone at the gate. An ambulance at the gate."

He reached down, swiftly lifting the young woman into his arms.

It was a crime scene; there should have been forensics, pictures, a search for fingerprints and DNA.

But life came first. And they had to move for this young woman to have a chance.

Lachlan was already on the phone, then leading the

way through the twists and turns in the decaying ruins to bring them to a gate. They heard sirens almost immediately.

The gate opened.

Paramedics rushed in and Mason relinquished the young woman to them.

"Still alive?" he whispered to a med tech.

"Just barely. We're in communication with Dr. Collier, one of our best who has studied this killer's methods," the man assured him.

"I'm going with you!" Della said.

"Then I am, too," Mason said.

Lachlan nodded to him and said, "We'll fan out. We interrupted him. I'll contact your team so they know what we're searching for and get every man and woman I can out here, searching."

Mason nodded.

They had a chance to save this woman.

And they most assuredly had interrupted Dante at his work.

That meant he would be angry...

And no one was safe.

Six

Della stood silently in the waiting room, not certain if she was glad that Mason was there with her or if she wished that he were still by Canongate, searching with the others for Dante.

But he was at her side when the doctor walked out, solemn-faced, and she feared that their victim had not made it.

"Did we get her here in time?" Della asked, dismayed that her voice was little more than a whisper.

"I have her stabilized and we're giving her blood transfusions. We're fighting the loss of the blood and the heavy doses of several different drugs in her system. She is stabilized. But I'm afraid it will be at least until tomorrow morning before she'll be able to talk," he told them. "I promise you, we will do everything that we can. Have you found any kind of identification for her?"

"There was nothing by her side and we were hurried to get her here," Mason told the doctor. "We didn't search her for ID. She may have been fingerprinted for a number of reasons so perhaps we can discover her identity through that method?"

"I've spoken with the deputy commissioner—your associate, the local detective inspector, spoke with him—and we're going to do everything in our power first to preserve life, and then to find the answers that may help you before another lass is taken," the doctor assured him.

"She needs protection," Della said.

"I assure you, our hospital—" the doctor began.

"She needs protection. Don't worry, Doctor, we will see to it," Della said sweetly.

Mason nodded; he already had his phone out.

But the doctor sighed. "Special Agents, trust me. Our entire city council is deeply disturbed, and the deputy commissioner has seen to it that not just one but two officers will be always with her, not just outside her door, but within her room. Rest assured, while I understand that you are especially qualified to seek this man, we are adept with care and law enforcement as well."

"We were not questioning your abilities, Doctor," Mason assured him. "Or those of law enforcement. It's natural for us to double-check each other. Thank you."

He set a hand upon Della's shoulder, leading her to the exit. Della smiled. She'd always thought herself the more diplomatic of their duo. But Mason had kept her from making enemies at the hospital.

"We didn't," she murmured. "We didn't check her for ID, we didn't take a single crime scene photo—"

"Life comes first," he said.

"I know. But—"

"Trust me. Lachlan is seeing to it that a forensic detail comes in—and that police are combing the streets, searching for him."

"He heard us," Della said. "He heard us coming. He collected all of his paraphernalia and disappeared—he didn't take the time to fold her hands." She hesitated. "Mason, where did he go? How did he disappear like that?"

"Well, we need Lachlan. All right, this much I know— many of the closes changed after the plague in 1645. Some wound up underground, some became like pilings for other buildings and I believe that there must be many twists and turns that not even the average Edinburgh resident might know about."

"We need to find Lachlan and... Mason, our new Scottish friend, Boyd Breck, might be able to help."

Mason nodded, offering her a dry smile. "Well, in that case, we need to let him find us—since I sincerely doubt the fellow is carrying a cell phone."

She managed a weak smile as well. "He'll find us, and perhaps—"

"Perhaps we'll meet others who know more," Mason said.

"And Brianna may be Irish, but she knows her history. It's just that she's not trained for the field and seeing as she's a lovely young woman and just Dante's type—"

"We need to keep her safe and we will," Mason said flatly. "So—"

He broke off because they were approached by an officer in uniform. "Special Agents Carter and Hamilton, I have orders from Detective Inspector Mackenzie to bring you to Canongate at your convenience. I saw that you spoke with the doctor and have headed toward the exit—"

"And thank you!" Della said. "We're ready."

The officer quickly had them in his car. Della took out her phone to call Lachlan, but the young officer was already doing so, assuring his superior that he had the two American agents and was bringing them to meet up and continue their search.

Lachlan was waiting for them at a corner.

"She's stable—we don't know who she is, and she won't be able to talk until tomorrow. The doctor told us there was quite a cocktail of drugs in her system," Mason told Lachlan.

"At the least, you showed your magic touch," Lachlan said, smiling at Della. "You saved that lass. I believe that now that she is receiving the proper care, she will pull through. But the rub! My people have inspected the area. No purse, no phone…nothing to help. And the worst of it is that we can't find him. How the hell the man disappears so completely and quickly is quite far beyond my ken."

"Are there maps of the closes, anything that tells what remains, what was buried?" Mason asked.

Lachlan shrugged and grimaced. "I'll get everything we have, but bear in mind, some building was done centuries ago. The plague of 1644–45 was horrid, and you must imagine the Edinburgh of that day to comprehend what happened. The city was built within old defense walls, medieval times, Flodden Walls, and naturally the city was built up—with the richest at the top, away from the smells of the street. Sanitation was nonexistent. Buckets were kept by residents and at a certain time each day, passersby could hear the 'Gardyloo!' That meant that the buckets were being emptied and the streets with narrow wynds and closes… Well, it wasn't nice, suffice it to say. Mary King's Close—named for an exceptional businesswoman of the day—wound up being bricked off, not because the Scots were exceptionally cruel but because they were desperately trying to contain the plague. Food was brought to the victims, plague doctors—you see the masks they wore at Carnivale in Venice and other places—were sent in. They didn't have the medicine they have today—though, as we've seen, new plagues can hit at will. Anyway, some closes are underground, some are private property, some lead to dead ends and some to public spaces."

"So your question is a good one," Della murmured. "How did he just disappear? And it's frustrating…he knows so many places, he's obviously been to Edinburgh before and—"

"And he came to Edinburgh because he does know it," Mason said. "We have to get every man possible and keep searching until we find out how he did disappear."

"Pardon," Lachlan said as his phone rang. He answered it and Mason and Della both watched as his expression grew tense as he listened. He ended the call saying, "Will do." Then, wincing, he looked from Mason to Della.

"What?" Della asked softly.

"Apparently while Dante wasn't able to finish his body display, he does believe that his latest victim died. He's gotten another missive to the paper. His letters and claims are growing increasingly bizarre. And his speed of assault is…"

"Last night and today," Della murmured.

"What did he say in it?" Mason asked. "His letter to the paper?"

"The deputy commissioner is sending it… It's in. I'll get it to all your people. Reading his words… 'Understand that he is me, truth is what is said. Dates have been read, but I am not dead, Jeanne St. Germain, time for refrain, 'tis true that I live, and your blood you will give.'" Lachlan looked up at Mason and Della again. "What in God's name is he talking about?" he asked.

"This one I know," Della told him. "And," she murmured, glancing at Mason, "I'm surprised Dante hasn't used it before. Jeanne St. Germain was—according to records—born in 1712, died in 1784. An alchemist, artist, adventurer and whatever else who supposedly gave grand parties throughout Europe during his lifetime, eating nothing—and existing on human blood. Voltaire claimed to have known him—whether they were both alive at the same time or not, as did royalty and others. He was educated, charming…and, supposedly, a vampire. Then, years and years after he was dead, a man showed up in New Orleans, giving his name as Jeanne St. Germain. 1902."

She glanced at Mason and he nodded, picking up the tale. "The story goes that the man claiming to be Jeanne St. Germain invited a young woman to one of his parties, but she *was* the party. He tried to bite her neck. Terrified, she preferred to jump to the pavement below. The police came—they found all kind of period clothing in his home, all of it stained with blood. There was no food to be found and certainly nothing—knives, forks or spoons—to eat with should there have been any food. So to those who want to believe, St. Germain was the immortal charmer of the 1700s in France who probably killed his way from elegant dinner party to elegant dinner party and, being immortal, appeared in New Orleans almost a century and a half after his faked death. To those who are more logical and scientific, he was a monster killer playing upon the name and reputation, just as Stephan Dante is apparently doing today."

"All right, maybe he wants the populace to believe that he's really a vampire?" Lachlan asked. "And, perhaps, make even those with intelligence and logic question their own minds. Lord knows, with social media these days, many have read ridiculous things and believed them! But what does that gain him. Does he really think that he's an immortal vampire?"

"No. He just likes killing and watching law enforcement run around like dogs chasing their tails," Mason assured him. "We need to meet. Plans, blueprints, anything that's known about the closes and wynds, perhaps ways to the underground… He's going to keep using whatever escape portal he's found. We need to find that portal."

Lachlan nodded. "What about…his latest victim?"

Mason was thoughtful. "He is moving quickly, but we are like dogs chasing our tails. Your people know Edinburgh—every officer out there is on high alert. We let them hold the streets, wynds and closes now while we research the closes. Once we have a better concept of how and where he might be finding his escape routes, we'll be back on it. And then—well, that will be the time to announce to the media that his latest victim is recovering."

Della cleared her throat. "Lachlan, the doctor said that she was being protected—"

"She is." Lachlan smiled at Della. "Please. We are competent. I have two officers on the detail by her room, another plainclothes officer in the waiting room, rotating duty…trust me. We are usually quite competent."

"I have no doubt. I just—"

"It never hurts to double-check one another. Don't be offended when I do it," Lachlan said.

"We're really hard to offend," Mason assured him. "So I'd like one last look at the area where we found our latest victim. A wander through the tangled closes there."

"Let's do it," Lachlan said. "Follow me."

They entered the alleyway that led to the area where Della had discovered the crevice that had led them to the young woman who was now in the hospital. But this time, they went into the open area through another narrow wynd.

As Mason went to inspect the area where they had found the young woman, Della found herself heading back to the broken crevice.

Dante had disappeared through another such opening, she thought.

It struck her again that he knew Edinburgh well, that he knew the closes especially well and that after Mason did his own inspection there, they needed to study any plans they could—yes, changes had taken place throughout history, but history might also show them what wasn't known today.

Della glanced back at Lachlan and Mason. They were intently searching the ground, murmuring together about the fact that they didn't need a killer's prints or DNA—they knew their killer. But some speck of evidence might give them a better understanding of how their killer was moving around and becoming invisible in such a small area.

Della left them to the task and turned and inspected the area of the little crevice again. It all had to do with eons of time, she thought—maybe going all the way back in geological history to when the area was formed by volcanic activity, to the fact that the Royal Mile climbed from Holyrood Palace to Edinburgh Castle.

She realized that almost directly across from the small crevice in stone that had led her to Dante's victim there was another. She hurried over to it and realized that she had enough room to slide through sideways. She did so.

This wynd was narrow and dark and she realized that it was slanting downward, leading beneath the earth— into the Edinburgh underground.

So many tales had been told about the closes.

She pulled out her flashlight, wondering if she was in an area that had been quarantined, where people had been forced to remain, fed and cared for but left to die.

The dark, narrow wynd seemed to stretch forever before her, as if it indeed led to a world of the deserted and damned.

But if Dante had come this way, where had he gone from here? Or had he slipped into this area and waited until no one was looking and...

No.

There had been a police presence in the close and

little clearing and on the streets since they had found his victim—interrupted his ritual.

She turned a corner ahead. The wynd led to another wynd or close, and this one was wider, graced with steps. She started that way and was then certain that she heard something behind her.

She swung around, drawing her Glock.

"If you're there, Mr. Dante, do come out," she said. "As you can see, I am all alone. I'm what you want? Come and get me. Oh, but, by the way, I wouldn't want to be with you for five seconds while I was alive—I promise you, I'd never be your bride for eternity."

Nothing. There was no answer. Her own voice seemed to echo in the darkness and there was nothing more.

And, of course, she knew she shouldn't be exploring alone. There was no way for a human being to see in every direction; if she and Mason had been nothing more than partners, it would have been stupid for them not to be working together in such a situation, because one person could be surprised far easier than two.

No one could see in all directions.

She started to hurry back along the corridor, going back to the very dark and narrow—keeping her grip on her Glock firm.

She couldn't shake the idea that someone was near her.

Watching.

But from where?

She had no answer and hurried back, hoping that Mason wasn't already concerned and calling reinforcements to find her.

But she hadn't been gone as long as she had thought. Mason and Lachlan were still down on the ground, but when she joined them, Mason looked at her curiously, a question in his eyes.

She pointed to the second crevice in the wall across from their first entry.

He sat back—he and Lachlan had literally been crawling on the floor—and arched his brow.

"You explored, naturally?" he asked.

"Not very far, really."

Lachlan stared at her, grinning. "Hmm. Maybe reincarnation is real and you were running around Edinburgh in a previous life. I didn't know there was more back there and if it's on a map…well, it will be an old map. It's all tricky. This is Old Town, so…some very old places, with the oldest structure in the city being St. Margaret's Chapel in Edinburgh Castle. Built during the era of David I. Many of these other buildings date back to the Dark Ages and the Middle Ages, many might have fallen into ruin and been rebuilt… We may need an army," he finished. "But—"

"I say we explore a bit further from here," Mason said. "And then…"

"Then we get a night crew on the streets," Lachlan said. "If he believes that he's made two kills but barely escaped the scene of the last, he'll be quiet tonight. Della, Mason, the two of you have been in the air way longer than birds flying south for the winter. I've been up all night—so have the others. We rest, order a wee bit of food—sleep. Tomorrow…"

"I think we'll probably start here, but—" Mason said. "We're in process of getting copies of all plans and blueprints," Lachlan promised. "And aye, we need to be on Dante 24/7, but we are human—and living—and need rest." He hesitated. "You are going to be the ones who find him—"

"We are going to be the ones who find him," Della corrected.

Lachlan smiled. "Which means we need to be sharp. Right?"

"No argument here," Mason assured him. He rose and Della saw that he'd put something in an evidence bag and was sealing it as he came to his feet.

"Lead the way."

Lachlan was up as well and she nodded and headed across to the second almost invisible opening in the far wall. "Narrow, very narrow!" she called back.

"Right. Pitch-black and narrow and leading into a great pool of ebony. Naturally, she followed it alone," Mason said dryly.

"Hey, honestly, I didn't go that far!" she assured him.

"Define 'that far,'" Lachlan said.

"Just down the slant and around the corner," Della said.

"There's a corner ahead?" Mason asked.

He knew, of course, that they were coming up on a turn; he had his penlight out.

"Funny!" she assured him.

They made the turn that seemed to lead back upward again, as if they'd traveled beneath something and come back up.

"Anything ahead up there yet?" Lachlan asked.

"More darkness, old stone…must be in a very old area—"

"People built up as years went by," Lachlan said.

"Okay…hit a wall!" Mason called.

Della and Lachlan aimed their penlights toward Mason—and the stone wall he had hit.

"So…this was just a mysterious underground close with a few weird crevices leading to it—and no way out?" Mason said.

"Not that I've spent that much time searching for deranged monster killers in the closes, but this is a new one for me," Lachlan said. "Yes, there are many dead ends in the closes. Yes…maybe we need to bring a specialist in on this, someone who specializes in very particular history, not just Scotland but Edinburgh, but not just Edinburgh, the closes. There must be someone out there who knows the twists and the turns and…"

"Found it!" Della cried.

She had only been halfway listening. At first, she'd been trying to use all her senses—wondering if she would have the sensation that she was being watched.

But she didn't feel it again…

Had someone been watching her? Stephan Dante? If so, why? Police and medical personnel had come, they had left, they had been gone…

Had he been watching the police? Laughing, because he knew what others didn't?

It hadn't been Dante, she thought.

Because Dante had managed to get another message to the paper. Unless, of course, he had arranged that message before he'd chosen his victim?

She didn't know. But she wasn't being watched now.

And she had found something. A break—narrow, barely navigable—had led into the strange dark and narrow space they had followed—under a street, under a basement, a shop? Who knew what lay above after twisting and turning and going up and down?

An expert, as Lachlan had said.

But she had found something, running her fingers along stone and brick. Low cracks, very low down where none of the penlights had shown them anything and where the path ahead had been stone and brick and walls and flooring.

"Here, here, here! Lachlan, I'm not sure, where are we—street level, or present-day street level, or are we—"

"Street level," Lachlan told her. "We went down, over and back up. This should be street level, still not far from where we met today."

"Halfway between the castle and the palace," Mason said, hurrying to Della. "I'm not sure what you've found, and if it's too small—"

"No, no, look! Hold the light for me," Della told him. "If you get down on the ground, you can crawl out here."

"Wait, I'll go—"

"Too late," Lachlan said.

And, of course, it was. Della had already shimmied her length through the low crack in what had once been a piece of brick wall set between stone walls. Trying to emerge on the other side, she realized that the hole she was escaping from had been hidden by foliage. Bushes grew right up to the wall, and just in case that hadn't been enough, someone—most probably Dante—had slipped a wooden slat advertising sign over the opening here.

Della pushed it aside and pulled and wriggled her

body the rest of the way through. She leaped to her feet, looking out to the street beyond—a bakery, a men's shop, a toy shop and an old medieval building with refurbished glass windows advertising that it was a doctor's office and that law offices could be found above.

Mason and Lachlan were quickly at her side.

"This is how he did it," Mason said quietly.

"All right," Lachlan said. "This is rather shabby on me, but... Well, seems that your American monster knows this better than me—a lad born and bred in Edinburgh! Did I mention the fact that I don't much like this joker?"

"Can't say that I'm fond of him, either," Mason said. "But here is the situation—we have lost him for now. Maybe Brianna or another tech, scientist, dentist or doctor has discovered our victim's identity, and by morning, we can speak with her. For now..."

"Blueprints! Plans, anything we can see!" Della told Mason.

"Your teammates were seeing to that, and, maybe even a bit sadly, seeing that our hacker friend has been locked up for charges. Time to head to the house," Mason said.

"Sleep for me," Lachlan told him. "Sleep for me. I was at the school all night and now...this man, this killer, this would-be king of the vampires, may strike again, but if so, I don't think that we'd have any more power than the many night shift officers we will have out there—"

"He won't strike again tonight. He believes that he killed at the play, and in the close. He's human, no matter what he claims. He'll be holed up for the night," Della said.

"How do you know that?" Lachlan asked.

Della wasn't sure how to reply. She didn't need to; Mason answered for her.

"If anyone knows this monster, Della does," he said.

"I've interviewed him," Della said. "And you're right. We're spinning our wheels here—"

"To our Euro-house," Lachlan said. "Your things are there—Edmund saw to that. And…" He paused, looking at his phone. "We have everything we have asked for at the house. The deputy commissioner has just texted to assure me he is doing everything we ask in hopes that we do capture Dante…quickly."

"Before he kills again," Della said, grimacing at Lachlan. "But you're right. Let's head to the house and…"

"Work—and sleep," Lachlan said. "And discover all that we can about the closes and wynds and all that goes bump in the night in this city!"

Della smiled at him and nodded.

"Lead the way," Mason told him.

They followed him out of the narrow grassy area to a wall with a gate—all part of the neighboring structure, a building as old as the others on the street. He had a car there, but before they reached it, Della stopped.

"It's him—he's here!" she said.

Mason and Lachlan both stared at her, anxious and hopeful.

Dante?

She winced.

"No, no, our wonderful fellow who was helping us earlier—"

"Dead fellow," Lachlan said.

"Yes, and he may—"

"Let's go!" Lachlan said.

The ghost of Boyd Breck was standing just inside the wall, leaning his spectral body against it. He nodded grimly as he saw them coming forward and pushed away from the wall to head toward them.

"Always careful, lads," he said, smiling at Della. "This lovely lass has assured me that there were a few more of you with the special sight, but... I always take care. Sadly, there's those who think that such folk need help, institutions, places where they might pathetically be locked away, and while time changes... Well, as we all know, some things within humanity do not change!"

"No, they don't," Mason said. "So thank you, sir—"

"Call me Boyd if you will, friend, I was no sir. Just a humble Scot, fighting for me people."

"Boyd, then," Mason said, "though—"

"'Tis just a title of respect, I do know."

Listening, Della smiled. "Given names are quite fine," she assured him. "Though you have our gratitude and respect."

He nodded. "I'd have sought you out, for I discovered here how he eluded me, but now I fear he will be onto other slips and cracks within the walls, and time has passed, and I do not know them all, though I intend to seek out friends among my kind. He was here, just moments ago, and I watched him as he saw you, but came upon him too late as he disappeared. Della, you went for your mates, and knowing you were safe, I headed to the streets, but... I was grateful to see that you were still here that I might tell you I will continue the search for other such ways and means the monster might travel here. And I was anxious! The lass he had in the clearing—"

"She is alive, Boyd. We believe that she will live. They are caring for her at hospital," Lachlan told him. "But we believe that he thinks he succeeded and for the rest of this night, at the least, he will delight in what he has done."

Boyd nodded. "Know that I am out here." He looked at Della. "Lass, take care. You are strong, and capable, and he may well have met his match. He knows that you are armed, a fierce warrioress, and still…"

"We're aware, I'm aware," Della promised him.

"There are two I spoke with earlier, friends who passed the earthly life near here, when the fever struck so many a few centuries ago. They know certain areas, for, before being struck with the fever themselves, they cared for those who were ill, bringing food and water to those quarantined and in need. I have informed them, Margaret and Hamish of the Douglas clan, regarding your talents. They may seek you out at some time, for they are searching other areas they know now."

"Thank you! We will be grateful to them, too," Mason said.

"Go then, for the living must do as the living must, and sleep is among those things they must do," Boyd told them. "I will be here when you need me."

"He has a base somewhere," Mason said. "He must sleep, too. We must find his base."

"I will be doing all that I might," Boyd promised them. He looked away into the distance. "I was at Falkirk—I survived that battle. It was 1296 when many of the Scottish nobles, including Robert the Bruce, sued for peace with Edward, so weary of war and the murder of our people. And 'twas 1305 when Wallace, betrayed, was so brutally murdered, and I was grateful when Robert the Bruce, Robert I, went to war again. Now I feel that I am at war again, and this war is one that we will win." He paused and nodded. "For now, I will wander on my quest." He grinned suddenly and looked at Lachlan. "Have you taken them to any of our ghostly pubs? We have one called Frankenstein, you know. Quite an intriguing place, good spirits, enjoyable entertainment!"

"Nay, I'm afraid as yet we've had little time for entertainment. But...in seeking our man, I promise, we'll visit many a pub," Lachlan promised.

"We even have one named for a famous witch," Boyd said. "Half-hangit Maggie—the pub be Maggie Dickson's. Lovely place."

"We will surely have to try it," Della said.

"We do have a sense of humor about our brutal past," Lachlan assured them. "Now—"

"I will take my leave," Boyd told them, turning.

He was quickly gone.

"Back to the house," Mason said. "We have help on the street, and now..."

Della was dismayed when she let out a tremendous yawn. "Sorry!"

"Sleep."

"Blueprints!"

"I will pick you up when you pass out on top of them!" Mason said.

"Della," Lachlan said quietly, "remember, Edmund,

Jeanne, François and Jon Wilhelm are at the house already, along with Brianna, working away, seeing what they may see."

"We are a team, yes."

"So onward to teamwork!" Lachlan said. "We have an unbelievable weapon that our man may not know about."

"Oh?" Della asked.

Lachlan grinned. "Brianna. Her expertise is any kind of tech, but she's a remarkable historian as well and knows far more than I do!"

"And she's Irish."

"We can be very mixed here, much like the States. Her parents grew up in Dublin—her father's parents were from Edinburgh. But her love for studying is remarkable and she has proven to be a priceless asset here, so…"

"We'll just be grateful!" Della assured him.

"Onward," Mason said. He winced. "Food would be great, too."

"Then food we shall find!" Lachlan assured him. "When this is over, I will take you on a pub crawl, I promise. For now…"

"We order in. Let's do it!" Della said, and they began to walk at last.

Yes, they had quite a remarkable team.

And still…

This one man, this one monster, was eluding them.

"Wait!" Della said suddenly.

Mason and Lachlan turned to look at her.

"We are an amazing team. And he is one man. But, as we learned with his help at the school, he seldom works as one man. We must remember that—find anyone he twists, coerces or bribes into helping him in any way. We are a team—but he creates teams as he goes, and we must break down whatever teams he creates." She hesitated. "He's out there somewhere, in a pub, a restaurant, a music venue...finding people. Finding those he can twist to his will."

"Ghost tours!" Lachlan said. He shrugged. "We are chock-full of ghost tours because, of course, a city this old with centuries of violence, witches, plagues...our ghost tours are very popular."

"Okay, so study blueprints, head out on ghost tours—" Della said.

"Go to the house, eat dinner, go to bed," Mason said. "We have our own team, remember, and team members can get out there!"

She nodded.

Because she knew that Dante was "dying" to kill her. She had to be alert, aware, as angry and ready to face him as she had been today.

And he had been there! Watching her!

He had known not to strike.

She had to be ready for when he did.

Seven

They were endless...the wynds and closes of Edinburgh.

Mason had spent hours poring over the many plans and blueprints Lachlan had procured for the team.

In retrospect, it was strange. While Jon Wilhelm and Edmund had been out in the streets, pub-crawling and looking, François, Jeanne, Lachlan and Brianna had been with Mason and Della at the conference room that had been created in the old Georgian house that was their headquarters. Food had been brought in and they'd started researching while eating. Each of them had papers, maps, blueprints and more spread out before them.

"So, so much to go through!" Edmund said, shaking his head and echoing Mason's thoughts.

Lachlan grimaced. "Aye, well...they know that the first people were here about 7000 BC—in this area with access to the Firth of Forth and the mainland because water was the best way to travel for our early ancestors—and excavations at Edinburgh Castle and Holyrood show that people were living there in that last millennium BC. Castle Rock has been continuously occupied, so say the archeologists, for at least three thousand years, so…"

"Not helping!" Jeanne said.

"What about access to all these areas?"

"The commissioner and deputy commissioner have given us free rein," Lachlan reminded him.

"Of course, I spoke with him," Jeanne said. "But… are his words good?"

"Beyond a doubt. Whatever we need, we will get. And hopefully before—" Lachlan began.

"Another woman is killed," Brianna said.

"The Edinburgh, or South Bridge Vaults!" Della said suddenly.

She looked around at all of them as they stared at her curiously. "Okay, I'm seeing in all these things before me that they were a series of chambers built in 1788— not quite so ancient—part of the South Bridge Act of 1785. Chambers in the arches…used first for shops, taverns and tradesmen and then, as many things do… downgrading to illegal distilleries, places for the homeless, gambling…and, according to this letter written in protest, a haven for body snatchers—though they don't think that Burke and Hare were holding any of their bodies in the vaults, but…"

"Underground ghost tours go through them every night," Lachlan said.

"Right, but there are so many chambers, closed off, iron gates… I think that… Hey, I'm an American fascinated by Scotland. I can go on a ghost tour!"

Mason grimaced at her. "I thought you'd been on a bunch of ghost tours."

"With Davey the Ghost—the best. Not a real ghost—"

"Davey the Ghost is known, not to worry. An incredible historian," Brianna said. "And I would be delighted to go on a ghost tour with you."

"Brianna," Lachlan said. "You're not a field agent—"

"And I have no intention of wandering off anywhere alone! I'd be with Della and, of course, we know that real field agents and amazing detective inspectors would be right behind us," Brianna said.

Mason looked down, thinking that there was far more than a casual game of Irish versus Scots between Lachlan and Brianna—whether they admitted to it yet or not.

Della looked at Mason, who in turn looked at Lachlan.

"There are many companies specializing in ghost tours of the underground. Easy enough for them to be ahead, and us to be behind."

"Not to mention the fact that Dante isn't going to grab a woman out of a crowd. I think we need to see what is down there—"

"We can explore anytime," François reminded her. "We have—"

"Yes, of course," Della said. She paused and sighed. "We can explore them anytime. I thought that going on a ghost tour… Well, I'm sure that Dante has, at some time, gone on one of the tours just as we are sure he's spent time in Edinburgh. He came here because of Edinburgh's history with ghosts and witches and body snatchers and more. I was thinking that it would be good to see the vaults the way that he saw them—and somehow, I doubt he had the help of the city."

"Tomorrow, early, we need to speak with the young woman Dante thinks he killed today," Mason reminded her.

"Of course, but…" Della began.

Mason glanced at Lachlan and François. "We'll get to the hospital first thing, and then we'll head to the vaults?"

Lachlan nodded, glanced at François, who nodded as well.

Then Lachlan rose. "I've now been awake forever, so it seems. I'm to bed. Mason, Della, forgive me if I'm wrong, but it was my understanding that one room—"

"One room is free for you to use," Della said quickly, rising as well. "It has been a long, long day."

"We're good for the night. I've spoken with the hospital and our young Jane Doe is resting well—the police have seen to it that no one has come in. They're also holding our young hacker and he will face charges, but we've noted that in our questioning, he truly had no indication whatsoever that he was being used so that a man might commit a murder."

"Good, then that is it," Mason said. He gave a mock salute. "Bright and early!"

Della joined him and they headed for the stairs, followed by the others. He noted that Brianna and Lachlan looked at one another as they reached the hallway.

They had separate rooms.

But they'd be sleeping in one.

He grinned and waved good-night to everyone, ushering Della on into the room they'd been assigned.

"I guess we should probably get married," he told Della.

She turned to him, grinning. "Was that a proposal? Oh, my God! How absolutely—unromantic!"

He laughed as well, drawing her into his arms. "But completely logical and professional, right?"

She made a face, smiling as she leaned into his hold. "Well…ugh, wait!"

"Ugh?"

"No, not you—just ugh on romantic right now. Like Stephan Dante and his displays…the beauty fast asleep, waiting for true love's kiss. Never mind. You don't have to be romantic right now."

"I was thinking a little romantically," he teased.

"You're not ready to keel over?" she asked him.

"I wasn't thinking about standing up, though—"

"No! And shower. We were on a plane forever, we went to see a dead victim, then—thankfully—a live victim, then we crawled around dark closes—"

"I wasn't crawling. I was walking."

"Correction! We crawled through the little crevices Dante is using for his escapes," she reminded him. "So, yeah, you're…ugh!"

"Oh, and you're a pristine daisy?" he inquired. He leaned low and kissed her lips lightly and tenderly. "Well, your face isn't too grubby," he told her.

She laughed, pushed away from him and started her evening ritual, setting her Glock and the little Baby Browning she kept in a sheath at her ankle on the bedside table. He watched her and she swung around. "Well?"

"My Glock goes in the bathroom with us."

"Even here?"

"Oh, yeah. Even anywhere."

She grinned and headed into the bathroom, stripping as she went. Watching her, he thought that while they could see the darkest sides of humanity and the world, he was one of the luckiest men alive.

Della was a beautiful woman with her rich flow of light brown hair, emerald eyes and incredible smile. God, as an artist, had truly created someone stunning in her. But it was so much more that made him love her the way that he did.

It was her mind, her passion and, naturally, it helped that they were both "gifted" in the same way, able to communicate on every level, to joke, to tease…and to respond to one another as partners in all things the way that they did.

He followed her. She was already in the shower, clothing in bits and pieces here and there. He slid in behind her, arms around her waist, pulling her against him for a moment just to hold her, to thank God that she was in the world, in his world.

She leaned against him. They felt the heat of the water.

Then she spun around, grinning. "Your knees! Especially grubby."

"I was wearing pants!"

"Somehow, the grubby went through."

"We can't all be delicate little princesses."

"Delicate! I'll show you delicate!" she protested indignantly. But she was laughing. "Maybe not in the shower—if I knock you out in here, you could get hurt and be totally worthless as an international law enforcement officer."

"If you knock me out?" he asked.

"All things are possible."

He let out a sigh. "I take it back. You're a kick-ass princess."

"And still a grubby one! No wait, no princesses!

Anyway…get the soap and let's get out of here—we're too big for this shower!"

It was a tiny shower. He grinned, grabbed the soap and got started—on her.

"Hey! You're dirtiest!"

"Why me?"

"You're a guy—guys are always dirtiest!"

"Oh, oh, oh, I beg to argue on that one!"

"Okay, maybe you're right. People get equally as dirty."

"And that can be taken in so many ways…"

"Yeah, let's not take it the grubby stone dust, spiderwebs, icky stuff way!"

They scrubbed, grinning, laughing and then, because it was a small space, he lifted her out, they half dried and headed into the bedroom.

It was good to be close as partners.

In so many ways…

A shower was good, too, in so many ways, touching, soaping, the heat, the sweet, sensual way that water and soap made the body hot and slick…

They made love quickly the first time, more slowly the second, and then talking faded and sleep swept around them. Sweetly.

He was too tired to even wonder long if Dante was with another victim.

Holding Della close, he found an incredibly sweet sleep.

When the sun rose, he woke. And the night had been restorative; he was ready for whatever the day would bring.

Ready to find, to stop, Stephan Dante.

* * *

Their second would-be victim appeared to be sleeping as they walked in, but her eyes opened and she sat up as she saw them. She was instantly wary, something easily understood after what she had been through.

Della spoke quickly, hoping that she was being reassuring.

"Please, don't be distressed. The doctor told us that you've been able to say that your name is Gwen Barney, that you're from Ohio and that you were staying in a hotel by the castle. I'm Della Hamilton and this is my partner, Special Agent Mason Carter, and we're first hoping that you're doing well, and second hoping that you can help us."

"You're the ones who found me, who saved me!" she whispered. "I'm so grateful!"

"We're so grateful," Mason said quietly. "And we do need your help."

The girl laid her head back on the pillow, her eyes closed briefly. Then she sat up again, shaking her head. "I was so stupid, but… I was with friends, but I teach government and history to high school kids in Cleveland, and I started talking to a guy at the bar at the pub. We were right on the Royal Mile and he'd been having quite a conversation with the bartender and I thought… I didn't think, I guess. The doctor told me…" She paused, wincing. "A woman was killed! He killed another woman just the night before, but I hadn't watched any news, and… I didn't know that there was a predator on the streets. He claimed that he was a history teacher for a secondary school in London and that he was here to study the way time has changed the streets of Edinburgh and how the closes became such intriguing places, especially those used when the plague was killing so many. He offered to show me some of the fascinating areas and it wasn't until…it wasn't until I left with him that I began to feel… I don't know. I believe I passed out, or… I wasn't drunk, but—"

"Gwen, you were drugged," Della said gently.

Her face wrinkled as she said, "I was so stupid! But he seemed like such an intelligent person, charming and courteous and—and I thought that I was seldom so lucky as to meet a man who was a true gentleman."

"He has charmed many people. Please, you mustn't berate yourself. He escaped from a heavily guarded facility in Louisiana and has taken many, many people by surprise, or through his practiced demeanor," Della assured her.

"I was still stupid," Gwen said flatly.

"You're going to be fine—"

"My parents are coming, and I will not leave them, I promise you. And a nurse was assuring me that there were plenty of policemen watching over me but that I probably didn't need to worry—the police didn't let anything about the attack be known, so he might think I'm already dead." She stopped again. "I did hear about this man before! But he had been caught in Louisiana… a man who thinks that he's a vampire. He's a monster. And—and he's still out there?"

"That's why we need your help," Della said. "You said that you were at a pub and he was already sitting at the bar. Describe him as you saw him."

"Um…fairly tall, clean-shaven, blue eyes, dark hair, great grin… He and the bartender were talking about a soccer match when we came in. Oh, we sat down at the bar and my seat happened to be the one next to his—"

"Did you travel here from the States with your friends?" Mason asked.

"Well, they're new friends. I belong to an online group and this was the first time we ever met—we were due to go to the castle…to explore and learn together," Gwen said.

"No one reported you missing," Mason said curiously.

Gwen shook her head. "They wouldn't have done so. Because we were just all here to explore Edinburgh. We were from all over—mostly Americans, a few Canadians and a few from the British Isles. But we weren't staying together and everything was loose… For those who wanted to do an activity, we just had a schedule and a time to show up if we wanted…and sometimes, we had a choice of activities, so…no one would know that I was missing. I spoke with the policeman in the room and he spoke with someone else. They know who I am, they have a statement from me…and I knew that you were coming in, and…"

She lay back again. Della glanced at Mason. The doctor had warned them that she was still very weak and that they shouldn't stay long.

"Did he really drink my blood?" she asked, pained.

"We're not sure what he does and no one knows what really makes him tick. I think his greatest pleasure is being a master manipulator," Mason told her. "Previously, yes, he has imbibed the blood of his victims and taught others to do the same. This is so important, Gwen. You are alive. And we really pray to stop him. What pub was it?"

"Something new, Grady Grant's just off the Royal Mile," she said. "The bartender he was speaking to and who served us is a man named Drake. And I could give you numbers for my friends, but it seems that everything of mine has disappeared, or everything that I had on me, my purse, license, passport, cards... Maybe he used my credit cards for something!" she said.

"No, I'm afraid not," Della told her. "As soon as the police had a name they could trace, their technical crews were searching...and, of course, they're busy checking security cameras along the mile. But you have helped us."

"I did?" she asked anxiously.

"We're on our way to Grady Grant's," Mason told her. "If he was speaking with the bartender, he may be able to provide something else. An officer will go into your room and get your computer—you were traveling with one?" he asked. He waited for her to nod and continued, "And we'll find your friends, make sure they're advised and see what they can tell us. Maybe someone you were with saw something that you didn't."

"Maybe," she said hopefully. "But you'll have to go to Grady Grant's later—way too early for a pub to be open."

"But we will get there."

"I wish I had more!"

"For now," Della said, "just get better!"

"Yes, feel better," Mason said. "And we will be back to see to it that you are doing better, and maybe by tonight, you might have thought of something more."

"Of course, thank you!" she whispered.

Mason smiled and led Della on back. The policewoman who had left the room when they arrived nodded and went back in. Outside the room, another officer was in a chair at the door. He rose, assuring them that Gwen was being guarded, lest the killer realize that he had failed.

"She's a truly lovely young lass, grateful she's alive," the man assured them. "Trust in us—we'll see to it that she stays alive."

They thanked him and met up with Lachlan, who had been speaking with the doctor in the hallway. Lachlan arched a brow at them but asked no questions, just introduced them to the doctor on duty, who assured them that Gwen was on her way to being fine.

"One more thing," the doctor said.

"Aye?" Lachlan asked.

"Catch the bastard," the doctor said, walking away.

Lachlan looked at Mason and Della. He sighed softly. "All right, then. François and Edmund are waiting for us at the vaults. Jeanne and Jon Wilhelm are going through all the security footage they can gather off the businesses near the close."

"Great. We need to get them into Gwen's room, too—she's going to have correspondence on it from the friends she met here—women who would have seen Dante and might have noticed something. We're grasping at straws here, but, hell, we need the right straw."

"Aye, we need the right straw," Lachlan agreed. "I think of other cases…Forensics seeking to identify a killer through prints or DNA, interviewing anyone trying to find out who a killer might be, following leads everywhere for an identity. We have this bloke's identity, but he disappears into thin air. In a country that's not even his own!"

"And we need to play on those weaknesses. Lachlan, this is your country. We're going to take it back from him," Della promised.

"For this, I have the car—we'll drive to our starting point," Lachlan said. "Della, what makes you so sure that Dante might be at the vaults or using the vaults?"

"They are, historically or according to legend, filled with corpses stolen or created by body snatchers. Playing with such stories is just—just what appeals to him. Just like managing to slip into a school—and kill a makeshift Snow White."

"You've interviewed him," Lachlan said.

"Oh, we've both spent a few minutes of horrifying time with him," Della said.

"What is equally frightening is the concept of what he gets others to do—as Della was saying, the man can create a team. In Norway, he convinced others to kill, to seek blood for their immortal lives. He had them convinced that he was the king of the vampires, and if they listened to him, they could be immortal, too."

"And people fell for it," Lachlan murmured. "Ah, well, we see daily what can be believed. Social media! Great to see distant family, puppies, pictures of wee cousins and so on… Quite frightening when we see the way that lies on it can travel across the globe into truth! And, of course, as Brianna can tell you, some sites that are truly heinous and criminal can be shut down—but they just pop back up a wee bit later. But can a man running in the underground, seeking places to kill where he can quickly disappear, get on the internet?"

"Oh, trust me, Stephan Dante can find a way to do about anything. Still, he will make a mistake," Della said. "Trust me, he is persistent. We will be more so. Oh! Where is Brianna now?"

"Working on security footage with your teammates and our technical department," Lachlan assured them. "She is disappointed—she wanted to go on a ghost tour."

"Maybe we'll get to it soon enough," Della said.

They reached the car. Mason slid into the back, allowing Della the front. As they drove, he looked out at the city.

If it weren't for Dante, he'd be seeing Edinburgh as almost magical, something of a fantasy. Old Town featured nearly ancient buildings in graying stone that were often adorned with the present-day painted-glass windows announcing businesses, passersby in business suits, often on their cell phones. In Edinburgh, the modern world and history meshed, fascinating in its appeal.

As they reached their entry point, Lachlan told them, "The vaults were closed sometime in the mid-1800s. Now the area north of the Cowslip arch is used for the ghost tours but if you go the other way, there is a wonderful venue where many elegant parties, big and small, are held. There are about one hundred and twenty vaults of varying sizes all together. Oh, in fact it was just the 1980s and 1990s that they were dug out, discovered by one of our rugby stars and then used by him to help a Romanian friend and player escape the Romanian secret police and seek asylum before the Romanian Revolution in 1989. Very little is known about the time when most of the shops and legitimate venues had left, but, of course, that was the bad times… Hey, big tourist business, ghost tours!"

"Of course—one hundred and twenty vaults," Della murmured. "Well, he's not hiding anything where people are working day and night—he always finds a way to drug or subdue his victims, and then he whisks them to a place where he can spend the time to drain them of their blood."

"Ghost tour side," Mason agreed.

As Lachlan had told them, François and Edmund were waiting for them to divide up and search the vaults. Lachlan explained what was commercial as in having events, and what was still commercial in the sense that the ghost tours, often with costumed "ghosts," made the most use of the space.

"So we start!" François said. "Edmund, you and I head to the far end?"

"Don't forget, there is more than one floor. And, seriously, a dozen ghost shows have been filmed here and naturally, the lights appear to be old gaslights and… Be warned, the vaults are meant to be eerie."

"Got it," Mason assured Edmund.

"I'll start up," Lachlan said.

"François and I will head toward the rear," Edmund said.

"Meet in the middle as you say," Mason agreed.

Della started off walking slowly with Mason as the others hurried on. As they entered the realms of the ghost tours, she agreed with Lachlan—if the ghost tour businesses had wanted "eerie," they had gotten it. The stone was aged and graying. The lamplights looked like something out of forgotten history.

The vaults had been deserted by shops and even the homeless for well over a hundred years, and they'd been left to look that way, haunted and decaying. There were strange little paths that twisted in different directions, and there were iron gates, strange doors in many styles.

They opened every door.

And for the most part, they looked in empty, decaying rooms, much like everything that they uncovered.

They were coming along, heading toward the middle, when they heard a startled, deep and guttural cry.

"What?" Mason shouted.

"Uh, just me!" François called back. "Wasn't expecting the skeleton!"

"Skeleton?" Della shouted.

"Just a prop! Found a room set up by one of the ghost tours!" Edmund called to them.

"All right, then…"

Della saw that one of the iron gates before her was ajar. She pushed it inward. At first, she saw nothing, the darkness in the tiny vault was so extreme.

But she heard something. Breathing.

She drew her Glock and quickly shone her penlight over the space.

"Mason!"

There were two women in the room, both leaning against the far wall, both young, one a blonde and one a brunette, and despite their lack of life or movement, it was evident that they were both attractive.

Della holstered her Glock and hurried forward, quickly kneeling by the women. Mason was at her side, seeking a pulse on the blonde as she did the brunette; they were both alive.

"Medics!" Mason shouted. His voice rang and echoed through the stone vaults.

The brunette's eyes opened and she stared at Della and screamed.

"No, no, we're here to help you. We're with the police and we're here to help you!"

The woman stared at her, blinked and said, "He's—he's gone?"

"No one is here. What did he do to you?" Della asked.

On the floor, between the two women, she could see needles and tubes…Stephan Dante's tools of the trade.

But it didn't appear that he had taken blood from either of them yet. Had they surprised him at his work again?

"Was he here just now?" Della asked.

"I—I—I don't know," she whimpered. "I…" She broke off, staring at the young blonde woman in confusion. "I don't know how I got here! I don't know who she is… I… Oh, my head! My head is still reeling…"

By then, Edmund and François had arrived with Lachlan close behind.

"Emergency help on the way!" Lachlan assured them. "Is he still down here somewhere?"

Della looked at the blonde again. "Please…is he here somewhere?" she asked.

The blonde shook her head, truly distressed. "I don't know what happened. I was with friends at Deacon Brodie's Tavern and everything was fine and Sally suggested a new place down one of the closes and we went and I ordered a drink and I looked up and…it was horrid! He was a monster… He was crinkled and his face was broken like in a—a zombie movie or… I screamed but I couldn't fight, and then—then I don't know! I looked up and you were there!"

"Lachlan! Get men down here, rip this area apart!" Mason said.

"We'll start," Edmund said.

"Front to back," François agreed.

"Up and down!" Edmund said.

But Lachlan did have a magic touch for getting help quickly. The vaults were rapidly filled with police, with medical personnel coming through. Della and Mason stepped out of the way, with one of the emergency techs saying quickly, "This lady will be fine. I don't know what this darker-haired girl was given. She has a pulse but weak and we're getting her help as quickly as possible."

"My head! My head is spinning," the blonde said.

"And we are getting you help!" the medic assured her. "Gurneys!"

The two women were quickly and cautiously moved. The emergency personnel were professional; they moved with both speed and empathy.

Mason suggested that François accompany the victims to the hospital and Della agreed, wanting to continue the search for Dante in the vaults.

"Once again," Della said, "no purses, fanny packs, phones…nothing!" It wasn't difficult to search the tiny vault. Once the women had been moved and the syringes and tubes bagged for evidence, there was nothing at all, barely even dust, in the vault.

Along with the others, she began searching again, checking where they had already searched, seeking anything in the damp, echoing places where, now and then, they had to stop to assure themselves that something left—a grotesque head upon a pole, a rubber body shoved up against a wall—had been intended as props by a ghost tour company.

They had been at the task for an hour when Della felt that she wasn't alone. Turning, she saw a woman who was watching her anxiously. In the murky gray of the vaults, it took her a second to realize that the woman wasn't living, that she was, indeed, dressed in period clothing with a tartan swatch over a tunic and dress with a sash about her waist. She'd been in her forties or a bit older when she had died, and she had a look of grave concern upon her countenance.

She remembered that Boyd Breck had spoken of other ghosts, Margaret and Hamish of the Douglas clan, and she determined that this must be Margaret.

And so she asked softly, "Margaret?"

The woman nodded gravely. "You are one of the seers Boyd has spoken of," the woman said.

"Della. Della Hamilton," Della told her. "And I am so sorry. Boyd told us that—"

"Aye, we helped with the plague, we died with the plague. A bitter time, and yet long ago, and a curse of nature and not that of man," the ghost told her.

"You know what is happening here," Della said.

"I do."

"Did you see him? Our human monster?" Della asked.

The ghost winced. "I saw him crawling about the close the day that you saved the young lass—I tried to follow. I failed."

"But you came here," Della said.

"I have sought him all over. Hamish is here, seeking the man as the living seek the man. I wasn't certain, but I thought that I had seen him near St. Giles, and I followed him and…again, he disappeared. But I believed that he had come to these vaults, and so… Hamish discovered the young women…"

"They are alive. He hadn't even started to draw their blood," Della said.

Margaret shook her head. "I looked…everywhere. Over where they have the parties, here, where so many traded—then gambled and stole and dragged corpses and more. I didn't see him. Just the young lasses…the one better than the other."

It was as she spoke that Della felt her phone ringing; it was on a conference call and it was François calling.

"Something is off! She's gone. The area is crawling with police, but they weren't expecting a lass who needed the hospital to disappear. I thought she was still on the gurney… She's gone!" François said.

"On my way!" Mason's voice came over the phone, echoed by Lachlan and Edmund.

"Yes," Della said over the phone, but she saw that Mason had already come to the door of the little vault; he wasn't going anywhere without her.

He saw Margaret Douglas, of course.

"Pleasantries later!" the ghost said sternly. "Go! Do what you must. I will be here—with living police, of course—and we will hunt and hunt…until our vampire fox and his vixen are caught!"

Mason nodded. He waited for Della, and they turned and hurried out as quickly as they could, meeting up with François where one ambulance remained.

That which the blonde woman had been in.

François was beyond distressed. "She just—disappeared! How? My God, my fault, and I don't see how…"

"François," Della said quickly. "We all thought that she was a victim, but Dante must have gotten to her! And our brunette… I think the blonde lured her to the vaults, that she learned to drug a victim and take them somewhere…private."

"So we have two vampires?" Lachlan demanded.

"Maybe more," Mason said wearily.

"It is what it is, Lachlan, and I feel your distress," Edmund told him. "We will find the woman—she won't be as talented as Dante at disguise and he won't give a damn about her—she failed him."

"Well, my police will tear this area apart," Lachlan said. "She has to be near. Monsieur Bisset, don't distress, we all assumed her a victim. If you would be so kind, I'll set up with my commissioner and you must speak to the media again, warning everyone about going anywhere with strangers. Edmund and I will stay here and search and—"

"Hospital?" Della said. "Maybe our brunette can help. And the pubs will be open. I want to speak to the bartender who saw Dante when he charmed Gwen."

"We'll head there now," Mason said.

"Take the car," Lachlan told them. He looked at Della. "The vaults…you knew to look here!"

"I'm afraid that we've been on the hunt for this monster too long," Della said quietly. "Deep in the earth… his kind of place."

"Let's go," Mason suggested, but then he paused, looking toward the street. "There!" he cried.

They all looked.

And there, disappearing into a throng walking along the street with a guide, was the blonde woman. She'd stolen a hoodie off someone, and her head was down.

But it was her.

They all began to run, Lachlan shouting for help from the police officers who were searching near the vaults.

Della and Mason had a head start.

Of course, the blonde woman saw them and took off, running up a grassy slope. Della circled around, running full speed, confronting her with Mason coming to stand behind the young woman lest she turn and bolt in his direction.

The blonde stared at Della, and she looked completely different. She had not been drugged, of course. She had feigned her distress and confusion.

And done it well.

Now she stared at Della and drew a scalpel from her pocket.

"No!" Della cried.

But to her horror and dismay, the young woman slammed the scalpel into her own chest, stared at it a second longer and fell as blood began to spew from her chest.

Eight

The Edinburgh police were efficient, good, professional, in fact, and in Mason's opinion, wonderful.

That didn't take away from the fact that the order of the day was changed. Della and Mason did not head immediately to the hospital, which, of course, might not have mattered too much on the timing side—the young woman, the brunette who had truly been a victim—had been saturated with sedatives and her system had to be cleaned out before she might make any sense whatsoever or even form words.

François remained at the hospital, ready to report to them when they finished with their interviews over the suicide of the blonde and the discovery they'd made in the vaults.

And when the paperwork was done, they learned that the brunette was Abby Holt from Glasgow and she had been reported missing by a call from her mother because she hadn't returned any texts or phone calls. She'd been due to meet up with cousins from Ireland for dinner that evening and since it wasn't yet evening, the cousins didn't know that she was missing.

Abby had grown up in Glasgow and knew Edinburgh. She was a good student at her university, fond of pubs but never one to drink to excess, and while she usually enjoyed places such as Frankenstein and those with history—like Deacon Brodie's Tavern—she loved to try new places. Her parents were driving in from Glasgow and would be there quickly.

But the doctors warned it would be evening before she was able to speak with police—or any members of the Euro team chasing the monster who had come to Edinburgh.

Security cameras found footage of Gwen Barney on the streets—heading into the close—with a man. A man who appeared just as Gwen had described him, Stephan Dante in one of his many disguises.

They also found footage of their unknown blonde woman sitting with a man at a table at one of the outside pubs on the Royal Mile; the two laughed together, held hands—and drank either Bloody Marys or tomato juice or...

Well, the pub didn't serve blood, so unless they had brought their own, Mason thought dryly, it was most likely Bloody Marys. Dante talking the woman into the fact that he really was a vampire, that he would live forever—and she could do the same. And she wouldn't really be harming anyone; being a sacrifice to a vampire also gave a victim immortality.

Mason and Della had just finished the last of the required paperwork when François found them exiting the station.

"We found her. The blonde. She's been identified, I

mean," he explained. "So very sad. Tragic, really. She has suffered from mental difficulties since she was a child. I spoke with her psychiatrist. She suffered from a rare form of schizophrenia and had been at a facility just outside the city when she managed to elude the doctors, nurses and security."

"And Dante managed to meet her," Mason said, shaking his head.

"Possibly in the streets of the city, or maybe even before. I'm starting to believe that he might have been in Edinburgh before he started killing in France, England and Norway. According to the director at her facility, Karen— sorry, her name was Karen Dougherty—received visitors now and then, and friends were encouraged since they helped those swinging into depression. I don't know this—but I do believe it's possible that Dante started here, planning, before he killed in other parts of Europe."

"And the States," Mason murmured. "What could he have said to her that would make her slam a scalpel into her own heart rather than surrender to us—when she hadn't killed yet and her mental condition would have helped her in court?"

"Maybe he convinced her that death was preferable to failure," François said.

Mason glanced at Della. He knew that watching the woman kill herself had been hard on Della; she was good at negotiation. She had talked killers into dropping their weapons, and she had slid into situations that were dangerous for her but that might save lives. While she was a crack shot and not afraid to do what had to be done, Della did her best to talk people down, to bring them in.

But Karen Dougherty hadn't given them a chance. She had killed herself swiftly.

She had tried to pretend, of course, to be a victim. She had tried to escape and nearly done so.

And then, so swiftly, taken her own life.

"We have a team watching all the traffic cameras and security cameras from around Edinburgh," François said. "The police are extremely professional and all of them, of course, want this madman caught as soon as possible. But it's difficult—Dante changes faster than a traffic light."

Mason nodded.

Della asked, "Has Karen's family been notified?"

"Well, there's another rub. Apparently, they gave up on her years ago. They've said that the city may do with her body as they pleased."

"Wow!" Della murmured, shaking her head sadly. "I can see why she might have believed in Dante, and even why she might have been so ready to die, fearing she might have lost her first real friend for failing him, as she surely saw it. And still, it's so tragic!"

"But you must remember, at least the innocent woman she was programmed to kill is alive," François reminded her.

She smiled and said softly, "Thank you. In a different way, Karen was a victim, too. So..."

Lachlan joined them in the hallway. "Jeanne and Jon Wilhelm are back in with our video experts. Edmund will join us shortly and I've summoned Brianna. Orders from on high. I'm to take you to dinner. The commissioner has made a strange suggestion. He thinks it might shake up our minds and he personally enjoys the food there. We have been ordered to go to dinner. Well, I guess my commissioner can't order you, or can he when you're here? I don't know, but as we must sleep to be useful and vital, we must also dine. So follow me."

Mason glanced at Della. She almost managed a smile.

Edmund joined them, saying, "Food will be quite lovely at this point! Shall we?" he asked.

"Wait! Brianna," Della said. "Where—"

"I'm here!"

Brianna came hurrying down the hall to the entrance to join them and they started out; Edinburgh was a walking city and it seemed that they were walking.

When they arrived at their destination, Mason looked curiously at Lachlan.

"Deacon Brodie's Tavern?"

Lachlan shrugged. "There's some good to be found here, too! May I recommend the steak and Nicholson's pale ale pie or the chicken and portobello mushroom pie? Or fish, or vegetarian, if you like."

"Food will be fine," Della assured him. "And it must be good—it looks quite busy."

"Not a problem. We have a reservation," Lachlan assured them.

They headed on in and were shown to a table. They read over the menu, deciding on a few of the specialties offered, as that way they might have a taste of many.

"Did you know that there is a Deacon Brodie's Tavern in Hell's Kitchen in New York City?" Mason asked Lachlan.

"Ah, but at this one, we're near to Brodie Close, where his family lived," Lachlan said.

"He was respected by day, a hardworking cabinet maker!" Brianna said.

"But he lived a double life!" Lachlan cut in. "Seems the man loved to gamble and had to find a way to pay his gambling debts. He also liked the lasses, and I'm not quite sure how many mistresses and children he had to support along with his legal wife and issue. But—"

"Two mistresses, five children," Brianna said.

"Of course she knows!" Lachlan teased.

"Well, it is quite the story," Brianna said. "He was deacon of a trade union and because of his position and because he was considered to be one of the best lock makers in Edinburgh, he had access to the homes and businesses of the richest of the rich. He used wax impressions to copy keys and he successfully led a double life for years. Then he organized a raid on an excise office, sure of himself and the time that people left—and the time that the night guard came on. But someone returned, the scheme was foiled, and at first, Brodie got away. He made it to the Netherlands! But he had sent letters to his mistresses and others involved gave names and he was pursued and brought back for trial, convicted and sentenced to hang. Even then, he constructed a metal collar, bribed the hangman and hoped to be brought down quickly enough to be revived. History says that he was not, though there are those who claim he was later seen in various places. Of course, his real claim to fame over other thieves through the centuries was created by Robert Louis Stevenson. The writer's father had owned furniture made by Brodie and Stevenson was fascinated. First, he wrote a play that wasn't well received. But then he wrote *The Strange Case of*

Dr. Jekyll and Mr. Hyde. Brodie went down to the ages in infamy!" she finished. She frowned then, looking from Mason to Della. "You have read the book, right?"

Della laughed softly. "Oh, yes, and seen a recent play, and it was quite excellent."

"Yes, at school, we were required to read the book and I found it quite excellent as well—chilling, but excellent," Mason said. "The most important question here is—are the pies really all that good?"

"Delicious!" Lachlan assured him.

The pies were delicious. And as they ate, Brianna regaled them with more tales—history, and what history could become in legend. When they were finished, Mason glanced at his watch.

The evening was wearing on.

"The bar," he said, looking at Della.

"The bar is actually quite extensive here," Lachlan assured him.

"It does seem as if we know all there is to know and that our problem is that finding and holding Stephan Dante is like trying to catch a fish in a vat of oil. But Gwen Barney was at a place called Grady Grant's not far from here. And according to her, Dante was having a conversation with a bartender named Drake before he turned his attention to her. We want to speak with the man."

Lachlan nodded. "Of course," he said. "Shall we join you, or do you feel that you will do better if we don't crowd and frighten the fellow?"

"I think we're fine," Della said. "And I want him to chat and feel comfortable, so maybe just two people. But, oh! The important things we are forgetting!" She lowered her voice, though Deacon Brodie's Tavern was alive with music and conversation. "As the fact that Karen had disappeared this morning came through to us, I had just made an acquaintance—a woman from the plague era whom Boyd Breck had told us about, Margaret Douglas. She was disturbed because she hadn't seen Dante, just the two women in the vault. Then, of course, we discovered ourselves as she disappeared that Karen was…an acolyte to Dante, following his instructions."

"Jon Wilhelm told me he managed to accrue such followers in Norway," Lachlan said. He sighed. "Today, though we weren't happy with the ending, we found one of the heads of Dante's hydra—and we can only pray that he hasn't had the time to gather more of a following. Still, we must—"

"Must sever the main head," Mason finished for him.

"And he must have others in the city helping him," Lachlan said.

"Else, where did Karen get her supplies to drain blood from a victim—and the scalpel with which she killed herself?" Della asked quietly.

"Now, there's an angle," Edmund said. "But," he added, glancing at Lachlan, "the forensic folks have all the evidence we collected. With any luck, they'll find something for us."

"With any luck," Della murmured.

"The check—" Mason began, but he was cut off.

"We've cleared it already," Lachlan assured him. "Brianna, it's time that we see you safely to our Eurohouse, and—"

"I will not be a burden!" Brianna said. "Lachlan, if I need to—"

"You need do nothing. They are keeping Gwen Barney and Abby in the hospital—we will speak with each of them again tomorrow. Day and night crews from the Scotland force will be doing all that they can to keep the streets safe. François has done another piece for the news—the city is warned."

"I'm beat," Edmund said. "And I'm suspecting that our American friends will be heading back for sleep again when they've finished their conversation with the bartender, Drake."

Mason nodded. "Oh, yes. And, of course, thank you! We truly enjoyed the pies. And the entertainment!" he told Brianna.

She smiled. "Aye, and 'tis true, so it seems. Everywhere, anywhere, in the world, we have infamous folk who are often remembered long after those who did good in the world. Scotland…oh, here there is a share! Deacon Brodie and worse—Burke and Hare. And—"

Lachlan cleared his throat and interrupted. "My dear lass, be so good as to remember that Burke and Hare were Irishmen working in Edinburgh!" He sighed. "Our most famous grave robbers. But at the time, Edinburgh boasted the most medical schools in the isles and perhaps beyond. Bodies were at a premium until a bill was passed stating that a person with legal possession of a body could allow dissection *if* no relative objected. That put a damper on grave robbing—and killing to get bodies before they went into the grave. The outcry over the murders—sixteen, so I've read—was so great that public opinion demanded legal action."

"Hey. We had Jack the Ripper," Edmund said dryly. "All the copycats—including the last."

"H. H. Holmes—or Herman Webster Mudgett," Della said, grimacing. "Among others, of course, but he was often considered to be the first serial killer with his murder castle and other escapades. He was suspected of killing between twenty and *two hundred* people."

"I've read the book *Bloodstains* by his great-great-grandson!" Brianna said.

"Of course she has," Lachlan murmured.

"Quite the book! When he discovered his ancestry and inherited Holmes's diaries...well, quite a good book," Brianna said. She hesitated. "And proof that we don't have to carry the sins of our fathers on our shoulders. And then again, as we've stated here, every nationality and ethnicity on earth can claim monsters."

"And we just have to find this one right now," Mason said. Standing, he waited for Della and assured the others, "Onward. Pity it isn't really like bar—or pub—hopping. We'll see you soon but won't wake anyone sleeping!"

The walk from one pub to another was short and easy. And yet, in the little distance, Della thought that Edinburgh was truly a fantastic place.

And she wished that they might be pub-hopping for real, as Mason had stated.

The spires of the several churches rising on and just off the Royal Mile were majestic and the city itself was beautiful at night, lit in many colors, alive and vibrant.

There might be a killer on the loose, but Edinburgh boasted a nightlife that could be bested by few places in the world, so it seemed. Lights blazed from numerous pubs and music venues.

They arrived at Grady Grant's and Della paused, glancing at Mason.

"A bartender?" he quizzed. "Take a stool and begin, if you will. Our man Drake will certainly warm to you before me."

"Don't be far."

"Not to worry—I refuse to be far."

Della slid onto one of the stools at Grady Grant's Pub and smiled at the man who was bartending, hoping that the good-looking young man was the bartender Drake—tall, blue eyed, with sandy-blond hair—who had served Gwen, and Stephan Dante.

He finished serving a couple down the length of the bar and came to her. "What will it be, lass, what's your desire?"

She smiled. "Are you Drake?"

"I am. Drake Sinclair. And you're an American. We have a full supply of all our finest Scotch whiskeys here, so what you haven't tried might be great!"

"I—I'm sure I would love just about any Scotch whiskey," she told him. "But I'm afraid I'm here to ask for your help."

"My help?" He looked truly perplexed. "Oh…are you trying to make someone jealous, or—"

"No, no, nothing like that," she assured him. As she spoke, Mason walked up behind her, truly confusing the young man.

"I'm not sure—"

"Two nights ago you had a man at the bar who spoke to a young lady next to him—"

Drake sighed. "'Tis a pub. Most nights I have a man at the bar, speaking to or hoping to speak to a young lady."

Mason leaned in. "Sir, this young lady was drugged—here, at this bar—and taken by the man next to her to be murdered. The—"

"The vampire?" Drake said, his eyes widening. "No, no, that fellow was friendly and very intelligent. He was all into Scottish history—which is what attracted the young lady. He was English, I think. He was fascinated by the way that Princes Street and the Royal Mile run all but parallel, telling me he loved Edinburgh because it was just about impossible to get lost! Oh, he loved the way that Old Town most often looked old while the shops along Princes Street might have had their window displays prepared by someone for the newest mall. Oh! He knew so much—more than I know, and I'm born and bred right here, in the city."

"Did he tell you about any specific places he liked to be?" Della asked him.

Drake thought for a minute, frowning. "Let's see… he had done a tour he'd seen online, something that he'd seen in a video. Started at Edinburgh Castle and then found something he said that many tourists never notice—the Witch's Well. There's a plaque on the wall near the entrance to the castle, dedicated to the many witches who were put to death there—a tremendous amount of so-called witches were killed, many of them after being nearly drowned at Nor Loch. Nor Loch doesn't exist anymore, got so very nasty that it became what we have today, the very beautiful Princes Gardens, between the Royal Mile and Princes Street. Of course, it had been man-made at the start—a defense for the castle, but neither here nor there, sad to say, we strangled and burned and 'douked'—dunked, nearly drowned—many a poor woman accused of being a witch in Scotland. With all the other many renowned sites in the city, I was somewhat surprised that he had such a thing for that, but...oh!" He stopped speaking, frowning.

"What is it?" Della asked.

He winced, appearing to be in pain, realization or acceptance.

"This killer...king of the vampires...does he really think that he's a vampire?"

"I think he likes to kill and to keep some people believing that he may be what he says and to keep law enforcement chasing him insanely."

"He killed the teacher at the school!" Drake said.

"Yes," Della told him.

"And the pretty young woman who was here..." Drake began, his frown deepening. "But—I keep news on here most often! I heard nothing about another murder. She must be all right—"

"He tried," Mason said. "We're keeping information about her out of the news. He delights in media about himself and we're trying to keep quiet, not letting out any information regarding the attack—other than to continue to warn women to be wary."

Drake nodded. "I swear, if he darkens this door again—"

"If he does, you probably won't know him," Della said. "He is a master of disguise. He will appear different, and he'll have a new accent."

"Right. The killer is an American. The Americans

let him escape. Oh, sorry. I understand that he committed murder to escape. Not to offend… Um…"

"We don't offend easily—it is what it is, and we must stop him again. But we have Scottish and international help to capture him again. Is there anything else you can think of?" Mason asked.

Drake was thoughtful, lifting a hand to beg for a minute when a man sat down at the bar a few stools down.

"He was fascinated by the witches and liked the area by the castle. But he also talked about Canongate— there are some old closes there, areas where the town was built over the town, so to say, with dark wynds and closes beneath the main streets."

"We are aware," Mason murmured.

"He talked about Arthur's Seat—that huge hill that was once a volcano. Well, I guess volcanic activity formed most of this area, but… Two things, aye. He talked about the Witch's Well, and he talked about Holyrood, the park and the palace and…oh! He was almost offensive, talking about the place where the Old Toll Booth once stood—People's Museum now, I think. As the Old Toll Booth, it stood near St. Giles and housed government offices, and a jail, where people were tortured and public executions were carried out. It doesn't even exist anymore, but…" He paused, wincing. "He did seem fond of places where people were tortured and killed. Oh! And the graveyards. He wanted to go on one of the ghost tours conducted at the graveyards. I mean, it's Edinburgh, you know—we're on every ghost nut's radar."

"Thank you," Mason said, presenting a card. "If you think of anything else—"

"So this is real. I mean, I've seen it on the telly, agents or whatever handing out cards." He hesitated and winced again. "I will, I swear it. I will call if I see him again, or if I remember anything else that may help in any small way."

They thanked him.

"You really do need to try some good Scottish whiskey!" Drake said.

"And we will," Della promised. "When we've got him!"

They left Grady Grant's Pub and their phones buzzed simultaneously. Della glanced at hers as Mason glanced at his.

"Lachlan. Just a message," Mason said, shrugging and glancing at Della. "They are all in for the night—police are on the alert. And…"

"Where do we start in the morning?" Della asked.

"The hospital. Gwen—and Abby. One of them may know something, or we may learn from Abby that she never saw Dante at all, that she found herself simply becoming friendly with Karen and… Della, we couldn't have stopped it."

Della nodded. She couldn't shake the image of the young woman stabbing herself with such violence and determination straight in the heart.

"Della, she'd suffered mental illness for years," Mason reminded her.

"All the sadder."

"Yes. But she did mean to kill Abby."

"I know. Just…"

"Right. But we move on."

"Of course."

When they reached the house, it was silent. They were working long, hard hours with an emotional toll as well as a physical one.

And sleep was necessary. She knew, too, that the rest of their team—Blackbird as well as Lachlan and Brianna—was grateful to have saved a would-be victim.

She turned to Mason. "You know what? Abby was totally innocent and deserved to live, but I do count Karen as one of Dante's victims as well. But I don't want you to worry. It just makes me all the more determined that we need to outthink him and take him down. It makes me—so angry! He is a true psychopath, heedless of who he hurts, who he kills. He is the worst of the worst!"

"Well, as we noted tonight, history has been riddled with the worst of the worst. But I agree with you. He is heinous and horrible."

"They never did catch Jack the Ripper."

"But we caught ours, and we will catch Dante."

She lowered her head and smiled. Mason didn't want to admit it, but if they were going to catch him, she was going to have to be the bait again.

He'd been holding a young woman hostage in Louisiana when they'd gotten him—because she'd allowed him to take her. The team had been in on it, of course, following. They had tramped through the bayou, with Dante certain that he knew the terrain better than anyone else. He knew it well, of course—he'd come from the area. But he hadn't counted on their team.

On Mason. Mason had managed to creep up and take a shot at the right time—shooting Dante's gun out of his hand. They had saved his would-be victim.

And she had survived herself.

But in her time as the man's hostage, she had probably come to know him better than anyone else might. He'd had a rough childhood, being the son of an unwed mother. Only his exceptional brilliance in school had brought him back into the sights of a well-to-do grandfather, but most of his inheritance had gone to taxes and he had used his mental capacity to turn to a criminal existence.

He'd been impressed with her—because he believed she could kill. She'd been instrumental in bringing down someone he believed had betrayed him—but she hadn't killed him and Dante thought that she should have.

"Stop," Mason said.

"What?"

"I see your mind working. You think you know Dante—"

"Better than most."

He set his hands on her shoulders, his eyes sharply on hers. "I know you, Della, and you're trying to figure out a way to reach him because you know that he is obsessed with you."

"He really hates you—you shot him. Which makes me wonder just how his hand and wrist are doing."

"Della, you're getting off point. We can't take chances. He knows that he risks us coming after you if he's able to get his hands on you. That would mean that this time, he'll be ready to kill you quickly."

She shook her head. "He doesn't want to kill me

quickly. He wants to watch my eyes as he bleeds me. I don't think that he believes that my blood will be special in any way, and I don't believe that he really thinks he's a vampire or that he's going to live forever."

"Della, at one time, he believed that you would reign with him—for eternity or a lifetime—but he thought that he could sway you to his way of thinking, that he could persuade you to become the killer he is, join him, reign as queen of the vampires to his king. And we do know that he has convinced dozens of people of the most ridiculous things in the world, so why not? But! He knows now that there is no way in hell you'll be with him. He can write all the poems he wants, but he knows the truth."

"Hey, chill, we have no idea of where he is and no, I wasn't thinking of doing anything. I'm just tired and… well, trying to draw on what I know about him to figure out where he might go next. In our conversation in the bayou, he never once mentioned Edinburgh or Scotland in any way. And it can't be like Louisiana—he didn't come from here and from what Angela discovered about his background, he had no connections with Scotland."

"Well, I think that our one theory is right—he did come here. And he probably watched every possible documentary on Edinburgh, found out about every little twist and turn of the past—and where he might excel at convincing people that he knew something special… and, of course, he can feign just about every accent known to man. Edinburgh's history, witches, ghosts, closes…Scottish vampires… I think he considers the city one of the best places to slide into being any person who might appeal to a targeted victim, where there would be plenty of people fascinated by its reputation for being haunted, for witches, the paranormal—and where those targets could be lured to come away with a man who could disappear into wynds and closes and underground because he could convince them that he knew a fascinating, secret place. And, of course, a place where he could arrange his displays—and relish all the media after."

"So how do we find him?" Della asked.

"Give me that question again in the morning!" he told her. "For now..."

He pulled her close and his lips moved down upon hers, moist, slow and then demanding. She responded; she was in love with him, and she loved him, two different things, really, and his touch always seemed to be magical.

She pushed him away.

"Shower!" she said.

"You and your showers!"

"It's been a long day. We're dirty."

"Hey, no dirty crawls...we're not that dirty, and this little dirty...um, I like dirty!"

"Showers," she assured him, in her lowest, sexiest, most teasing voice, "are fun."

"Okay, you got me there. Shower!"

Showers *were* fun.

And nights could be beautiful, always restoring her faith in the world.

There would always be Dantes in the world.

But there would also be those with amazing integrity, strength and caring in the world as well.

And it didn't hurt, of course, that he was an amazing lover, and that melding together was a closeness she couldn't imagine with anyone else in their world—or beyond.

And the great thing was that physical exertion did lead to sleep. Held in his arms, Della felt the ticking of her mind slow…

And sweet sleep claimed her. Tomorrow would come. And with it, of course, another chance that Dante might strike.

And another chance that they might find him again.

Nine

"She told me her name was Holly Ferguson," Abby Holt said. "She was sitting with an elderly man when I came into the café—they were at a table right next to mine. I'd been doing some work from school, but I couldn't help overhearing them. They were talking about the vaults and the ghost tours and he was telling her how they had recently discovered some etchings on one of the walls that have explained more about the way that they were finally effectively deserted—even by the homeless and the criminal element of society."

"And history is part of your curriculum at university?" Mason asked her. He and Della were alone with the young woman. Her parents had arrived and stayed at her bedside through the night; they had been grateful to see Mason and Della, thanking them over and over until they were finally convinced to go for coffee.

"Who does this kind of thing?" Abby's mother, Marlene Holt, had asked.

"The woman is dead—the police told us that she killed herself rather than surrender, remember?" Abby's father, Joshua Holt, a tall, gray and distinguished-looking man, had reminded his wife. "I don't think of myself as a vindictive man, but it hurts me not in the least that a woman who would kill others is out of this world, God forgive me, but 'tis the way I feel!"

They'd assured him that they understood and that no, he wasn't a horrible human being, and finally convinced them that it was okay for them to take a break, grab coffee or tea and something to eat—and they'd promised not to leave until they had returned, despite the policewoman assigned to watch over their daughter and the many police in the hospital.

"I love our history!" Abby whispered. "Who could ever figure that such a thing might be dangerous." She let out a long sigh, turning to look at Della and Mason as she added, "I knew not to trust any man! It didn't occur to me that a friendly blonde might be dangerous! I mean, in a fight, I could have taken her!"

"Well, that's what we need to know. How did she get you to the vaults?" Mason asked.

"Take your time, please, tell us your story at your leisure and how you remember everything," Della said, smiling gently and taking the young woman's hand.

Abby Holt was a victim Dante would have happily chosen for himself. She had shoulder-length, soft brown hair, lovely amber eyes and a sweet smile. Somewhere in her words, he felt that she was a young woman who loved the world, looked for the best and was truly curious and excited about new experiences—and who longed to trust people rather than think the worst of them.

"Right," Abby said, looking into the distance again, squeezing back when Della gently squeezed her hand.

Della was great with people. When they needed to be reassured, she was reassuring.

When attacked, in reverse, she could be a formidable tigress.

"So the elderly gentleman—she said he was her grandfather—when he left, she just looked around and she saw that I was next to them and had probably heard what they were talking about. She smiled at me and said hi, and I said hi... She asked where I was from and I told her Glasgow and she was excited, telling me that Glasgow was a great city, filled with industry, young people, excitement...but she loved Edinburgh for its history, and I agreed that it was fascinating. We started talking and then she was sitting with me and we had more coffee. She told me about her grandfather's discovery, how they hadn't closed it down yet and that we could see it—if I had the time, of course. I was excited. So excited! I couldn't wait to tell my friends what I had done while waiting for my cousins..." She paused, shaking her head. "I remember walking, feeling dizzy...and she told me to sit." She frowned. Then she looked at Della. "I think...I think I might have been in a car! And then...nothing. I remember nothing at all!"

"You were drugged."

"I have been told," Abby said softly. She let out a long sigh as she leaned back. "I think that I am so wise and careful! But I never would have gone anywhere—or even had a cup of tea—with a strange fellow. She just... She was a small blonde woman. But I was such a fool, so very stupid!"

"No, you were a normal human being, interested in

history and decent to your fellow human beings. It's sad that—" Della began.

But Abby interrupted her, frowning.

"She killed herself. She wasn't shot, she… They told me she managed to stab herself, hard! That she had serious mental problems… I'm sorry, but still grateful that I'm alive. Her poor grandfather, though."

"That man wasn't her grandfather," Della said. "He was her teacher."

"Oh, dear lord! That was him—the vampire? The king of the vampires?"

"He is no king of anything," Mason said, determined to hold his temper while he explained. "He is a devious murderer—who loves to charm, coerce or bribe others, to do his best to play on delicate mental patients like Karen and create others like him," Mason said. "He's truly a master of disguise, and though we'll never know, he probably convinced Karen that he could give her the decent life she never had and that even if she killed you, it would be better for you, do something for your eternal life. We can't be sure exactly what he says to any one person. He sizes up and judges those he intends to use and goes with whatever he believes will work with that person. Our hearts are with her, too, but we are also incredibly grateful that you are alive."

"Thank you!" she whispered, and she smiled. "I'll be okay here. I've always been lucky. I have wonderful parents. And while my mom has a nephew and niece in town now, she refuses to leave my side—except for you!"

"Well, we have police on duty, too, but I understand your mom," Della assured her, glancing at Mason.

They had gotten what information they could from Abby, which, of course, wasn't much. And they had promised that they wouldn't leave until Abby's parents returned.

When her parents walked back into the room they looked anxiously at Abby, apparently seeing that she was none the worse for her conversation with Mason and Della.

"We'll be taking her home with us, that we will," Marlene assured them. "They've suggested one more night here and we're glad to do whatever is needed for our lass."

Joshua Holt gravely thanked them again and they managed to take their leave, thanking the young policewoman on duty. But as they were about to walk down the hall, Della paused, looking at Mason.

"One minute," she murmured. "I think that we should…"

For a moment, he wasn't sure what she was worried about. Then remembering the fact that Karen had gotten a scalpel and drugs and paraphernalia for bloodletting somewhere, he understood and nodded.

"I doubt seriously that it's the hospital," he said. "But we can never be too safe."

She nodded and turned quickly around. From the hallway, Mason watched as Della spoke to the young policewoman and then to Abby and her parents. She joined him back in the hall, smiling grimly.

"I just thought that necessary."

"Good call," he assured her. "And while Edmund came by here already to see Gwen Barney, I think we stop in there, too."

"Good call!" she returned. "I believe that Gwen's father was due to arrive."

"Edmund told me that he had arrived, and he, too, spent the night."

It was easy enough; Gwen was on the same floor, just in another wing of the hospital. Her condition had been more serious and had required intensive care.

As Lachlan had assured him, they found a policeman seated in a chair by the door and when he nodded for them to go in, they discovered that a policewoman was reading on one of the hospital guest chairs while an older man was next to the bed, holding Gwen Barney's hand.

He quickly rose, seeing them, and introduced himself as Harold Barney, Gwen's father, and they in turn said they were just stopping by to see to her welfare and, of course, if she'd thought of anything else to tell them. Mason winced as the man passionately thanked them for saving his daughter's life—he'd read all about Stephan Dante, the king of the vampires.

"Stupid idiots at that facility, letting him escape!" the man said.

"A few dead idiots, I'm afraid," Mason said. "You can't imagine how devious this man is and, well, sir, honestly, doctors and anyone in law enforcement have to abide by the law."

"Should have shot him right between the eyes!"

The young policewoman in the room cleared her throat. "Sir, we're not allowed to be judge and jury, here or in the United States," she said quietly.

"Where there are laws and there is human knowledge," Barney said. He waved a hand in the air. "My girl had to come here—to Edinburgh—to be attacked by an American monster. It's deplorable."

"And he is a monster," Della said lightly. She smiled, trying to ease the tension in the room. "But! While we're here and because he is a devious monster, we want you to be watchful. Of course," she added, smiling at the young policewoman, "you are truly being guarded by Police Scotland, Edinburgh Division, one of the finest forces I have ever worked with. But this man is devious, so take grave care with anyone who comes in and…"

The young policewoman was up. "I will double-check food and medications," she vowed.

"Thank you. No threat out there that we know of, just…"

"Aye, be safe," the policewoman said.

"You know," Gwen called from the bed, "I am in here!"

She managed with her dry assertion to make them all offer each other grimaced smiles. Della walked over to the bed.

The girl smiled at her. "Thank you and all my watchdogs!" she said.

"Did you think of…anything else that might be helpful?" Della asked her.

"I wish!" Gwen told her. "I heard about the strange events yesterday. The other young lady—they said they couldn't use names on the air—she's all right?"

"She will be all right."

"But the other is dead. I can't help but be sorry for her. It sounds like…" She winced, shaking her head. "How can someone so horrible pretend to be so charming and courteous? That young woman was mentally disabled! Oh, I know that I'm not God, and I'm not horrible, but I think that the punishment given Wallace would be good for him—I wish he could be hung, drawn, quartered and cut to pieces!"

"And I so agree!" her father said.

"Well, we need to get out there," Mason told them.

"Like trying to catch the wind," Gwen murmured.

"Ah, but the wind has been harnessed to serve mankind!" Mason said. "In this case, we need to serve mankind by finding and harnessing him. We'll leave you be. Take care."

"Oh!" Gwen said. "I did think of something!"

"What is it?" Della asked her anxiously.

"Thinking today, my head clearing... Well, he had a contact lens bothering him. And I thought it curious that when he took it out to clean it, that his eyes were brown and the contact was blue. I guess people do want to change the color of their eyes and at the time, I thought nothing of it. But...maybe, I know he's hard to find, but maybe his eye is still bothering him, if that helps you any."

"It may, Gwen, thank you," Mason told her. "It just may. We have people watching footage from cameras all over the city and while it might be hard to recognize him in one of his disguises, they may note someone poking at his eye while sitting at a café or even walking in the streets."

"Any little detail," Della added softly. "And, of course, just be watchful and careful."

"Of course! And we'll be heading back to Ohio just as soon as we can!" Harold Barney assured them.

They smiled, said goodbye and headed out.

"I'd hate to tell him," Della murmured.

"That monsters can and have existed in Ohio, too?"

"Yep." Della glanced at him. "Let's head out. I believe François—with Lachlan—was doing another news conference, doubling down on the warnings out there."

"And maybe Dante will be quiet for a day," Mason said. "He's failed twice."

"But he doesn't know what is going on—not completely, at any rate. We never mentioned Gwen Barney on the news, though there was media on-site so fast and there were so many witnesses when Karen killed herself, he must know that she failed."

"We never really know what he knows," Mason reminded her. "He saw us at the close—he probably saw the ambulance at the close. Whether the news reported anything or not on Gwen's state of being, he may know just about anything."

Della nodded. "I'd like to go back to the close," she said.

"Hoping to find our dead friends and find out if they've seen anything more?"

"Exactly."

"All right. Lunch on the Royal Mile—we'll keep watch while we eat. Then we'll head to the close and see if we can find Boyd and perhaps meet Hamish Douglas." He'd stopped at he spoke, pulling out his phone to text their group about Gwen's description of Dante's eye problem and Abby's assertion that she'd met Karen after Karen's "grandfather" had left the café. He also wrote that they were heading to get a bite to eat, and then back to the close.

Lachlan wrote back that he'd meet them with Edmund and Brianna. Jeanne, François and Jon were just returning from having gotten something to eat, and they were heading to Forensics to see if anything had been found regarding the tools they'd uncovered when they'd discovered the young women at the vaults.

Karen's tools—procured for her, Mason was certain, by Dante.

The Devil's Advocate, Lachlan texted.

Mason saw that Della had quickly put in a question mark, adding So you're the devil's advocate, or…

The Devil's Advocate. Great midday meal. 9 Advocates Close—think you can find it?

See you there, Della messaged back.

"You know, I wanted to make sure that everyone had the tiny bits of information we had, but when it got to Lachlan and lunch…we maybe should have just called!" he said.

Della grinned. "I like it. Sounds like fun. So let's bring up our maps…"

Lachlan and Brianna were there when they arrived. They'd secured one of the outside tables, and though they weren't on the Royal Mile—Mason wasn't sure if it mattered or not—a team of Lachlan's people were watching the activity from cameras all over the city.

"Sorry, not at all sure why, but Devil's Advocate seemed right for the day," Lachlan told them. "Not to mention lovely food."

"Lovely food is fine," Mason assured them.

"It is lovely food," Brianna agreed. "But not to worry. Next time, I'll take you to Angels with Bagpipes!"

"That will be great, too," Della said.

"Now, don't be having more faith in the Irish than a good Scotsman!" Lachlan said. But he grew serious then, asking about the hospital and Gwen and Abby.

"Gwen's dad is fierce," Della said, wincing. "He's down on America—we let Dante escape. And he's down on Edinburgh—it happened here. He wants to go home and to take Gwen home. Will he be able to do that? Abby's home is just Glasgow, but—"

"None of that is up to me," Lachlan said. "I believe we've gotten from them what we can—if Dante is caught and goes to trial here, she'll be needed by the prosecution. But you know how that goes—trials can take a long time."

"Please don't say *if* he's caught. We must catch him," Della murmured.

"And so we must. First…hmm. They have three hundred Scottish whiskeys here, but, alas, we're on duty. To food then." He looked at his menu for a minute and then looked up at Della. "You're hoping to find one of our dead friends? Not to worry, I know that all here are aware that some souls remain."

"I'm willing to bet that everyone on this team sees the dead," Brianna said. "Why else would they have put us together?"

"Well, Edmund was in charge of the investigation in England, Jon Wilhelm in Norway, Jeanne had worked cases in France and François was assigned," Della said. "And, customarily, you don't just start a team investigation by asking others if they speak with ghosts. Because, if they don't—"

"You let them think that you're joking and have a sense of humor," Lachlan advised.

"Sometimes, with a man like Dante at large, it's not easy to have a sense of humor," Brianna reminded him.

"Ah, well, I shall ferret out the truth!" Lachlan said. He grew serious. "Della, I am with you. This is my home, a place I love dearly. I feel as if a monster is at the gate—because a monster is at the gate. Lunch for sustenance, and then…the search."

They ordered, with their waitress terribly disappointed that they were Americans and not trying one of the many, many whiskeys offered. But while they didn't explain what their work was, she understood the concept that they'd come back when they weren't working.

The food was, as Lachlan had promised, very good.

So far, though, he'd managed to avoid the Scottish national dish—haggis. Traditionally, various organs and spices and grains cooked in a sheep's stomach, but, of course, as with all things, different places and people had their own variant.

When Lachlan had suggested he try it, Mason had smiled and said that the chops looked delicious.

Edmund, having just arrived, had gone for fish and chips along with Della.

It was when they were just finishing that Brianna turned to Della and said, "You seem to know Dante better than anyone else. Just from an interview?"

Della looked at her plate for a minute. "He had young women hostage in a cabin on the bayou. We devised a plan where he'd find me…and take me to them."

"We were all close, all connected with ear buds," Mason said.

"But you...spent time with him. Is he brilliant—or crazy?"

Della let out a breath. "Yes, both. I have never seen such an extreme narcissist before. Did he have a bad childhood? Yes—but no worse than many others. He learned in school that being brilliant brought rewards. And when he wasn't receiving what he thought he deserved, he devised new ways to get it. Through all this, he learned to use charm when it was necessary, to use bribery when it would acquire his desired ends, and... our coworker Patrick, who is an agent and a psychiatrist, says that the power he has is akin to that of a cult leader. At first, a picture may be so beautiful you can't help but reach for it, and then you realize what will happen to you if you don't keep reaching. Also, through his many years, he has, of course, enlisted other men and women who are simply as criminal as he. Somewhere along the line, he began to love to kill. But while he prefers his killing to be an art, he will kill anyone in his way."

"But he can't stay invisible. He has his failings, like every man," Mason said.

"But he really wants to kill Della!" Brianna said.

"And I'm willing to bet that he'd just love to kill Mason, too—with no fanfare. Mason shot his hand," Della said. "That's another reason I'm curious now. I'm wondering how well his hand and wrist recovered. Lots of tiny bones. But, of course, as we've seen in Karen and our young hacker, he finds the people he needs. Sometimes, he convinces them that he's real, that he can give them eternal life with all power on earth. Sometimes, he pays them."

Brianna shuddered. "We all know he's here now. I have to admit, if I were you two, I'd be back in the States, grateful another law enforcement agency had to deal with him."

Della shook her head. "First, catching monsters is what we do. Second, there's no peace in wondering at what point in your life you have to be looking over your shoulder."

"Then again, that's every day in law enforcement," Edmund commented. "And, of course, you people have it worse—it's still the wild Wild West over there in America. Everyone—and everyone's mother—has a gun."

Mason shook his head. "We aren't political. I don't make laws, I uphold them. Most people don't care if others have a gun for home protection or to hunt— they hate it like hell that getting one can be so easy and they don't understand why any peaceful citizen needs a semiautomatic. But again, we make a fine point of staying out of politics. Dealing with monsters is enough."

"Agreed!" Brianna said, lifting her glass of tea. *"Sláinte!"* she said, offering up a typical Irish toast.

"Sláinte agatsa!" Lachlan replied, lifting his glass.

"What he said!" Edmund agreed, lifting his glass as well, as did Mason and Della.

"She really said it the Irish way, but… Scottish Gaelic, Irish Gaelic, not that far apart," Lachlan said with a shrug. *"Sláinte*—'health.' *Agatsa*—'to your health as well.'"

"And may we truly all keep our health!" Brianna

said. "So we're going to the close and wynds where Gwen Barney was found, barely alive," she said.

"We're going, you're not. I'm getting you back—"

"Lachlan, please. I'll stick to you like glue, I so swear!" she told him.

Mason understood them both and he decided to step in.

"Brianna, we know that you're as passionate about stopping Dante as the rest of us. But we've all been through training. Would that save our lives at all times? No. But if we're worried about your safety—because you haven't had the training—then we'll be risking ourselves more. Does that make sense?"

She nodded. "Just please…if anything… Let me be the first to know. I'll go back and start searching all the live cams we've managed to get feed from."

Lachlan softly said, "Thank you."

Mason wasn't sure if it was said to him or Brianna or both.

"And we're armed," Della said quietly.

"Of course," Brianna murmured. She frowned. "Do you think he's running around Edinburgh with a gun? How would he get one? Not on a plane…and they aren't easily available here."

"No matter the law, criminals will find a way," Mason said. "I seriously believe that he came here before he started his killing spree—theory, yes, but a good one, I think. He may have even known Karen before—possibly visiting her at her facility when she was seeking treatment because they encouraged visits from friends as a way to fight depression. And while he was here or in the UK before, he might have found a way to get hold of many weapons—and his blood-letting equipment—and then stashed them back then. We can expect absolutely anything from the man."

"Absolutely anything," Della murmured. "He combines so many terrifying qualities—as I said, he is a narcissist to an extreme. He believes he is owed the world, he is brilliantly cunning, can take on any guise and can oddly revert to what I felt was a schoolboy pique."

"So we stick together," Mason said firmly.

"Together," Edmund echoed.

"Time is wasting!" Lachlan said as they heard the boom of the cannon that was fired every day—except for Sundays, Good Friday and Christmas Day—sounding the one-o'clock hour. "All right, then. We are paid up and all set. On our way. I'll get Brianna back and catch up," he told the others.

They split, going in different directions. As they walked, Della turned to Edmund. "Oh! I had meant to get online and see how François managed the press conference."

"He did brilliantly, of course, gracefully dodging questions he didn't want to answer, carefully warning our populace to be careful in the extreme—and on the lookout. We've set up a tip line, but, as you can expect, it's already being bombarded and some people think that Dante is everyone from the postman to one of their in-laws."

"And he well might be," Della said quietly.

"Well, not a father-in-law a woman has known for years," Edmund said, smiling.

They reached the close that led to a turn and then an

angle downward against the wall where they had come upon the low courtyard and then the stairs that led up and down into darkness. They heard Lachlan shouting for them when he arrived, and he joined them.

"This really is underground, eh?" Lachlan murmured. "So many times, they build over what was there already. This ground allows for it because, of course, volcanoes formed the region. If you get into geography, the British Isles floated around a bit before man arrived, but then... Never mind! Geography is not my shining talent."

Della was frowning. "There's someone here," she said softly.

They all tensed before she added, "It's Boyd. Boyd Breck. I thought he might be keeping his vigil here. Boyd!" she called.

The ghost stepped out of the shadows, coming toward them, studying them all.

"Della, lass, and friends," Boyd said.

"All looking for the monster," Mason said.

Boyd nodded. "Strange activity here," he said. "Come, I'll show you."

They followed him to an extremely narrow wynd. The path led to an archway. Through the archway, they discovered a tiny room.

Mason didn't think that he'd have ever found the strange bit of brick dividing the wall at the rear of the room. Nor would he have known to press it if it weren't for the ghost.

"There. A group of young lads came down here late last night," Boyd told them. "I followed, and of course, they were up to no good, the lot of them. They were smoking the weed, they were. But I noted one of them seemed a bit older and I saw him…here. Now, I can't be doing it m'self, but give the brick there a solid push!"

Mason stepped forward to do as the ghost had said.

The brick gave way, pushing back to expose a canvas sack, the kind available at grocery stores, or markets here in Edinburgh.

He opened the bag.

"Supplies for our monster," he said, looking at the others. "Needles, tubes…medical bags. Dante does have a supplier, right here in the city."

"Well, when he comes for this, he will wonder what has happened," Lachlan said. "We'll get it to Forensics right away. Maybe they can find fingerprints or DNA. If we can get close to one of his associates, we might be able to get close to him."

"We'll need to watch the close *closely* now," Della said. "Because he will come for this!"

"Twenty-four-hour surveillance," Lachlan promised. He looked at the ghost of Boyd Breck. "We are in your debt. Truly, we are grateful."

"I will be grateful when this war is over, and grateful for the living serving now," Boyd told them. "I, too, will keep watch. You will know where to find me."

Mason felt the vibration of his phone. He was surprised that it was working beneath the ground as they were, and when he drew it out, the connection was fading.

But he could see that the call was coming from Brianna and was probably to them all.

"We need to hear this," he said, "heading up!"

Della was close by his side as he nodded his thanks

to Boyd as well but hurried back along the path, seeking a connection.

He was still in the close when he saw that he was out of the dead zone. He quickly read the text that Brianna had sent.

"Forensics department was finally able to trace the make and model of the scalpel that Karen used to kill herself. They were sold to an area hospital—where Abby and Gwen are now."

He looked at Della.

Edmund and Lachlan were coming up behind her.

"We've got to get to the hospital, fast!"

"What…?" Lachlan began, but he was studying his own phone.

He looked back at them after reading the message, shaking his head.

"Police are there. Dante may be getting supplies somehow, but the women are protected, double guarded. Dante couldn't just walk in—"

"Not Dante," Della said. "Someone who could pose as a nurse or an orderly or even a doctor. Someone he has threatened or bribed, or perhaps even paid. Call your people, Lachlan, warn them. No one comes in, no one gives them anything, and let's get there, please!"

Lachlan moved with the speed of light, leading them out as he spoke on the phone. He spoke quickly and curtly to a policeman at the hospital, and then to Dispatch.

They needed a ride.

It was amazing just how quickly he got them to their destination.

Mason just prayed that they were in time.

Ten

"Gwen's room, Abby's room," Della murmured as they reached the hospital. But she paused and turned to Lachlan.

"We need to be discreet about what we're doing—"

"My officers have known that," Lachlan assured her. "So we split, two to Gwen's and two to Abby's?" he asked.

Della looked at Mason and let out a breath, speaking quickly. "I'm thinking one and one and that the others need to be casual, speak with the staff, find out if they've seen anyone new. I'm afraid that if Dante does have an accomplice at the hospital or someone who knows the workings of the hospital and has slipped in, he'll kill someone else because he won't want Dante killing him—or her," she said.

"Right," Lachlan said. "I'll do staff, Edmund can help me." He turned to Edmund and added, "These two already have a rapport with Gwen and Abby."

"Fine by me," Edmund said.

"And so we go!" Mason said. He glanced at Della

and she knew that he didn't like splitting away from her even here—even in the hospital with so many police on duty and moving about as well.

But he knew that they needed to split. And he knew that they worked because they were both careful, did have one another's backs—and knew when they had to move.

They did. At least Gwen and Abby weren't on different floors. When they reached the floor, Mason said, "Gwen."

"Gwen. Good, you get the vindictive dad and I get Abby's parents, who are lovely!" she said.

"Oh, wait!" he teased.

"You called it!"

He made a face at her and went in his direction. She hurried on to Abby's room. Two officers were in the hall and greeted her and she asked about the care that Abby had received that morning—if anything unusual had happened and if they knew or had seen the hospital personnel with her before.

Abby had been seen by the doctor who had been with her the day before, and the only nurse who had been in had been the same nurse she'd had the day before as well.

"I believe they're planning on discharging her this afternoon," one officer told her. "The doctor wanted to assure himself that her system was cleaned out and check with Mackenzie to see if it was all right for her to leave with her parents."

Della thanked them and hurried on in.

Abby was sitting up and smiling. Her parents were

in chairs on either side of the bed. They rose to greet Della, asking anxiously, "Anything?"

Della smiled. "We keep following leads. I'm afraid we don't have him yet."

"But you're here for something," Marlene Holt said, glancing at her husband.

"Maybe, maybe not," she said cheerfully, but she paused and shrugged. "I understand you might be leaving later today or this evening."

"Home to Glasgow," Marlene Holt said. "If the police think it's safe!"

"It will be safe," Joshua Holt said firmly. "I have friends with a private security firm. We'll hire our own since... Not to be offensive, but since the police seem incapable of catching one man, well, I shall be taking things into me own hands!"

Della managed another smile. "You can never be too safe."

From the bed, Abby spoke up. "I would have said that it was possible to be *smotheringly safe*, but...now, if Dad wants a guard on me day and night, I'll be fine with it!"

Joshua looked at his wife. "Marlene, luv. I do trust this lovely lass who saved our girl. Perhaps we could—"

"Della, can you stay a wee minute?" Abby asked. "He doesn't care for the tea or the coffee they have on the floor and there's a café—"

"I will be here!" Della promised.

"Thank ye, lass!" Joshua said. "Marlene?"

"We'll not be long," Marlene promised.

"I have time—we're fine," Della assured them.

When they were gone, she smiled at Abby and took a seat by her bed, facing the door to her room.

"What's really going on?" Abby asked her.

Della shook her head, but she decided that telling Abby exactly what they were afraid of was better than accepting whatever reaction she might draw.

"Seriously, we may have a problem," Della told her. "Very smart forensic people discovered that this hospital received orders of the scalpel Karen used on herself."

"And so…you think someone who works for the hospital is involved?" Abby asked.

"Maybe and maybe not. Maybe just someone who knows their way around this place. Honestly, it's probably Gwen Barney who is in greater danger, but I'm afraid that the media captured the events when Karen stabbed herself in public, and the killer most probably knows that she failed with you and so… Well, we just want to be extremely careful."

"Thank you!"

"Of course."

"Should I leave the hospital?" Abby asked worriedly.

"If the doctor and Lachlan say that you are discharged, and they see to it that you're safely home, it might be the right move. Police Scotland, Glasgow Division will take over, along with your dad's private security. I think that will be fine."

Abby leaned back. "What if you never catch him?" she asked miserably.

"Oh, Abby, I promise you, we will catch him."

"Please, please, catch him before others die!" Abby said.

"Oh, Abby, we are doing everything in human power to do so, I swear!" Della promised her.

Abby looked up again. "Of course, forgive me." She

smiled. "My dad is overprotective as it is in life! Though now...oh, Della, I'm so scared!"

"And that's understandable."

The door opened and one of the officers looked in, staring at Della.

"A nurse to see to Miss Holt's IV," he said.

The way that he was looking at her, Della knew that this was a nurse that he hadn't seen before.

The nurse entered the room, a young man with a good smile, soft brown hair falling a bit over his forehead but netted in the back.

His scrubs were right. The fresh bag he carried for her intravenous appeared to be legitimate.

"Fresh saline, lass, get you all hydrated just right," he said to Abby. "Excuse me, miss," he said to Della. "If you could give me a minute?"

Della rose, but she didn't leave the room. "Saline?" she asked.

"Yes, she's been receiving saline, helps flush the toxins out of the body!"

"I don't think so," Della said.

"Pardon, miss, but—"

Della swiftly grabbed the bag from him, asking for his identification.

"My badge! You see my badge on my shirt. I'm— I'm Jenson Ledger, and if I don't do my duties, you'll be giving me quite a problem with my superiors!" he protested.

He hasn't remembered the name on his badge! Della thought. *That means that somewhere there's a real Jenson Ledger, and this man has done something with him and taken his identification.*

"We'll call your superiors right now," Della told him, heading toward the hospital phone at Abby's bedside.

"No!" Abby screamed.

But Della had known that he was behind her. She swung around, catching him with a blow to the chest before he could get his hands on her.

He cried out in pain, falling back. One of the officers was quickly in the room, cuffing him, and Della said, "I'll call Lachlan—"

"On his way, mum, on his way. Garson called him when we let the fellow in. We did so knowing who you are, of course, and thought it best—"

"We caught him in the act," Della said. "Thank you." As she spoke, she approached the man who was now cuffed and staring at her with hatred.

"Where is the real Jenson Ledger?" she demanded.

"I am Jenson Ledger!"

"No, you're not. You couldn't even remember who you were supposed to be before. The real Jenson Ledger wouldn't have needed to read his name badge," Della said. "Tell me. Where is he? Let's pray he isn't dead. That will be all the worse for you."

The man tried to spit at her; she stepped back quickly. The officer was outraged, about to wrench the man violently about, but Della lifted a hand.

"No, it's all right. He's a lackey. He's not capable of hurting us, but I guarantee that bag is filled with something other than saline. I ask again—where is the real Jenson Ledger?"

"I don't care what you do to me! My master will rescue me!" the man cried suddenly.

"More likely, you're safest with us—I know your master and he kills those who fail him," Della informed him.

Lachlan arrived as she spoke, staring at the man, looking at Della and his officers, and asking, "Abby is fine?"

"Abby is fine!" Abby called from the bed.

"And these fellows played it magnificently with me," Della assured him. "We need the bag of 'saline' analyzed, and he's stolen a real nurse's identity. He won't tell me where he is, Lachlan," Della said.

"It will go all the worse for you," Lachlan told the man in cuffs. "We will find him. Staff and police are already on a search. Help us, lessen the time you'll be locked away!"

"You don't understand! You can lock me up with a million chains. My master can break them all! He is immortal and stronger than anyone—"

"No," Della corrected. "He's only as strong as the pathetic fools who fall for his lines. Where is Jenson Ledger?"

Lachlan's phone buzzed and he drew it from his pocket, answering quickly. He listened, smiled and told their culprit, "We don't need your help. We've found Ledger. And you...well, you won't see bars for a bit. We're going to need to have a good conversation with you. Didn't you hear? Come now, you must have seen the news! A lass killed herself yesterday rather than face the wrath of your master, and you are such a failure!"

"Probably torture him endlessly," Della said. "I mean, what a failure!"

"No, no, I tried!" the man protested.

"But you failed. He doesn't accept failure," Della

said. "Oh, well. Maybe we should let him get to you—worse than anything the law allows us to do. But then if you helped us…"

"They tried to stop the master before! They surrounded the master with iron gates and walls and he lifted his arms and escaped. He will always escape, he is all-powerful and immortal and—"

"That there is the biggest pile of shite I think I've ever heard!" one of the officers exclaimed.

His words caused the man to frown and go dead still. He suddenly looked confused. "But…he did escape! He told me—"

"That he lifted his arms and the gates and the walls fell away?" Lachlan asked skeptically.

"He is the immortal king!" the man said weakly.

"No, he threatened and coerced and bribed—and killed—people. People like you. That's how he escaped," Della said flatly. She moved forward, warning Lachlan, "Abby's parents are coming down the hall."

"Get him out of here, please," Lachlan told his officers. "Bring him to the interrogation room at Euro-house. Don't leave him for a second."

"Aye, sir!" the man who had cuffed their culprit said.

Della thought that the man might scream and protest as he was dragged away.

He did not. He went quietly.

But too late. Joshua and Marlene came into the room, demanding to know what had happened.

"I don't know what the bloody hell went on here, but my lass is coming home!" Joshua said. "Please, sir!" he said to Lachlan.

"Mr. Holt, she was safe here, because we are here,"

Lachlan said. "But I've spoken with the doctor and the Glasgow police. You may take Abby home. There will be an officer in front of your home until Stephan Dante is caught. You'll make sure that he or she and your private security are aware of one another at all times. One of my officers will leave the hospital with you and drive with you—a car will follow."

"Yes, and thank you, sir!" Joshua said. He looked at his wife, and then at Della.

He suddenly turned and hugged Della tightly. "Thank you!"

"Of course!" Della said, wincing and smiling at once as she gently disentangled herself. "Of course!"

"Now, get out there and get him!" Marlene ordered.

"Wait!" Abby called.

She hopped out of her hospital bed, but she was still attached to her intravenous—one that was delivering the last of a real bag of saline into her system.

Della moved to her and accepted another hug, telling Abby, "Thank you, and be safe!"

After that, she managed to hurry out of the room, leaving Lachlan behind to set up for her safety.

"At least we have someone alive, someone who has been in touch with Dante," Mason said, looking at Eurohouse as he and Della exited the police car that had brought them back. Edmund would be shortly behind them, along with Lachlan.

The man—real identity still unknown—waited inside for them to question him. His fingerprints had been taken. They expected that he'd be in a system somewhere and were just waiting for Forensics to get back with them.

Mason glanced at Della and smiled.

"I was okay the whole time!" she assured him. "The officers were right on it. If I hadn't been there, they would have stopped him. They knew he wasn't usual staff."

"He didn't try to clock you?" Mason asked her.

She shrugged. "He did. Abby screamed. But I knew he was behind me."

"Idiot didn't know not to tussle with a girl who went through every kind of training known to man?" he teased.

"He is an idiot. Maybe I shouldn't say that. I'm thinking mentally impaired, or perhaps the victim of abuse... He wants desperately to believe in Stephan Dante. Maybe he feels that God failed him and his only choice was looking in the other direction. Whoever he is, Dante should have kept him as a supplier and not expected something out of him that he wasn't able to do."

"But he would have done it, Della," Mason told her. "Pretending to be a nurse and changing an IV bag isn't like having to stab or shoot someone. It would have been murder, but not the kind where you have to look at a victim and get violent. We'll never know, my love, because, thankfully, you stopped him."

She smiled, but her smile faded. "That's what I'm afraid of."

"What?"

"I'm afraid that Dante knows a way—always—to get his hands on weapons, even in the United Kingdom. And I know you worry about me, but seriously?

Mason—you shot him. If anything, he's going to try to shoot you in cold blood."

"He's too busy keeping his identity secret," Mason told her.

"But if he's cornered—"

"He's going to try like hell not to get cornered. We have to start outthinking him. And maybe this follower of his can help us in that direction. He knows you— he doesn't know me yet. I think I should start—you'll know when to come in."

Della nodded.

They didn't have to key in the code at the gate; an officer had been standing on the porch and he hit the button by the door that allowed them to open the gate.

The officer nodded grimly as they reached the house, telling them, "He's in there with Officer Mulvaney."

"Thank you," Mason told him.

They entered the house and Della walked into the observation room while Mason walked into their small interrogation setup, aware that she'd be watching—and that she'd instinctively know when to join him.

"Oh, now they send in the big bloke, eh? No more the smaller lass, eh?"

Mason studied the man at the table before thanking Officer Mulvaney, who had been standing like a statue against the wall in the little room, arms crossed over his chest.

The officer nodded and left.

Mason looked at the young man, still in scrubs, sitting at the table. He was young, in his early to mid-twenties, hair a little wild over his head for a nurse, but otherwise, few people would be the wiser, seeing him walk into a room as if he belonged there.

"I am the big bloke, though personally, I wouldn't tangle with the smaller lass myself."

"A few kilos of pure wiry muscle, eh?"

"Something like that. So what's your real name?"

"I'm Jenson Ledger—"

"Oh, come on, stop with that. The real Jenson Ledger was found on the floor of the supply room where you left him. Oh, and be grateful. He's going to live. Now, you may still be charged with accessory to murder—"

"I didn't help anyone kill anyone!" he cried.

"You supplied equipment that was used in a murder—and attempted murders," Mason said, taking the seat across from him at the little conference table in the room.

"No, no, no. Do they charge the gun manufacturers with murder when someone is killed?" he demanded. "No, no…"

He sat back suddenly and said, "Doesn't matter. He will rescue me."

"Oh, please," Mason said. "If he were to rescue you, he'd only do it to kill you."

The man looked down. He wasn't sure at all.

"So how did you meet Stephan Dante?" Mason asked.

"Stephan Dante?"

The man was truly confused.

"Your master. What did he call himself when he met you? And when did he meet you?"

Frowning, the man said, "He's just…Master. I—I don't remember when. Maybe a month ago…maybe more! But he—he was magical! He told me to quit tak-

ing the stupid pills they had me on…pills that made me
feel like a zombie! He taught me that…"

His voice trailed.

"He taught you what?" Mason pressed.

The man was silent for a minute.

Mason leaned forward. "You need to understand this,
and I know that you're uncertain now and that you must
listen very carefully. Help us. That's your only help. Your
so-called master doesn't accept failure and he's aware
that when failure happens, he's at greater risk. His way
out of that is to make sure he leaves no witnesses—he
kills those who would have helped him. So. We can help
you. Just as we kept Abby safe from you, we can keep
you safe from him. But you must help us."

The door opened and Della walked in, taking the
chair next to Mason's and looking at the young man.

"Mark Hudson," she said quietly. "Mason, we do
need his help, and we need to help him in return. Mark
saw his father strangle his mother when he was ten.
He has never been able to make friends and his living
relatives were on his mother's side and thought that he
might be a horrible human being—that's the way they
saw his father. Mark! You don't have to take on the
sins of the past. Mason, he has a record, but only because of petty thievery. There is a chance that you can
have a life, Mark. Real help, not just like the help you
received from a pill pusher. I'm afraid that you will do
some time for stealing from the hospital— Oh, Mason,
he never worked for the hospital, he was a deliveryman
and drove a truck, and just helped himself to supplies as
he unloaded. And, of course, he studied the hospital."

She looked hard at the man she had identified as

Mark Hudson. "He knew the hospital because he spent a few days there when he attempted suicide, an act that was really a cry for help, but then, as happens, he slipped through the system. Mark, we know all about you. We even understand how a man like Dante was able to offer you something that you never had—a purpose, a purpose that would offer you a life and friends. He was your 'master,' but he was your friend. And he promised you much more."

Mark Hudson leaned back, wincing as if he was in extreme pain.

"Where do you meet him? Where do you leave the supplies that he wants?" Mason asked.

Mark Hudson winced again and sighed.

Della answered for him. "He leaves whatever his 'master' asks for down in the close. Now, things could go two ways. Maybe Dante didn't see us, maybe he'll go get the last supplies you left him behind the brick— and believe that you failed him there, too! Then again, maybe he saw us, and he won't go back into the close and try to see what's behind the loose brick. Either way, you have really not done what he's asked of you, and knowing him—oh, and trust me, I do know him—he won't want to just kill you. He'll want to torture you and drink *your* blood."

"Mark!" Mason added. "We can and will help you. We will keep you alive, and while you face charges, we can see that you are really helped and that the charges are as lenient as possible. You haven't asked for legal help but we will get it for you!"

"Please, help us," Della said very softly. "Mark, when he kills people, they are gone. They suffer, their families suffer, and they don't get any kind of immortal life, it's all just brutal and painful. Please, please, we need you. I know that you've suffered, and truly, we're so sorry. But don't hurt others. Please, help us and help them."

"I…" Mark Hudson leaned forward, his head in his hands, and he sobbed.

Mason glanced at Della and he knew, as she did, that they needed patience.

"Would you like water, some tea, some coffee?" Della asked gently.

He nodded. "Water," he managed.

Della rose. But as she reached the door and opened, Mason saw that Lachlan was there, ready to hand her a glass of water.

She took it silently and set it before Mark before taking a seat again.

"You have to get me far, far away!" Mark said at last. "Where he can't get me!"

"We will keep you safe, I promise," Della said gently.

Mark nodded, wiped his face and took a long sip of the water. Then he winced and began speaking.

"I have no concept of time, really. I met him here, at a pub. I'd seen him the night before, sitting at the bar. The night before… I couldn't help but notice that people—people seemed to flock to him so naturally. Lasses flirted, trying to get near him, blokes joked, bartenders wanted to serve him. I—I wanted to be like him. And he cared! He listened to what had happened to me through the years and I told him about the times I'd gone for help…about the pills I was taking. And he said that was wrong, the pills were just keeping me down and when I said that I wanted to be like him, he told me that I could be, but that others in the world didn't understand, I would have to swear an oath of secrecy. He explained to me that most people didn't understand. Then… I didn't see him for a while, but then, at the same pub, in the afternoon, I saw him again—I had stopped for lunch while I was on my rounds. I was thrilled to see him, a friend who wanted to talk to me, and as we talked, he told me that he was the king of the vampires, and when they'd tried to lock him up, he'd proven it, closing his eyes…escaping. People didn't understand that when he took the women he bled, he was giving them a different plane of life, way better. Drinking blood would cure my soul, do more for my brain and my being than any stupid pills. All I had to do was help out with a few supplies now and then and he would provide all that I needed, that in time, I would become immortal like him. If people just understood, he told me, they would all want to be with him, to let him drink their blood, to become…strong! Live forever, with friends, with strength. And I…"

"You…?" Mason prompted.

"I told him that my truck was right outside, I could get him a few of the things he wanted right then and—and I did. And he told me he'd need more, and that there was a loose brick in a tiny wynd off a close…"

"And that's where you were to leave him more supplies," Della said quietly.

"Yes. And…I still don't know, I mean…is he a vampire?"

"No. He's a man who enjoys killing and getting others involved in his murders," Della said. "But we understand—you believed him because you needed to," she said softly.

"Maybe," he whispered.

"When did he tell you to kill Abby Holt—and Gwen Barney would have been next, right?" Mason asked.

Hudson nodded. "He told me… He told me that while it would take them longer to reach his special plane of existence, they would get there. And I wouldn't have to hurt them—he seemed to know that I couldn't… um, stab someone or smother them or… I don't know. He said they'd just go to sleep and start their journey. They were special because he had chosen them and they would get where they needed to be if I just helped him."

"Thankfully, you didn't kill them," Della said, her voice encouraging.

He nodded.

Mason glanced at Della. They'd stopped one "supply train." But there had to be others, others, like Karen, who might not be squeamish at all about bloodletting.

Hudson seemed to respond to Della's gentle touch. He nodded at her, a sign that she should keep going.

"Dante gave you friends, right?" she asked.

His head was down again. He nodded. "I told you, people—people liked him. And the lasses… I never went out, but Dante said he was grooming a few for me."

"But you hadn't dated anyone yet—and he hadn't asked you to drug and bleed anyone yet?" Mason asked, keeping his voice as low and even as Della's.

Hudson shook his head. "No, he said that he'd been telling people about me. He was just back and he'd see to it that a lovely lass was on my arm soon enough."

"When did you last talk to him?" Della asked.

"The night before last. Night, early morning, some-time in the wee hours. We…met in the crypt in the close."

"Crypt?" Mason asked.

"Oh, right…the crypt was his secret. So many things were built over it through the years… There's a—a place in the wall where the top is open right near the loose brick, and if you crawl over, you're…in an old, old crypt. Maybe during the plague people used it… The master…um, Dante…said it was his secret. There was a church there at one point, but, you know, as churches or congregations get bigger, land is deconsecrated and the church moves and sometimes I guess they got their dead and sometimes they didn't. Dante loves the crypt. He told me…for a vampire, it was home. He was excited by the fact that there were no records that described it—maybe they tried to move their congregation and didn't have the money to take the dead…who knows? But Dante said we needed to keep watch, it was a matter of time before an archeologist or historian from some-where discovered it. That—that's where I met him." He was moving his forefinger on the table as he spoke, as if seeing the crypt in his mind and making a mental map of the loose brick—and the crypt.

"This is incredibly important, Mark," Della said. "Do you know of any specific friend who might have been helping him, supplying him with things he might need?"

Mark was silent, thoughtful.

"One bloke seemed a bit of a tight mate. I met him just briefly."

"Do you know his name?"

"Angus."

"Angus…what?" Della asked.

Mark shook his head. "I don't know. I swear, I don't know."

"Do you think you could describe him to a sketch artist?" Mason asked.

"I could try. But…" He stopped speaking, looking from one of them to the other. "Can you really keep me safe? You say he isn't a vampire. But…he has a strange power. A strange power over people. It's so very hard, almost as if he touches someone…they become part of him."

"But not really," Della said firmly. "You're not part of him. You have yourself back now, and we're going to keep you safe." She rose, looking at Mason. "We'll see to it that we get you something to eat, and then a few of the officers will see that you are kept safe!"

He nodded. Head down, he murmured, "Thank you."

"Thank you," Della told him. "And the officers will see that you get legal help," she assured him.

He looked up at her, much as a beaten puppy suddenly given a treat.

"Thank you," he said again. She nodded and headed for the door.

Mason followed Della out, smiling grimly at her. "You were really kind to him."

"Mason, he's a mess."

"A mess—willing to kill two women."

"To bring them to a higher plane," Della said. "Yes, he's a mess. But I don't think that he's evil, and with the right help—"

"Not drinking blood," Mason said dryly.

"Real help!" she said. "With the right real help, he may one day get to have a life."

"He will do time."

"Yes. But he will do time with help, I believe," she said. She stopped just outside the door and turned to him.

"He's so broken, Mason. And, of course, I always wonder…can broken like that be fixed? Sometimes, yes, but sometimes, I wonder if people are just so broken that they turn into men like Stephan Dante."

"There's something in Dante that is far more than just broken," Mason said. He gave her a real smile. "Mark Hudson isn't a narcissist. He's squeamish—and I don't think he's really all that sorry that we caught him. And there is a chance for him."

"Thanks!" she whispered softly.

Mason nodded as they joined Edmund in the observation room and Lachlan returned with his men to take Mark Hudson into custody, giving them instructions to do as Della had promised—keep him under guard from any, and all, around him except for their known officers and guards, since they knew that Dante could find different ways to strike. He asked as well that a sketch artist be brought in so that they might get an idea of their unknown Angus.

When the officers watching over Mark Hudson were gone with him in custody, Mason said, "Okay, so…let's go find that crypt he's talking about."

"It is night," Lachlan reminded him. "I have the area crawling with police. I hate to think that we brought this Euro team over here to work 24/7 when we do have a competent force."

"Nothing at all against your force—we have found Police Scotland, and the Edinburgh Division, to be one of the best, seriously. But…" He paused, glancing at Della. "His words were like a spur and we're not going to sleep until we find it."

"And how—" Lachlan began.

"He was drawing on the table with his fingers as he spoke," Mason said. "From where we found the brick that moved and gave us our cache of medical supplies, I believe I know where to go."

"He did say by the brick," Edmund reminded Lachlan.

"All right. I'm going to get Brianna searching for someone named Angus who might have a record while she, François and Jeanne are still working together on video footage. Of course, they must all be going blind by now, but… I'll let them know that they can come to the house and eat and sleep when they feel the need."

"Not alone," Della murmured.

Lachlan smiled, looking at her. "Well, François may be the Interpol liaison, but he seems a man who can handle himself and Jeanne is a French detective, meaning he's had himself a wee bit of training, too. So you mean Brianna. And not to worry—you might have noticed that while she is an amazing asset, I keep her off the field."

"Of course," Della murmured. "I'm sorry, of course."

"Back to the close!" Edmund said. "Perfect timing! Dark as night—oh, it is night—and into a dark close with narrow wynds seldom traveled."

"Edmund," Mason began. "If—"

"I am not sitting this one out!" Edmund assured him. "Bring it on, I am eager! That spur that will steal sleep is settled in me as well."

Mason smiled. They headed out, and soon reached the close.

As Lachlan had assured him, the entire area was being heavily patrolled. He spoke with one officer who assured him they were being vigilant, but that thus far this evening, they had seen nothing that seemed suspicious in any way—or anyone who might have been Stephan Dante.

They started into the close, traveling the open area, following twists and turns—heading downward, upward and downward again.

And then into the darkness, and the area of the brick.

Eleven

Della was the first to see the opening that Mark Hudson had described.

It was easy to miss, since the wall there was a stretch of centuries-old brick, so darkened by age that they seemed to run as one, except that...

Knowing what to look for allowed her to see it.

"I found it!" she cried.

A little jump gave her a handhold and she hiked herself up. The wall was thick enough that she could sit at the jagged top—though it was rough and uncomfortable—and shine her light down.

There appeared to be a broken tomb formed from brick in the center of the room, with the walls lined with...

Catacomb-like shelving along the walls.

"This is it!" she said again.

"Wait!" Mason cried.

But she was already leaping down, carefully squatting as she did so, lest she break a leg.

"Right behind you!" Mason said then.

A second later he was beside her, having landed a bit more easily because of his height.

Lachlan and Edmund came down as well. They all flashed their lights around and Lachlan said, "Well, it is a crypt. Here. And...I don't think a tour guide in the city knows about it. I didn't know about it...and it isn't in a single plan or blueprint I've ever seen."

Even with their lights, there seemed to be a haze in the small, confined space. Time had not been gentle here. The "shelves" were composed of old stone, all of it dark and jagged with age. In areas, it had broken through and jumbles of bones and bare bits of fabric or metal remained with the remnants of lives lived long ago.

There was no cover on the bricked tomb that might have been one of many at one time, but now remained alone. Glancing in, Della winced—they had truly found a spot which the finest of Hollywood set designers might not have imagined for the creepiest horror story possible.

She couldn't help but feel a chill herself.

She glanced into the broken stone tomb. The cover had long turned to bits of brick and fallen in upon whatever coffin had existed, now decayed and, like the shelves of bodies, a jumble of bones, a piece of metal here and there, and fragments of fabric.

"So lovely. This is where a vampire hangs out," Lachlan said. "I am going to have to inform the city—this is a site that needs to be appraised by our finest academics. Except..."

"Dante," Edmund said. "If this is where he meets his followers, then..."

"It's been here, untouched, for centuries," Mason

said, grimacing at Lachlan. "Are a few more days going to matter?"

"That I leave to our commissioner," Lachlan said.

"He won't come back here," Della said. "What we need is…"

"Why won't he come back?" Lachlan asked.

"Because he won't keep to one place too long. He knows that damaged people are the ones he can convince to be his followers, aiding and abetting him, but he also knows they're damaged—not trustworthy." She shook her head. "We didn't let out any news about today, but the hospital was on alert, employees know what went down, and you know how that goes—a friend tells a friend tells a friend and then it's huge on social media. But say he didn't know. He knows that someone might slip—might fail him—at any time. I believe that he'll be moving on. What I hope we might find is…something. A clue to who he is using now or maybe even who he is targeting next."

"One way or another," Lachlan said, throwing his light around the tiny crypt, "this is an incredible archeological and anthropological find."

"It's more than that!" Della exclaimed. "Oh, dear God…"

Against the far wall, behind a pile of broken brick and stone, a body lay on one of the low ancient shelves.

But it hadn't been there for hundreds of years…

Just, perhaps, months…

Rats had been at the remains. But a rich swatch of hair remained. Skin still stretched over bone, and clothing, darkened by the very dust of the air, remained almost intact, loose over areas where the body decayed and bone remained.

Her face…

Her face had been gnawed by rats or whatever other creatures the darkness and the close allowed. Spiders had created a world of webs around her.

Della didn't jump when she felt Mason at her side, his hands gently on her shoulders as they both looked down upon the victim.

He had killed her some time ago. In between his early practice kills in the United States and the time when he had begun his murder spree in Europe. And while decay had set in, the coolness of the vault had helped preserve parts of her despite the damage done by rats and more.

She had been a fairy-tale kill. She had been left, bloodless, Della was certain, but lain out in beauty, her hands, with bones now protruding, folded upon her chest.

Della had seen enough. She turned away.

"Lachlan—"

"No signal down here—I'm heading up to call the medical examiner and a forensic team," Lachlan assured her.

"I'll back him, just in case," Edmund said.

The two of them were quickly back over the wall. Della looked at Mason, feeling ill at first, and then feeling her anger grow.

"How he must love this place!" she said, her voice filled with emotion. "And there is something we can now really thank Mark Hudson for. He can't come back here. Dante can never come back here. At the very least, we have taken this much from him."

Mason nodded. "Something…anything. But we need to take so much more from him. Find him and take away his ability to ever do anything like this to anyone—ever again. No matter what it takes."

"Agreed. Lachlan has people on the way. And I don't want to stay in here any longer," Della said. "Give me a boost."

He did, making it easy to crawl up the wall, and jump back down. As she did so, she felt the air change, and looking along the strange little wynd she saw that one of their new spirit friends was on his way.

"Where were you?" Boyd Breck asked worriedly.

Mason leaped down beside her. "Ah, the two of you together," he said. "But—"

"It's an old crypt. You didn't know about it?" Mason asked.

"If I'd known I would have shown you! Ah, but there were long years in this city when things changed and changed again, and…that's how he's disappearing. He knows things that I don't, which is quite sad on me part. Seriously, I do apologize. But I wasn't always about—"

"Not to worry, please," Della told him. "You have done so much for us already. You led us to the brick, we found a cache of supplies, we've surely stopped something evil because of all the help that you've given us."

"Have ye now?" Boyd said. "I am grateful." He shook his head, looking at the brick. "There is surely much more lost to time. My day…so bloody and brutal. I lived to see Robert take the crown. For that, I am grateful. And you must understand the truth of it. Alexander III of Scotland died in 1286, leaving no direct heir, and the nobles of Scotland asked Edward I of England to help them choose a proper leader, and instead, Edward I, who also became known as the Hammer of the Scots and Longshanks, decided that he would choose a king for the Scots of his liking, but that the nobles owed their fealty to him as overlord. They had to bow to him, including the man he made king. In 1292, he set John Balliol on the throne, still commanding everything in Scotland himself. The nobles finally became angry, allied with the French, went to war, went into retreat, John Balliol abdicated and Edward I continued to rule, despite a council set up by Scottish noblemen."

Boyd paused, as if to take a breath, or perhaps to wonder if they cared at all about his speech. Della was about to assure him that she wanted to hear whatever he had to say, but his story was picked up by a feminine voice.

Brianna was coming toward them along with Edmund.

"Then!" she said. "Along came William Wallace, a man who many say, 'loved his country more than his life.' Here's the thing people don't understand now. Bruce wasn't horrible to Wallace and never betrayed him. He just didn't fight with him and they most probably never even met. But remember how affiliated the families of nobles could be—the senior Bruce, our good king's father—fought with Edward I in the Holy Lands. Anyway, 1297 came around, William Wallace began his campaign, Marian—wife or sweetheart, not sure—was murdered by the sheriff when he escaped after sacking a town, and Wallace went back and decapitated the sheriff and roused the people to fight. He went on to soundly beat the English at Stirling Bridge, was made Guardian of Scotland—and made a mistake taking on the whole British army at Falkirk in 1298."

"And Wallace went into hiding at that time," Boyd said.

"I know! Blame it on the English!" Edmund said wearily, giving them a dry smile.

"Well, Edward was a jerk!" Brianna said.

"Okay, hmm…"

Brianna, grinning, ignored him.

"And Edward stamped down hard on the Scots! Oh, he was up against major opposition, but Comyn—the man Robert the Bruce or his men murdered in a kirk for being a traitor or because Bruce was ambitious—"

"I don't know what lay in the man's heart and soul," Boyd interrupted.

"None of us knows another's true motives. But Comyn had taken his men and deserted Wallace on the field, perhaps seeing a battle lost at its start, or to save lives? Well, it's all up to speculation."

"Even with me. A man who fought—and fought," Boyd said.

"So," Brianna continued, "it's believed that Wallace went to France—the Auld Alliance existed between the two countries—seeking help. Some believe he went on to Rome but by 1304 he was back in Scotland, harrying the British. In 1305, a Scottish knight loyal to Edward betrayed him near Glasgow, he was tried for treason—he knew that they would kill him tortuously, but he denied the charge. He said that he couldn't have committed *treason* against Edward because he had never been his subject, never sworn allegiance. That didn't fly. He was then stripped, dragged through the streets, hung, disemboweled, castrated and drawn and quartered with those quarters sent to Newcastle, Perth, Stirling and Berwick while his head was spiked upon London Bridge. Oh," she added, looking at Boyd, "now it is believed that when Robert the Bruce learned what was done to William Wallace, he was beyond furious. All Scots were growing weary of the horror inflicted upon too many by Longshanks' rule—and the taxes they were forced to pay to such an overlord as well. Robert the Bruce might have been tied to a feeling of obligation to old noble and family connections at one time, but after the execution of William Wallace, he was going to be king of Scots—the Scots, as in the people, not so much the land, but the people—or die in the trying for his country!"

"Ah, leave it to an Irish lass to know this history!" Boyd said.

"And then people married people and the royalty of one kingdom became the royalty of another and then another and then…whatever," Edmund said. He shrugged, smiled and looked at Boyd. "Now we all agree Edinburgh is a fantastic and beautiful city and we need to stop real, human and current monsters, like Stephan Dante."

"Aye!" Boyd agreed.

Brianna nodded. "My knowledge of history doesn't help here!" she said. "I knew nothing about this at all and I loved exploring and…oh! A medical examiner and a forensic team will be here any second. Thank God,

and I don't know how they do it. Seeing that body…
does things to my stomach!"

"I shall be a perfect ghost, silent as they arrive!"
Boyd promised.

"I need a lift up," Brianna murmured, looking at
the wall.

"Alas, I cannot help!" Boyd said.

"Here," Mason told her, lifting her by the waist to
reach the opening in the wall.

"Thank you!" From the top, she looked back down
at them. "You're not coming up?"

"I've already been in, thank you!" Della told her.

She had barely spoken when Lachlan came upon
them, nodding to Boyd in a way that gave away nothing about him being there.

He was followed by a young woman who was introduced as Dr. Caitlin Alexander, and Della had to wonder if she had simply been on duty—or if she had been
called in because the position of the body demanded
someone who was agile and could crawl the wall without injury.

She was followed by a team of four from the forensics department, all of whom were introduced—and
then crawled over the wall, passing their equipment
up and over.

Lachlan looked at Della, Mason, Edmund and the
ghost.

"I thought we had long nights before. This one…"

"May well go on forever," Mason said quietly. "I'll
head up and inform the rest of our team—"

"Done already," Lachlan assured him. He glanced
at the wall and shrugged. "Jon Wilhelm, François and

Jeanne are here, speaking with some of the police up on the street. They escorted Brianna—she is sick with determination." He sighed. "We found someone our monster killed—and the crypt is also an incredible historical find."

"It is good when the past is learned and remembered," the ghost of Boyd Breck said quietly. "We all need to learn from the past, from our cruelties to one another. Though I fear you'll not see real peace and caring in your day, either. Perhaps humanity will never see such a day. But it is not a bad thing that we keep hoping." He paused, looking at the four of them. "And it is a good thing that there remain those who fight monsters."

"Thank you, and thank you for remaining among us," Della told him.

Boyd nodded. "If you'll excuse me, I shall see this wondrous—and heinous—discovery myself." He turned and then hesitated and told them, "I will find Margaret and Hamish Douglas and maybe a few others—someone might have known this was here, and they might know of other such places."

"Thank you, Boyd!"

"The medical examiner and the forensic team will be in there awhile," Mason said. "There is nothing else we can do here now."

He was right, of course. Della looked at Edmund and Lachlan.

"Maybe we should head back," Edmund said. "By tomorrow, we will have a sketch of the fellow Mark Hudson said was close to Dante, and we may get some leads on that. Dante will discover that his cache is gone if he hasn't realized that already. And he will know that his personal crypt is gone, and—"

"He'll be furious—he must have truly savored meeting people in that long-forgotten crypt. A vampire, resting in a crypt. What could be better?" Lachlan asked dryly. "I—I need to stay. I'll get the medical examiner's preliminary report and whatever Forensics might be able to give us."

"You can surely get those in the morning, too," Edmund suggested.

But Lachlan shook his head. "I am the face of Police Scotland, Edinburgh Division," he told them. He shrugged. "I'll come as soon as I can. When Dante discovers all this…"

"That his favorite place of death is no longer available to him and he's lost a supply chain?" Edmund asked.

Lachlan nodded.

"He will be furious. He will strike again. We're going to have to hope that his fury causes him to make mistakes—and that we can find him before he finds a new place to kill," Mason said.

"So apparently, Jon, François and Jeanne have headed back to Euro-house, hopefully to get some sleep, maybe having discovered something," Edmund said. "We'll get some sleep, too, and be ready to head out in the morning."

Lachlan nodded. "Go, please. I'll need your team behind me, come the morning!"

They headed out, nodding to the policemen and women they passed on the way in the street. An officer asked if they wished a ride; Della suggested that they just walk.

She pulled out her phone to check for messages since they'd been underground, asking as she did so, "What time is it? I haven't the faintest idea."

The street was busy enough—cars were on the roads and people still walked in duos and groups on the pedestrian stretches.

"It's just eleven," Edmund told her. "Pubs are still open for an hour. Is anyone hungry? We could stop quickly. And since you're going to sleep, you could taste a good Scotch whiskey."

"A nice whiskey could be good for sleep," Mason said. "Della."

She had been staring at her phone. She looked up at the two of them saying, "Check your phones. François just sent through the image the sketch artist created from Mark Hudson's description of the man he knew just as Angus."

They both paused to look at their phones.

If the sketch was accurate, Angus, like Mark Hudson, was young. He was tall, a brunette with hair that had loose curls that dangled over his forehead.

And more.

Della was certain that she'd seen him before.

"What is it?" Mason asked her.

"I believe that he was at a table near us when we were at the pub, Grady Grant's. He appeared to be with two young women about his age. I wouldn't have thought anything of him. He and his friends were eating, shepherd's pie, I think, and drinking beer. I can't be sure—"

"He may haunt Grady Grant's Pub," Edmund said.

"If we're stopping for a bite, we might as well head for Grady Grant's."

"There is a plan," Mason said. "It would be something, wouldn't it? If we just happened to take a table next to a person of interest."

"We do need to eat," Della agreed. "And we can check in with our bartender, Drake, and see if he's seen anyone who might have been Stephan Dante again."

"Would Dante go back there—when he probably knows that Gwen Barney is alive and that she would have told police where she met the man who attempted to kill her?" Edmund asked.

"Oh, he would. He wouldn't look the same. He might go back as he was when he was with his follower Karen as a grandparent figure," Della told him. "That's the thing. I know that our team and the police crews are staring endlessly at video footage, and since Jon, Jeanne and François know this man, they are the most experienced in his many guises and still… We know that he has to be moving around, but none of them have seen him. He is a narcissist to such an extreme, he has no doubts at all regarding his talents to change like a chameleon."

"You would know him, though, right, if you saw him, no matter what his disguise?" Edmund asked her. "After our intriguing foray in Louisiana…"

"Yes. I think I would know him—even in a Santa suit or a character creature in a giant head," Della said. "Well, maybe not anything that severe, but he'd certainly be noted walking around Edinburgh."

"Onward," Mason said. "But I'm going to try to

reach Lachlan and let him know where we're going. He may want to join us if he can finish up."

They waited. Mason's eyes widened with surprise as Lachlan answered the phone. When Mason ended the call, he shrugged and said, "Well, that's good. Lachlan and Brianna will be joining us. Onward to Grady Grant's."

At the door, they were assured that the kitchen was still open when asked for a table for five, but as they were seated, Della saw that Drake was at the bar and that there were a few empty seats.

She walked over, remembering that Dante had once taken on the guise of a bartender.

That made her wonder about Drake, and yet...

He had seemed honest. And as if he wanted, in truth, to be helpful.

"Special Agent Della Hamilton," he said, and he looked truly pleased to see her.

"Hi, Drake," she said, sliding onto a stool for a minute to speak with him.

"I know. You're finally going to try one of our delicious Scotch whiskeys!" he said. He leaned on the bar, shaking his head. "You probably do need one—the tension in the city is palpable."

She smiled. "You know what? I'm here with some colleagues, dinner, but—"

"Dinner? It's after eleven o'clock. At night," he said, grinning.

"Yeah, well, we have some strange dining times," she told him. "But I'm going to go and sleep from here, so I'd love to try a good Scotch whiskey. Your suggestion?"

"Ah, hmm, now that's a difficult one when I don't

really know your tastes, dear lass. Sorry! Special Agent Hamilton."

"'Della' is fine, and 'dear lass' will do just as nicely. Please, anything you suggest."

"Ice? I suggest neat."

"I bow to your knowledge."

He poured her a shot from a bottle he selected off a shelf. "It's a Macallan, a rare one, sherry oak aged—shh! You can't afford it, but it seems Edinburgh can't afford to be without you, so…just…hmm, shh! And we'll keep it to one."

She smiled, taking a sip. She wasn't accustomed to hard alcohol and she wasn't sure if it was delicious, or something that hit her palate like a burning jolt. But she smiled and thanked him, assuring him she could never do more than one.

He grinned at her. "Hits like a brick, eh? But you didn't come up here to have a whiskey or to flirt with me, though the latter would have been quite nice," he said, but then he grew serious. "Did—did you get him? Has anything happened? Please, tell me hasn't…"

"I'm afraid we did find a victim, one who has to have been missing awhile," she said. "But thanks to you and a bit of other help along the way, he hasn't—hasn't another victim now. I was curious as to whether you've seen him again or not."

He shook his head. "Not that… I can't study every customer in here, though, of course, as a bartender, stereotypically, I listen to people's problems and I'm a good observer. Right? But we do get busy. Still, if I saw him as he was that night, I would have known him. According to what I've seen—recapping the press conferences given by a Frenchman with Interpol named Bisset—"

"François Bisset," she said.

"He is with you."

"Integral part of our team."

"Well, he warns that everyone must be wary of strangers, people they don't know—not just men, but women."

"True."

"Then what...?"

"I can't tell you about an ongoing investigation. But we also heard from someone else Stephan Dante met at this pub that he has a friend named Angus. Do you know of someone named Angus who comes in here?"

He leaned on the bar, close to her, grinning. "Do you know how many Scotsmen are named Angus?" he asked her.

She smiled. "Right. Like the name John Smith?"

He glanced down the bar. He was getting more customers. "I will try hard to remember. I can look at credit card receipts, but I can't do it now—"

"If you like and your manager agrees, we can send our technical department in and collect recent receipts," she said.

He nodded. "I'll see to it if you want to come by in the morning. The place is owned by a man named Grady Grant. And Grady will be willing to do all that he can in any way, I assure you. He was horrified and so angry that anyone could hurt such a beloved teacher."

"Thank you, Drake, and our thanks to Grady Grant as well."

"This is my city. Pleased to help in any way, I so swear it, lass. Sorry, Special Agent—"

Della laughed. "It's okay! I like the word *lass*. Makes me feel younger!"

He grinned, she reached for her bag to pay for the drink and he waved his hand in the air, whispering, "You ne'er had a wee drink here! Head to your table!"

"Oh, wait!" she said, pulling out her phone and drawing up the sketch that had been done of the man Mark Hudson had seen with Dante. The man she had seen here, and hoped they might find through the credit card receipts.

"Do you recognize this man?" she asked.

"Sure. He comes in now and then."

"Do you know his name, or have any idea of which receipt might be his?" Della asked.

"He sits at the tables most of the time and he pays with cash. But he comes in kind of regularly—not every day, but now and then."

"And have you seen him with Stephan Dante?"

He grimaced. "Maybe? I'm not always sure who is talking to who, who walked by and said hello in a casual way…maybe."

"Thank you, Drake. If you should see him—"

"Call you. Yes, I have the card, and I will call you right away."

She thanked him again.

"I promise, and for now…you should join your friends."

Della did so. Mason rose and pulled back her chair; Brianna and Lachlan had arrived and she was speaking enthusiastically about the discovery. She smiled as Della took her seat and then said, "I feel so horrible. I can't help but be amazed at such a historic discovery, and yet…"

"The medical examiner thinks she'll be able to tell us much more once there has been a proper autopsy," Lachlan said. "For now…the amount of decay may prevent us from knowing what kind of drugs were in her system, if any, and, of course, the odd way our victim decayed while bits of her were preserved—because of the temperature of the crypt and the enclosure, and then the creatures who took their nibbles upon her—"

"She can't give us anything but an approximation for time of death?" Mason asked.

"So…so sad," Brianna murmured. "And oh! I started searching for men named Angus—"

"But Edinburgh is filled with men named Angus, right?" Della asked.

"It is a common name here," Brianna said. "But we've already got the sketch moving across all news sources, and not to worry, the wording on everything has been careful—we're just seeking him as a possible witness to cases with which we are seeking any help."

"We had to be very careful," Lachlan said. "There is always a crazy person in the room somewhere who might think that us showing a picture of a man means that he is a monster and they might try to take the law into their own hands."

"Of course," Della said.

"We ordered several meat pies, by the way," Lachlan told Della. "Mason said you were easy."

"Easy," Della said dryly. "Great!" She smiled sweetly. "Maybe not quite as easy as him!"

Mason leaned toward her, grinning. "How is our friend Drake this evening?"

She shook her head. "I honestly believe that he'd help us in any way that he could. He's going to verify with his manager and turn over receipts because there are dozens of Scots named Angus, so he may have been in here. I suggested we could do the research on his customers easier than someone trying to set up for a pub. Oh, and he has seen the man that Mark Hudson described for us—comes in frequently, not every day, but now and then regularly. He doesn't know if he saw him with Stephan Dante or not—pubs can get busy. But he will call us the second he sees him if he should see him."

"It sounds as if he truly wants to be helpful. Handsome fellow," Brianna commented. "But hasn't Dante pretended to be a bartender?"

"Trust me, I would know Dante now, that close," Della assured her.

Lachlan leaned in toward Brianna. "You like the bartender, eh?" he teased.

"Seems handsome and charming, and, of course, I'm merely observant," she said sweetly, smiling at Lachlan.

"Oh, good lord, you two!" Edmund said. "Get a room."

"We have two of them," Lachlan said, grinning. "Some people seem to be lucky and they get to share one, which…" He paused. "I was always of the understanding that field agents weren't to be in the same unit or team, but…"

"True usually, but not with the Blackbird division of the Krewe of Hunters," Mason said. "And since we are all 'seers' or whatever anyone chooses to call us with our strange talents, you'll understand."

"Special, yes," Lachlan said. "And, of course… in truth, we're fine, because Brianna and I aren't the same—I'm field and out there, and she's not."

"Different areas—other members of the Bureau are more than welcome to be partners or married as long as they aren't in the same units. I understand," Mason said. "We have to be impartial in the field, saving all life, and if we care more about a loved one…"

"They believe that innocents could die," Lachlan said.

"I believe," Mason said. "But with your unit, or with Blackbird…"

"The thinking there is that it might be worse for partners pretending that they're not getting help from the dead, or for partners to think that they're crazy, or—" Della began.

"Wait. You didn't know about me and we still don't know about Jon Wilhelm, Jeanne or François," Edmund said.

Della and Mason looked at him, and then each other, acknowledging his words.

"I must say, you two were quite the surprise," Della said to Lachlan and Brianna. "And I don't know because Jon and Jeanne were working the cases in their countries when this all began. With François…hmm. I believe that Adam Harrison—the founder of the Krewe—knew of him and selected him specifically."

"Maybe we should just ask," Brianna said.

"And make it be a joke of some kind if they think we're crazy," Edmund suggested.

For all that had happened, dinner began a strangely pleasant event, all of them managing to enjoy talking with one another, laying out the truth in many personal areas.

Edmund told them about the makeup artist in London who had been so helpful as they had tracked down their "Jack the Ripper," and admitted he'd been attracted to her—except that Sean had been more than smitten and he'd stepped aside.

It wasn't easy, doing what they did, being him, and finding someone.

And Brianna laughed and told him that he was even cuter than the bartender, Drake. But she was smitten herself already, and still...

"We have to find you someone to love!" she said.

"No, no, no, no, no!" Edmund groaned. "No, let's solve this thing and..."

"But you need help!" she told him.

"No! No, thank you. When something is right, it falls in," he assured her. "You know, when the right woman comes along, we'll...mesh!"

They finished the meal and Mason asked for the bill, telling Lachlan that Blackbird had to pick up some of their own expenses, as much as they appreciated Police Scotland.

But Della didn't move for a minute. She searched the pub, looking at every face she could see.

Their Angus wasn't there; she was certain.

"Hey," Mason said gently. "We're all exhausted. Let's get some sleep. Tomorrow will be crazier than ever."

She nodded. "Right. Okay."

They left the pub and returned to Euro-house.

"Well, seems our Norseman and our two Frenchmen

are sleeping," Edmund said as they set the alarms and locked up. "But…"

"We do need to just ask them if they have any friends who are ghosts," Della said.

Edmund nodded. "Tomorrow—hopefully, we'll have a good meeting for an early breakfast, and then…"

Mason laughed. "'The truth is out there!'" he quoted.

"So good night," Lachlan said. "And at the least, we have a lead—Angus!"

"Good night," Edmund told him. "Oh, and it's okay. We all know. Get to your room. Just one room, and…" He swung around, grinning at Brianna. "No! No help, okay, I'll solve my own romantic life."

She shrugged and grinned.

Della was smiling as she and Mason walked down the hall, ready to retire to their own room. But she didn't have a chance to say a word once they were in.

Her phone was ringing and she picked it up quickly.

It was Drake on the other end.

"He's here!" Drake said. "He's here—your Angus just walked into the pub!"

Twelve

The rest of their Blackbird team might have been sleeping when they'd come in, but the minute Mason headed out to the hallway, he heard other doors opening.

He quickly explained the situation and Lachlan asked, "Should I get the police to stop him and hold him?"

"No, we'll get back there. Have them observe and follow if he leaves and only accost him if they have to—he may be meeting someone there," he told Lachlan. "We all go back in, but in pairs, just as patrons, looking for a beer or a whiskey. If he's meeting Dante by any wild chance, we'll want to give him time to do so."

"He's seen my face—everyone has seen my face," François said, "when I've done the news conferences."

"Right," Mason agreed. "François, stay back and coordinate anything we get from here. I'll have Drake make sure that you can tap into the security camera—there are two, at least, I saw them tonight."

"Some are just for show," François reminded him.

"I think these are real—one was aimed at the bar

and the till and the other covers the floor. Grady Grant must be an upright citizen. Earbuds, everyone, keep in close contact and François can advise us regarding anything that we can't see from our positions. The rest of us, let's move."

"I can go in with Della, two girls chatting it up after a night on the town," Brianna said.

"Brianna, you're not a trained police officer, your job description is tech analyst," Lachlan reminded her.

"I can help in this situation!"

But Jon Wilhelm cut in. "Lachlan, we'll be back at the pub, surrounded by your officers—at first just observing one man we have no call to detain other than that he's spoken in a pub to Stephan Dante. Two beautiful women just out on the town…almost real, and it was real a bit ago, all of us just having our dinner. Trust me, if there was any danger to her here, I promise you, I promise you, I'd be the first to give you my support. Mason?"

"We should be fine. Brianna, stick to Della—"

"We can try this," Della said. "Brianna and I go in alone. We will have you four behind us, Jon, Edmund, Lachlan and Mason—hanging close. Dante knows us if he sees us, so I'm going to ask for a table on the side in the dark, and then you four can slip in and keep watch from the corners of the room. We'll observe what Angus is doing and, hopefully, be in strategic positions if Stephan Dante does come in." She took a breath. "And don't forget, Dante can look like anything, so study people as you see them."

"Lachlan, I know my position. But I also believe that

I can be a real help now, surrounded by this team and Police Scotland. Please, we need to catch this man!"

"All right," Lachlan said. "And we do need to move, or he'll be gone before we get there."

They moved as a disjointed group toward the pub, talking in their little groups, appearing like any other late-night friends, enjoying the cool, crisp air and the beauty of the Edinburgh night.

Mason and Lachlan moved toward the side of the door, Lachlan leaning against it and Mason telling him, "We'll pause just a minute. Dante isn't in there now, we know—the bartender would have called Della. But he would have called her, too, or your policemen would have called you, if Angus had left the pub."

He could see through the glass in the doorway. Della and Brianna were in, chatting with the hostess, who remembered them.

He didn't know what they were saying, but the smiles on all indicated that Della and Brianna had probably told her that they'd enjoyed the place and just wanted to come back for a few last-minute drinks to chill out before last call.

She led them to a perfect table, to the far side of the bar against the wall. It was a sound position for Della—she could see everything going on in the dining area, at the bar and at the door.

"We're up next—head to the side bar," Mason told Lachlan.

Of course, the hostess recognized them, too. Mason wondered if she wasn't thinking that perhaps one of the couples had maybe gotten into a bit of a scrap after they'd left, but as she looked at him, Mason said, "So, my friend, we've business to discuss and I believe the ladies might be planning a spa day."

"Well, you are our American visitors. We do all that we can!"

"But we don't need a table," Mason said. "We'll grab those bar seats just to the side there. Thank you!"

"Certainly, gents!" she told them.

Mason and Lachlan took their seats at the bar. A young, pretty woman was working now behind the bar with Drake, but he smiled at her, probably said that Mason and Lachlan were friends, and moved around to help them, saying, "The usual, mates?"

"Aye, great!" Lachlan told him.

"In position," Mason said into his earbuds.

"Three fun blokes moving in for a nightcap," Edmund assured them.

And they could hear as Jon Wilhelm walked in talking about the amazing and very cool way the Shetland and Orkney Islands managed to contain so much culture from both Norse and Scottish history, while Jeanne reminded him that the Scots and the French had been allies for years—that Mary, Queen of Scots, had nearly been Queen of France—and Edmund reminded them that he was an Englishman, not to go picking on the English.

Della pretended to smile at something Brianna was saying, responding to her with a message for all. "Our Angus is sitting at a table just behind us, chatting with a young woman. I have studied everyone in here, but there is no sign of Dante."

"Let's just keep our eyes on him," Mason said. "And be patient and wait."

They waited. In their groups, they pretended to laugh and chat, listen and enjoy their shots of good Scotch whiskey.

Drake came back by, leaning casually on the counter and asking, "That is him, right, the man in your sketch?"

"We believe so. And thank you."

"No thanks needed. I want the monster out of my city," Drake said. "I—I have a younger sister. I want a world for her that is safe, which, of course, I guess I can never create, but while I might just be a bartender... Well, I don't overserve, I watch out for the ladies here and I insist on long walks and rideshares when someone comes in tipsy. Aye, my business is selling the whiskey, but I'm rather fond of living, I am, and I work for a man with the same ethic, so..."

"Trust me, Drake, a bartender who cares that people don't die on the roads when they leave and that no one, man or woman, is harassed, is damned valuable in society!" Mason assured him.

"Heads up!"

They heard Della's voice coming through their earbuds.

"Angus's friend went to the restroom," Della said. "We just saw him slip something into her drink."

"We can take him down!" Lachlan said.

"No, no, we need to wait, to see..."

"To see?" Lachlan demanded. "He's spiked her drink! In good conscience, we can't let her drink that!"

"Della, can you do something before she gets back?" Mason asked.

"That I can. Subtle and swift!" Della promised.

Mason could see the tables by the side reflected in a

mirror at the bar. Della murmured something he didn't hear to Brianna, got up and headed to the back table, followed by Brianna.

"Tony!" Della said.

"Um, no, I'm not Tony," Angus said, looking confused.

And maybe just a little worried.

"Sorry—"

"No, I'm so sorry!" Brianna said, pushing just in front of Della—allowing Della to switch her glass of whiskey with the one on the table as she kept the man's attention on her. "So, so sorry, my friend is in from America and she'd met my brother just once and I have to say, you look so much like him! We're so sorry—we didn't mean to intrude." She turned and looked at Della, who smiled; the deed had been subtly carried out. "Ask me next time!"

"Of course, of course, and, sir, I am so sorry!" Della said. "We'll just slink back to our own table now."

"Um, no harm, no foul…nice to meet you. Maybe I'll see you in here again."

"Maybe, when you're not on a date," Della teased.

He turned a little red. "Mates," he said. "We're just friends, pals. Anyway—"

"She's coming back—his date is coming back, let's not cause them any trouble!" Brianna pleaded.

"Right, right, back to our table!" Della said. She offered Angus a charming smile and the two women headed away, making it back as Angus's date made her way to join him again.

"Got it," Della said.

"We should arrest the bloke this minute—since it

would be quite illegal for any of us to give him the strong right to the jaw the bastard deserves," Lachlan said.

"I'm going to slip by and flirt, switch glasses again, and send that one out to one of your patrolmen, Lachlan, get it taken in for testing," Jeanne said.

"Eye out for Dante," Mason reminded him.

"Indeed."

They watched and waited, pretending to chat all the while, as Jeanne approached Brianna and Della, feigning a pleasant conversation and curiosity, then shrugging and leaving.

"Now, that was real, my friends. Pretty women like that wouldn't be wanting an older fellow such as myself, though they might well be sweet and polite," Jeanne said, shrugging as he joined Edmund again.

"You're not that old," Edmund said, shaking his head and grinning.

"Ah, but not a young stud like you, *mon ami*," Jeanne said. "Experienced, extremely dignified and certainly, for a slightly older woman… Well, as you might have noted as we've worked, I do not suffer from inferiority."

That made them all smile, a good thing, because waiting was both tense and tedious.

"You don't want to just take him?" Lachlan asked Mason. "He was drugging her—obviously, his intent is less than honorable."

"I want to know if Dante has turned him into a killer, or if he was supposed to procure her as a victim for Dante, since Dante does know we are on the streets looking for him. And since François has given news conferences with warnings but not describing the victims or whether they lived or died, he certainly knows that we are truly onto him. But...I am beginning to wonder if he'll walk in here or not," Mason said.

From the house, over his earbuds, Mason heard François say, "Watch it—something is happening. There was a crowd outside the door, extremely tall woman just turned—she's heading toward Holyrood. She has her phone out. Long blond hair—nice dress—but it's not a woman, it's Dante, and...he has his phone out."

Mason was already up. He saw that Angus's phone was sitting on the table and that it was ringing. The man answered it quickly, frowning as he did so.

When he finished the call, he set the phone down, scowling as he looked around the pub.

Eyes narrowing as they lit upon Della and Brianna.

"Dante," Mason said, rising.

"Right," Della agreed. "He just warned Angus to get the hell out. Now someone gets to stop him. He's out there!"

Lachlan had given up pretense. He was putting out a call to all officers.

Angus was already out of his chair muttering something to his date.

"Why, you cheap cowardly bastard!" the girl cried.

"We're going to need her," Mason said quickly.

"Right," Lachlan said. "I've got Angus and the girl. Go! Go, get Dante!"

Mason took off running, aware that behind him, Lachlan was already on his way to stop Angus.

No need. Della had been ready.

A strategically placed foot in his path, and Angus went down hard on the floor.

Della stood with Brianna, waiting for Lachlan to come and cuff Angus. Of course, the man protested, he raged against police brutality and fought as Lachlan dragged him to his feet, all to no effect. Lachlan had ethics and his ethics had been severely affronted the minute the man had tried to drug the young woman's drink.

And, coming here, they had, at the least, discovered the plan. Angus was a good-looking young man, too. His job was to find victims, flirt with them, buy them drinks, leave them in a drugged state—and turn them over to Dante.

She heard François muttering through the earbuds. "He shouldn't have tried to be a woman. He was one ugly woman!"

Della almost smiled, but the young woman who had been with Angus was hysterical, wanting to know who he was really and what was going on.

"You're all right, right, lass?" Brianna asked her worriedly.

"I… He was so nice! He asked about my home, said that he loved Toronto, that he'd been several times… Just casual, down-to-earth, so nice!" the girl said.

Her panicking wasn't going to help any. Della glanced at Lachlan and said, "We can pray we have Dante, but… we need to know so much. May we bring them to Eurohouse?"

"We only have the one interrogation room," Lachlan reminded her.

"We won't put her in the interrogation room," Della

said. "We'll just sit with her in the parlor area and talk...
I think she needs to calm down and I don't think there's
that much she can give us. We need Angus in the parlor. And we can pray they get Dante—Mason and a
score of officers and Jon and Jeanne and Edmund are
off after him, too. He is an ugly woman, I imagine—
how far can he get?"

She wished she believed her own words. Dante could
change in the wink of an eye. Of course, if Mason could
get close enough, he'd know the man—no matter what
he was wearing.

But officers might not, and since the city of Edinburgh did offer an amazing nightlife, the streets and
venues were still filled with crowds.

Crowds within which Dante might just disappear.

"We head back," Della told him.

He nodded, lifting a hand and summoning a few of
the officers who had come into Grady Grant's ready
to respond.

"Euro-house," Lachlan said. "The young lady and
Angus here and..."

He paused, looking around. People were mostly out
of the chairs.

The hostess and staff were just standing still, as if
they'd been frozen in motion when the upheaval had
started.

"Get them out!" Della whispered to Lachlan, refer-
ring to Angus and the girl. "I'll deal with everything
here!"

As they cleared out, Della stepped into the center of
the room. "It's all right, everyone, just carry on, please,
police business, but all set now!"

She turned to look at Drake, nodding her thanks to him.

"Drinks on the house!" Drake called.

Amazing. That seemed to set everyone back into motion. But before she could reach the door, a young couple stepped in front of her, pulling their phones out. "Miss! We're vloggers! Can you tell us what was going on here tonight? Seriously, we're both extremely popular influencers and—"

They were raising their cell phone cameras up to her face.

"No! I'm so sorry. Ongoing investigation, no photos or video, please!"

They didn't have to agree. She was nothing if not fast and she slid around them in a second, then realized that Brianna wasn't with her.

She spun around, avoiding the young American vloggers, caught hold of Brianna's elbow and hurried her on outside.

An officer was waiting for them.

Soon, they were back at Euro-house. The girl was sitting nervously on the sofa and Della believed that they needed to start with her—and let Angus worry awhile. François had been sitting with her and he, in his gentle and diplomatic way, had tried to put her at ease. As Della and Brianna came in, he rose and said, "Della, Brianna, I'd like to formally introduce Miss Louisa Blackwood, a student here from Toronto."

"Thanks, François," Della said, indicating that they should all sit again.

Louisa Blackwood was just Dante's type—an extremely pretty brunette with soft brown eyes, young, innocent-looking—a perfect Snow White.

"Louisa, may I use your given name?" Della asked, taking a seat by François.

"I… Yes, of course," Louisa murmured. She'd been crying, and, naturally, she was distraught. "I—I don't understand what happened! I was in the pub with friends a few days back and we met Angus and chatted and when we were leaving, he said that he'd love to see me again, and I told him that none of us were going anywhere except in a group and he—he said we could just come back to the pub and have a drink and talk! Such a nice guy—he told me that he'd just gotten out of university and that he was working for his father who was a sports agent and he was learning how to do a lot of crazy traveling and so… It was nice to have a friend in the city, just a friend, so that when he was home…we could just meet and talk. I wasn't stupid. I didn't intend to leave the pub with him…and… I never… I don't understand, I mean, what happened? Why did he suddenly jump up? Why did you send him flying to the floor, what did he do? We were just sitting there, having a whiskey!"

"You weren't just having a whiskey. When you went to the ladies' room, he drugged your drink, I'm afraid," Della told her.

"What? No, I drank it when I came back and I'm perfectly fine. I don't get drunk—"

"You drank my drink," Della told her.

"What?"

"She switched them before you got back from the bathroom," Brianna said quietly.

Louisa frowned. "He was…drugging me? No, you must be mistaken. All my friends like him, he's a great guy, friendly and sweet and a gentleman. I can't imagine that he's ever had to coerce anyone for…uh…for sex. Why would he drug me?"

Della took a deep breath. "Louisa, our partners and a score or more police officers are out there now looking for the man who has had Angus under his spell or in his employ—the murderer who likes to think of himself and put the press out there that he's the king of the vampires."

The girl turned an ashen color of white, gasping for a deep breath.

"No… I…"

"I'm afraid it's true. If you would have finished the drink he bought you as intended, you would have done anything that he said. And he would have walked you out and handed you over to a man named Stephan Dante, that would-be king of the vampires, and you wouldn't have even been alarmed at first because you would have believed that you were being introduced to Angus's very tall sister and just heading somewhere to pick something up before they saw you safely back to your home," Della explained.

"Oh…" Louisa let out a sound of distress, still not wanting to believe.

François suddenly stood up, excusing himself. Lachlan stepped out from the observation room, heading toward him, saying something quietly.

"What?" Louisa cried. "What is going on now?"

Lachlan turned to look at her. "We got the report

back. Rohypnol, among a few other things in the cocktail. Miss, you are a very, very lucky girl."

Louisa shook her head. "But..."

"Louisa, none of this is your fault," Della assured her. "I know that you were trying to be careful, that you wouldn't have gone anywhere with this man alone. Not on purpose. What we need from you is to know everything about the way that you met, how you met, how you made your plans."

"I—I told you. We go to the pub frequently. They are so good there to young women! I don't mean with free drinks, I mean...well, they watch over people. My friend said that Mr. Grant—Grady Grant, the fellow who owns the place—has three grown daughters, and that makes him...not mean, not weird, or anything, but even the guys like that it's such a safe place where people can flirt, sure, fine, and have a good time, but...no one gets attacked there, no one gets so drunk they'd be...date-raped there and...anyway, one night, we met Angus. And he was nice to all of us, but not icky, if you know what I mean. He joked, he laughed, and I told you...we just seemed to hit it off. He even told me that he understood how women in Edinburgh needed to be careful of strangers, that we'd stay there, we'd just have drinks there..."

Tears suddenly welled in her eyes and she exploded with, "He meant to give me to some sick son of a perverted bitch to kill me?"

"I'm afraid so," Della said gently. "Can you tell us anything else you know about him?"

"Everything he told me is probably a lie," she said. "But his name is Angus Crawford, he's twenty-five years old and he lives on the outskirts of Edinburgh. He loves art and history and he said that when things had calmed down and he knew me better, he'd show me anything at all that I wanted to see in the city of Edinburgh."

"It's okay, we—we want to see the good in others," Della said, and rose. She glanced at Lachlan and knew that no one had heard back from Mason, Edmund, Jon or Jeanne—or any of the officers on the street. They were still searching.

Despite having appeared as a very tall and ugly woman, Dante had managed to slip by everyone again, so it seemed.

Lachlan had taken a go at Angus; it was her turn.

"I'll go," she murmured.

"I'll be in observation," Lachlan said.

"Wait!" Louisa cried, distressed. "What do I do?"

"We'll be with you for now," Brianna assured her. "François and I are right here."

"What then? Is Angus really a monster working for a monster?" Louisa asked. "I'm scared, I'm so scared, I don't want to be alone, oh, my God, he was going to kill me!"

"We'll see that you're safe," Lachlan said, setting a hand on Della's back to steer her toward the interrogation room.

Louisa was still going on as Della nodded at Lachlan and went in, taking a seat opposite Angus.

He had a good bruise on his forehead and his hands appeared to be scratched. She hadn't caused the scratches—he must have gotten those resisting arrest.

"American!" he spit out. "You don't have rights in

this country. But you know what? I'm going to sue you. You—and everyone. I'm going to sue you for damages, for assault, for—"

"Well, you will be doing so from a nice place of incarceration, I'm sure," Della said. "We had the substance you slipped into Louisa's drink analyzed. Date rape. How pathetic. A guy like you? Ah, come on, but, you know, maybe…bad breath? You're not bad-looking. Then again, this wasn't for you, was it? The city is on guard, and most women are on guard and very careful. And for some reason—he's bribing you or threatening you or you are truly one of the idiots who believes he might become a vampire and live forever—you're drugging girls to get them to Stephan Dante."

He went silent, looking away.

Then he stared at Della and said, "You've killed her now."

She frowned, looking at him. "Louisa is alive and well and sitting—not drugged—in the parlor."

He shook his head. "Not Louisa."

"All right, you have a chance here. I don't know what you're talking about. Enlighten me."

"He'll kill her!" Angus said.

"Listen to me. Your only chance to save whoever this is that you're talking about is to tell me what's going on!" Della told him firmly. "Let's start with this—you're not an idiot. You know that drinking blood isn't going to make you a vampire who can continue to serve his vampire king and live forever."

"No," he admitted softly.

"You aren't doing this for money."

"Dear lord, no, never."

"Then…Dante is holding someone. And threatening to kill them if you don't bring him the women he wants. Does he know that you think he's an idiot, or…"

Angus leaned back. "The lass he has is my sister! Mum and Da were killed in an accident nearly a decade ago. Rosie was just a wee thing, nine years old. I had just turned eighteen, but my mum's sister helped and together, we raised Rosie. She's my sister, and dear as my child!" he whispered. "She just turned eighteen, a sweet and beautiful lass, smart as a whip in school, always listening to me…"

He paused, head lowered, tears stinging his eyes.

She knew that the man wasn't lying.

"All right. Tell me what happened."

"I—I had just heard about the teacher killed at the school…and the news had come from America that Stephan Dante, the king of the vampires, had escaped. I write under a pseudonym for several online magazines… I found that I was good on social commentary when I was young—I needed a way to be a brother and a father for Rosie. I—I had been interviewing a fellow who was working on a project for the Edinburgh Film Festival and when I got home…"

He stopped speaking again and shook his head.

"Maybe God will take us both, because I—I would have traded a life for Rosie's! The life of another innocent, except that—that—you stopped me, and now she will die, but…"

He broke down in sobs.

"Please!" Della said very gently. "How did you know him, how did he get Rosie?"

"He—he was in Edinburgh before, claiming to be

an actor. I met him one night… I had once wanted to act myself, I show up as an extra in friends' projects… and there was a group of us one night and I met this man…said his name was David Cunningham. He was exploring Edinburgh. I guess he explored it, all right! He came to my home…all before he apparently went on to kill across parts of the UK, France and Norway. But when we heard the news that Stephan Dante had been arrested in the States, I had no idea that Stephan Dante and the man I had met as David Cunningham were one and the same. But I came home…and Rosie was gone, and he was there. He told me that she was safe, but that I had to do what he wanted. He'd let Rosie talk to me on the phone so that I'd know that she was okay, but in exchange for her…"

His voice trailed again.

"You had to bring him another woman?"

"Two," Angus said miserably. "Two—for one," he said.

Della frowned. "Have you given him someone else?" she asked.

He shook his head. "Tonight would have been the first time I did this for him. I had to…prep. Because women are careful. But God forgive me, he was at my house right after he killed—killed the teacher, and he assured me that I'd find Rosie just as beautiful if I didn't find a way to bring him the kind of women he wanted. So I had to cruise the pubs, meet the lasses he'd like… make sure that I was not threatening and… I would never have to kill anyone. Just…"

"All right. He did let you talk to Rosie, though, you must realize, in the end, he would have killed you both," Della said quietly.

"You fight against that. You believe because…"

"You have to believe," Della said. She leaned forward. "All right, listen to me. He told you to get out—he probably knew that we were in there, though he may not know that we had you for trying to drug that young woman. Still, Rosie is in incredible danger—"

He started to sob again.

"He's going to kill her!"

"Not if we can get to her first. And men are out there—"

"They aren't going to get him. He knows Edinburgh. Every nook and cranny and there is so very much in this city that is underground."

"True. But we just have to find Rosie," Della said. "When you spoke to her, what did she sound like? Did you hear anything besides her voice, or… Did you record by any chance? Experts might be able to determine where he might be keeping her by what they can hear in a recording."

He shook his head. "I just…I just wanted to hear her voice. And I did. And she was scared, so terrified. She said that it was dark, there were spiders, she was so scared, but she didn't know! Rosie didn't know that he wanted to get someone else for him to kill—she thought that he just wanted money. Rosie—Rosie would have found a way to kill herself so that I wouldn't hurt anyone or cause someone else to be hurt or to…die. That's how sweet a human being she is!" he said desperately.

"All right, this is important. Listen to me and close your eyes. Think about the call, what else you might have heard besides your sister's voice," Della said.

"I was so desperate to hear her voice…"

"Think. We need to find her, to get her back for you," Della said. "Please, please, listen to me. Close your eyes and concentrate."

He did so at last, wincing.

Concentrating.

"In the distance, muted bagpipes."

"Good. Good…"

"The train! A train…there was a train in the distance, but it sounded strange, too, as if the sound was muffled, as if…"

"They were underground?" Della asked.

He nodded. He looked up at her again. "I may be a monster. I may belong behind bars for the rest of my life. But not Rosie. Please, please, find her! I'll help in any way possible, I'll tell you anything that I can remember at all, I'll be bait… I'll…"

"He called you. We have your phone, of course. And he ran after he warned you that we might be in the pub," Della said. She let out a breath; she needed to speak with the others, but one thing was expedient—finding Rosie Crawford before Stephan Dante could drain her of her blood.

"Listen to me, you have helped. And we will do everything in our power to find your sister. Sit tight for a minute, we may have to put a plan into action. All we need to do is get a few things in the proper order and… please, believe me, we will do everything humanly possible to find Rosie."

"Alive," he whispered.

"Alive," she agreed.

Rising, she headed out, hoping that Lachlan was

already planning what she was planning...unless, of course, someone had managed to corner Stephan Dante at last, the would-be vampire who still managed to be as slippery as an eel.

Thirteen

"Della?"

Mason was walking down yet another narrow wynd when his phone rang. He, Edmund, Jon and Jeanne were keeping contact through the earbuds; the team at the house had taken them out.

He cleared an ear to speak with her.

"Conference call!" she said. "Everybody on?"

One by one, they agreed.

"Anything on Dante yet?"

"No," Mason said flatly, and his word was echoed by Jeanne, Jon and Edmund.

"All right, we have an idea. Lachlan and François are with me. Brianna is waiting with Louisa while we arrange a protection detail for her, and we've been talking with Angus. Dante is holding Angus's sister hostage, threatening to kill her if he doesn't provide him with victims."

"Is he lying—" Mason began.

"Not lying!" Lachlan said. "I want to put him back out on the street—giving him back his phone. Brianna is going to do an underground video—which will go viral. One of our officers who works undercover is going to describe the horrible debacle where the police arrested a man just for sitting in a pub. Then we'll have a shot of Angus on the street. When he sees it, Dante will contact Angus, who will assure him that he didn't give a thing away, that all he wants is Rosie alive."

"I'm not sure—" Mason began.

"We've got nothing and his sister is out there and we need to find her!" Della said.

"Angus is agreeable to this?" Mason asked.

"He is agreeable to anything that might save his sister. We've already gotten his phone set up for a trace if Dante calls and everything that can be done to triangulate Dante's calls is being done. And we need to start a new search, guys, a desperate search. Angus thinks that he heard bagpipes in the phone call—"

"Bagpipes? In Scotland?" Mason asked dryly.

"No, no, listen! There's a place by the train station where there's a piper every day. We need to get on it, now. Right now. We need to find Rosie Crawford. Lachlan has been drawing up a concentrated plan for the police and, of course, us, and…"

She stopped speaking. For a minute, there was nothing but dead air coming to him and he frowned, saying her name. "Della? Della?"

"I'm here, I'm here, sorry! The paper received another note—probably received in the afternoon, just discovered by the graveyard crew. Another poem. And I think it means we would be right on to search any underground area by the train station—listen to this!

"Ah, the bonny, bonny banks, so many here, sounds
of the pipes,
Drawing everyone near.
A sweet bed to rest upon, as we all know,
Brings a strange kind of life to those who know,
The center of all, should you hear this call
For a bride is still a living doll."

"He's talking about Angus's sister?" Edmund asked.
"But he was just using Angus—"

"And this might have been a threat aimed at Angus,
if Dante was afraid that he'd back out on his promise.
But the 'center'—train station! He's been by the station and heard the pipes, too. Please, I've spoken with
Lachlan. They'll get every man out. You're not going to
get Dante now—he was gone in the first seconds—he
knew he had to run when he called Angus at the pub.
He was running even as François saw him and called
us. Please, all, we must find Rosie Crawford. We have
to stop Dante. Now! She will be his next kill if we don't
reach her."

"We'll meet you at the station," he said. "Edmund,
Jon, Jeanne?"

They all agreed.

They ended the call.

For a minute, just a minute, he paused, looking
around the now-empty streets.

Stephan Dante wasn't a vampire; he wasn't any kind
of immortal creature.

He was a man.

One who learned the ins and outs of Edinburgh better than he knew the structure of his own face—which

he knew damned well, too, considering the ways he could change it with makeup and putty.

He'd been dressed as a woman! According to François, he'd been an ugly woman, tall, but in a maxi-dress, wearing a shawl, strolling by the pub and then pulling out his phone before heading down the street.

And no matter how quickly they'd been on him, he'd turned off before officers had come after him, even before he'd finished his call to Angus to tell him to get the hell out.

The police had combed the many closes and wynds off the main streets; he, Edmund, Jeanne and Jon had split and gone in every direction. And, after hours of the search, when it had grown truly late and the streets were all but empty, they still had nothing.

Well, not nothing.

He had discovered Dante's discarded dress and shawl in one of the wynds. Dante had tossed it while running, not even bothering to bury the evidence that allowed them to see his path to his disappearance.

Unless that had been on purpose, something to taunt them, to show them how perfect he was—so that he could enjoy their chase and laugh at their failure.

Della was right. Dante had barely had a moment's chance—but he had known how to twist his way through the city so that he could doff his garb, blend in with others and probably disappear beneath the street level, heading to one of his underground hideouts.

Maybe heading to where Angus Crawford's sister was being held.

He turned, striding toward the train station. Della was right; the location was central. And while he couldn't hear him now, a piper played near it—perhaps several pipers because it did seem that no matter the hour, they could hear the distant sound of those pipes.

Reaching the station, he found Lachlan handing out assignments to his men. Della was there with him. "Brianna and François are at the house—François is wired to Angus Crawford. He has headed out and for his own apartment off Price Street. Plenty of police guard following undercover, and Brianna's video about outrage, suing and police brutality is going viral already."

Mason nodded. "All right, then…what path are we taking?"

She showed him the map Police Scotland had provided with what was known of the nearby closes and wynds.

"Some of the tinier wynds just connected houses, often for clan members who held land in the area hundreds of years ago," she explained. "I'd like to start heading down here…this way. It looks like all the houses have several levels and that there are tunnel wynds below some of the charming planted pathways… Anyway, shall we?"

"I'm going to have Edmund, Jon and Jeanne working with the officers I'm sending on the New Town side," Lachlan said. "If you and Della head that way—"

"That way is right where the piper stands," Della said. "We're on our way!"

Della was truly on a mission. He watched her as she moved ahead, first passing by streets that were wide and busy by day, turning down a close and pausing as she found a wynd within that close, one that zigged and zagged and wandered between homes and apartments or flats.

She paused for a moment, frowning, and turned to face him.

"What?"

"Just marveling at your ability to look fresh and like a bolt of fire when it's now way past one in the morning," he told her.

"Hey, we're all hanging in there!" she said. "We have to, right? And look, old steps, and a sign—Do Not Enter. That would be an invitation to Dante!"

"Yeah, and maybe we should be glad that they have laws against guns here—in many a neighborhood back in the States, a frightened homeowner could wake up and shoot us."

"Mason—"

"I'm walking, I'm walking! I want to find her, too!"

They moved around the barricades and down the steps.

Once again, they were moving into darkness.

"This is on the map," Della murmured. "Parts of the street ran down here once, but it leads into a dead end at a building… Hmm, and it's been abandoned, the city intends to do repairs, shore up the walls…" She paused. They were both shining their lights about, but in the abandoned area when they'd moved beneath the beautiful night lights of Edinburgh, it was dark.

"Hmm," Mason murmured.

"Hmm?"

"Kind of sad—well, I mean beyond the obvious sadness and tragedy of life around Stephan Dante. But Edinburgh…beautiful, rich in heritage… Hey, I love going to Camera Obscura and World of Illusions, Holy-rood Park, Princes Street Gardens…"

"You're not enjoying the underbelly of the city?" she teased. "No, I understand. I was a kid when my parents brought me to Camera Obscura and World of Illusions! I was fascinated—tricks of light and so much more and the view of the city from the roof…"

"And your mom was sketching everything in sight, I imagine."

"Told you—she is an amazing artist and my father is an exceptional marketer. Hey, how many people have dads who are way better at social media than they are at my age," Della said lightly. "Anyway…"

"You know that you're really proud of your mom. She's an exceptional artist."

"I know—and I'm proud of them both."

"There!" Mason said suddenly, looking at his own phone—at the dark, time-darkened stone and brick before him, and at his phone again. "That's supposed to be a solid wall, Della. There's a wynd… No, it's not even wide enough to be a wynd. Two bodies can't get through."

"One can at a time!" Della said, sliding through the strange opening in the ancient walls.

"Hey, you know—" he began.

"I'm a crack shot and I'm armed," Della reminded him.

"Yep. But biologically, I'm supposed to protect—"

"And you do," she assured him.

She stopped suddenly and he plowed against her.

"Dead end?"

"No...big empty space," she murmured, stepping aside to allow him room.

He joined her and they stared around at the emptiness in front of them.

"Nothing," Della said wearily.

But just as she spoke, they heard something. A voice, a cry, barely a whisper or moan in the air, as if it was coming from...

A box.

"She's here!" Della whispered. "Somewhere!"

They both looked around. It appeared to be nothing but empty space surrounded by the walls and the very narrow opening. No stairs led up and no stairs led down.

"Where? Circle, quietly, we'll listen, and...every few feet we'll take turns shouting out."

"Right," Della agreed.

She started slowly to the right, listening, pausing, starting again.

"Rosie! Rosie Crawford! Are you here?" Mason shouted.

They both paused, looking at one another. It seemed they could hear the cry again, but they couldn't tell where it was coming from.

They started walking again. The ground seemed to be nothing but dirt, but sliding his hands over the walls, Mason couldn't find anything that remotely resembled a secret door of any kind.

But there had to be something.

Because Rosie Crawford, or another victim of Dante's, was there. They could hear her.

"There's another level!" he said suddenly. "The ground...there's something in the ground somewhere—

that's why her voice sounds so weak and strange. She's still beneath us!"

He fell to the floor, sweeping dirt and gravel aside with an energetic vengeance. Della was quickly on the ground a few feet from him, wildly doing the same, her penlight held between her teeth to better see the ground right in front of her.

He sat back, drawing out his phone and dialing Lachlan, hoping that his call would go through.

It seemed a miracle from beneath the ground, but it did.

"We found her, I'm almost positive. But we need help. Send reinforcements."

"On their way," Lachlan promised him.

"We followed—"

"I know where you are. I pinged your phone."

"Great! We can hear her—we can't find her."

He and Della kept at it until six of Lachlan's men flooded in to join them. With all of them working, one of the policemen soon cried out.

"Here—here—I found a latch!"

The man had finally found something. And pulling it was easy enough. What had looked like earth was a wooden cover, scratched out and covered with the dirt and gravel to blend in with the ground.

Lifting the latch drew the cover up, and with police lights shining everywhere, it was easy to see a short flight of stairs that led to a level below.

Mason hurried down the stairs, warning that there were broken and treacherous steps along the way. He heard wood cracking but it was Della right behind him and she quickly caught herself before the step could give way.

They came to a far smaller space that resembled that above.

Except that this space wasn't empty.

A young woman, a gag tied tightly around her mouth, was bound to a heavy wooden chair. She tried calling out again in her muffled voice, tears springing into her eyes as she saw them all.

Della ran to her, ripping the gag from her mouth, while two of the officers quickly worked on the ties binding her to the chair.

"You're safe, you're safe now, it's all right!" Della assured her.

"My brother! Is my brother okay…? Oh, my God, he said that he was going to kill him first so that my blood would be richer…my brother…"

Mason had his phone out, quickly telling Lachlan that they had found Rosie.

For a moment he feared that they'd made a mistake, that despite the guard, their attempts to draw Dante out through Angus Crawford might have been too dangerous.

He couldn't help a moment's fear that they had found the sister just to lose the brother.

"Lachlan, we've got her," he said quickly. "Hospital, I think, but we'll get her there quietly—as quietly as we can with the amount of law enforcement we've got on the streets. But I think that we should pull Angus back in—he has to know this, anyway, and they should be together, and somewhere that is really safe, though."

"On it. And the officers watching over Angus have

reported that he's fine, no approaches, and his phone hasn't rung thus far. Angus is alive and well and thankfully, so you're telling me, so is his sister. Not a bad night's work. Wait. It's morning. We'll meet up at the hospital. This is worth a call in the wee hours to the commissioner. We'll plan from there." He was quiet a minute. "Is she always that good?" he asked.

"Pardon?"

"Della. She knows this man—she doesn't know the city the way we do, but she knew when Dante wrote his little poem where to go."

Mason smiled, looking at Della. Rosie Crawford was up, clinging to her as Della gently held her and assured her.

"She is that good!" he told Lachlan.

Thirty minutes later, he was reminded of his words at the hospital when they brought Angus Crawford in to see his sister. The two clung to one another, sobbing.

He set his arm around Della's shoulders as they watched.

"Sometimes," he whispered, "all this can… Well, you know. Suck so much. But sometimes… Well, this is an amazing moment."

She turned and smiled at him. "A beautiful moment! And when we get such moments…"

"Yeah," he said lightly. "The sucking part is worth it!"

"Will Angus be charged for trying to drug his date, not to mention hand her over to a serial killer?" Della asked quietly.

"That's not going to be up to us and I'm glad," Mason said. "Police Scotland and the courts here will have to decide on that. But…we owe Drake some thanks—this part of this case came out all right."

Della nodded. "Yes, but…"

"Dante is still out there." He shook his head. "I understand Angus—he was trying to save his sister's life. But it amazes me, no matter how someone explains the psychology, that he is able to coerce—no, charm, I guess—others into believing his whole vampire thing. I know, I know… But hey, we've worked through the night. Let's let them deal with this as is right, and… we'll head back, get some rest and then try to decipher his next move."

"What about the media?" Della murmured. "For most people here the day will be starting, and we need to have something out there."

"When Lachlan is finished here…which I believe he is about to be, we can speak with him. I'm not sure if we should have him tour our successes, or…"

"My opinion?" Della said. "I think that we let the media know that law enforcement was grateful to find a young woman who had been kidnapped and put out the warning again that everyone must be vigilant, because there is a killer on the loose, and again, put up the sketches of Dante—"

"Only François recognized him when he was a woman—and thank God he did," Mason reminded her.

"It can't hurt. His disguises can't all be that elaborate."

"All right. I agree. We'll run it by Lachlan, get François speaking with the media…and should we have breakfast and just keep going, or try to sleep?" Mason asked her.

She rubbed a finger over his cheek. "Sorry, dark smudge of dirt. You kind of look like hell."

"Wow, thanks. You're not all that…pristine yourself."

"I really do want to do some of the amazing things Edinburgh offers without crawling around in the underground dirt," she said.

"Okay, so…sleep?" he asked.

"I think I'm too keyed up," she said with a sigh.

"Okay, back to Euro-house, you get first shower and I'm not even coming up until you come down because, well, you know, showers can just be too much fun. And since we're both wide-awake, I think we need to look at everything and see if there isn't some way to determine his next move. He's been working this nonstop."

"So have we."

"Right. And he knows now that we talked to Angus Crawford, that we've rescued Rosie Crawford, and worse—we found his crypt. The news of an intriguing discovery beneath the streets of the city will go out. I think he might have even wanted us to find Rosie, to let us think that we're on his trail when he's already planning something else. We've destroyed part of his fantasy—he won't be meeting anyone in a secret burial chamber. And that will infuriate him."

"Let's head back then, shall we? And get started."

Mason nodded. They both took a minute to watch as Angus Crawford sat by his sister in her hospital bed, holding her hand.

They needed to meet, to throw out every concept, every idea, listen to one another and hope that in the discussion, they could guess Dante's next move.

Because one thing was certain.

Dante was already planning it.

Fourteen

As it happened, they weren't the only ones with insomnia. At the house, they followed their plan.

Della was glad that she was able to take the first shower—it made her smile to think that Mason wouldn't come up because even though they'd been up twenty-four hours, there was no help for it—they were all, she was certain, filled with far too much adrenaline.

The hot water was wonderful. Washing away the dirt was like washing away the darkness, almost like washing Stephan Dante out of her mind for a few brief minutes.

But after a few minutes with her hair and body seriously scrubbed, she stepped out, dried and dressed for the day, ready to let Mason come up.

He was heading up the stairs as she was coming down.

"François has been working with the police and the media, and I think we're good—pretty much exactly what we discussed. We're all gathering at the table in the kitchen, bit by bit. Seems like no one wants to sleep, but everyone feels as if they've been rolling in a mud pit. Shower was good?"

"Shower was hot and delicious," Della said.

"Even without me?" he teased.

She grinned. "With you, hmm. Maybe it would have to have been a cold shower!"

Grinning, he moved on past her and she hurried downstairs. Arriving in the kitchen, she found François, Edmund and Jon setting some of their food supplies on the table, including cereal, eggs and toaster waffles, while Lachlan sat at the table, studying his phone.

"Choice is yours—coffee there, tea there," Lachlan said, looking up and pointing to the carafe of coffee on the counter next to the teapot. "And...toaster is over there!"

She smiled, pouring a cup of coffee. "Whoever did this, I love you!" she said.

Edmund grinned. "Hey, we Brits do drink things other than tea."

"And gin, right?" she teased.

"Can't stand the stuff," Edmund told her. "I'm with the Scots on this one—whiskey is a much better drink."

"Unless you ask Brianna," Lachlan said. "And she'll tell you that the only really decent drink in the world is a Guinness."

Della smiled, taking her coffee to the table, looking over her breakfast choices and opting for a bowl of cereal.

"You are in Britain," François said. "We should be having eggs, ham or hash, an extensive meal to get one through the day."

"You're eating a bowl of cereal," she pointed out.

He shrugged. "I didn't say what I'd like, just what one might expect."

Jeanne joined them then, looking fresh and dignified and nodding to the others as he headed to the coffeepot. He sat and joined them at the table. Only two places remained empty, one for Mason, and one for Brianna.

Lachlan looked at Della. "You are remarkable, you know. Figuring out where this man might be, listening to his stupid poems and following the clues in them. But you... He wanted to kill you, right? Or, still wants you to be his bride. But I understand that after your foray in the bayou in Louisiana, he probably will prefer you dead."

"Lachlan," Edmund said, frowning.

Della waved a hand in the air. "Yes, I'm sure he wants me dead. And Mason. He may be having a little trouble with his hand. Mason shot a gun right out of his grasp. Yes, he wants me dead. But he wants everyone in his way dead—after he's finished with taunting and torturing them."

"But his victims...he drugs them. He doesn't torture them, he just kills them," Jeanne pointed out.

"True. He isn't sadistic in his vampire kills, but he enjoys psychological torture," Della said. "He relishes the idea of throwing out clues and watching us follow him but being just a step behind him every time."

"He doesn't really want you to be his vampire queen, even in the dark recesses of his mind?" Lachlan asked.

"No—and I don't think it was even a way for him to seek a psychological excuse for his killing if he was caught. It was his 'thing,' his chosen creation. Maybe, in his way, his means of living forever as a killing legend. What he did believe was that he could twist anyone, that he could turn me into a killing machine. Oh, and I might have mentioned before, I was instrumental in bringing down one of his old enemies, but we didn't kill him and, apparently, Dante wanted him dead." She shook her head. "He does have a few sides to his personality. Sometimes… In the bayou, I almost feel as if he acted like a five-year-old, angry that I didn't want to play his game. And sometimes, he displays cunning and reasoning that is truly terrifying."

As she spoke, Mason came back downstairs, also clean, and freshly and professionally dressed. He stood behind Della for a minute, his hands on her shoulders, before taking his seat.

"We will find him," Mason said.

"Curious," Jeanne murmured.

"What's that? Well, besides everything about him," Lachlan asked.

"Last time," Jon Wilhelm said, absently stirring sugar into his coffee, "he killed in one country and skipped to another. But he's still here."

"Because we have so many levels, places to hide?" Lachlan asked.

"Because he still has a plan," Mason said. "We need to figure out that plan."

"Well, we have managed to be here, all of us, except—" Jeanne began.

"Brianna?" Lachlan asked. He smiled ruefully. "She isn't in my room. I guess she was the one smart member of our twisted team—I think she's getting some sleep. I figured I wasn't going to wake her until we needed to do so."

"All right. So?" Mason said.

"He's going to send a taunt to the media again," Jeanne said.

"They just got one, and I'm assuming it was planned for this morning. But—" Lachlan began.

"I almost wonder if we were supposed to find Rosie," Edmund said.

"With a clue like that?" Lachlan asked.

Jeanne looked over at Lachlan. "He knows Della is here. And I think he may even be fascinated by the way that Della reads him. He loves killing, loves perpetuating the king-of-the-vampires myth, but he also loves a cat and mouse game, and no matter what we've accomplished, I believe he thinks that he's winning now."

"We can't just wait for him to strike again," Lachlan said.

"He made no attempt to contact Angus Crawford when he was released yesterday with the video about the police making such an unjust arrest?" Della asked. "Sorry. I saw him at the hospital, but we just watched as sister and brother were able to see each other."

"No. And we tried to trace the number that had called his cell when he was at the pub to warn him that we were out there," Lachlan said. "We found the phone. It was a prepaid and, yes, he ditched it right after he called Angus."

"All right," Della said. "He has a place out there. He made plans to come here long before he did—we know that. He planned his escape just as meticulously—he had a man to rig the cameras there, as he did here. He had people in line to provide him with false ID, and with an airline ticket. But while we've taken what I think might well be the place most important to him—the crypt—he has somewhere else where he has his makeup and clothing so that he can change his appearance. He may have other people here in the city who are helping him because he's brainwashed and drugged them, or because he's threatened them. What we need to do is find his main hideout."

"So," Lachlan said. "We simply tear apart the entire city, go down to every level in existence after the past thousand years or more and…we've got him."

"We need help," Della said, remembering what Edmund had told them the night before. "I think that we need to get out there and see if Boyd Breck has come across anything more, or perhaps the Douglas couple who died in the plague, Hamish and Margaret."

She saw that François and Jeanne quickly looked at one another. Jon Wilhelm frowned and looked down at his plate.

"Have you met them yet?" Della asked Jon.

He looked up at her. "Have I met…dead people?"

"Aye, exactly," Lachlan said, staring hard at him.

"Really?" Jon asked.

"Really," Mason said.

Jon Wilhelm then looked around the table. "Have you met the dead of Edinburgh?" he asked.

"I just told you, we need help from them. And we've met a few—an old, old warrior named Boyd Breck, and a lovely couple, Hamish and Margaret Douglas. They helped feed those stricken with the plague—then died from it themselves. Boyd is pretty cool, too. He fought under Wallace, and when Wallace was executed and

Bruce took up arms, he fought with him, too. He was able to see Robert the Bruce crowned as King of Scotland."

"And they've helped?" Jon asked.

Della nodded. "I think they could help more. And if you've met anyone…"

"Helen MacIntosh," Jeanne said suddenly.

They all looked at him and waited. "She was arrested for being a witch. The poor woman knew how to swim, so…she was tortured and put to death, near the castle and the Witch's Well, near that incredible thing, Camera Obscura and World of Illusions. I almost forgot what I was doing to go in and see the place, but…" Jeanne paused, shaking his head. "She promised to be on the lookout for anything odd for me, but… Well, her suggestion is that which we already have."

"And the problem being that many of the wynds and closes lead to private spaces and since some families have owned those properties for decades…there could be anything going on in basements that were once streets," Lachlan said.

"We all see the dead. When they choose to be seen. But…is this real? Is this a test?" Jon asked. "It's a secret I've kept for so long, afraid…"

"This is Blackbird, formed as the international arm of the Krewe of Hunters, all among the slim percentage of a percentage of the population with this gift or curse," Mason said. "With us, please, don't just speak to the dead—introduce us all to them!"

Lachlan let out a long sigh. "Well, that's that, then. Edmund, you were right. Ask, and you will get an answer. But—at this moment—we seem to have nothing from the dead or the living."

Jon cleared his throat. "What about Brianna?" he whispered, as if the woman might have super-hearing powers as well, something that Della had to admit she'd seen—in the Krewe.

"Yes," Lachlan said. "And that's why…"

"Why it's so important we have a tech analyst with us?" Edmund asked, amused.

"That, and, of course, the incredible way she works with us all," Lachlan said. "And…"

"It might be why you two have something that goes on beyond special," Jeanne commented. "This is all good to know. Thank you. If we had just all spoken sooner. Ah, *mais non*! We learn as children not to speak. Across the world, people with such claims are like…"

"Like a human monster preying on others to convince them he can make them immortal," Mason said dryly. "All right. Seems we fan out again."

"I will be out there—I am this gifted," François said. "I will be in connection with the main offices and the media all the while and keep everyone posted, out there, as I would be in here."

"François and I know Helen—we will wander the area nearest the castle," Jeanne suggested.

"I keep thinking that we need to go to the same area except that today, a host of archeologists and anthropologists will be there along with city leaders. Maybe a bit more toward the Holyrood area," Della said, looking at Mason.

"Between there—and where we found Rosie," he said.

"François, with me?" Lachlan asked.

"And Brianna?"

Lachlan shook his head. "We'll have her coordinate from here, just in case there are any communication snags. And she'll keep us abreast of anything that comes out from the media. Or if Stephan Dante has pulled another stunt—or sent another message to the media. She isn't a field agent, nor an officer specially designated to bear arms... She never has worked the field before, and she shouldn't—by job definition and procedure—be working as anything but an analyst. And, of course, there is still a crew searching the cameras for him constantly."

"But they won't know him. Not the way I know him," François said. He sighed. "I believe I am most useful here, watching. Nothing against others, we've just been on the hunt and... Jeanne, perhaps you and Jon Wilhelm can work together and Edmund—"

"Edmund and I will search the Holyrood area, heading uphill," Lachlan said. "And if all is agreed... Oh, we should tell Brianna."

"I will be here. Let her sleep. When she wakes, she can help me, and she will be quite a help," François said.

Lachlan rose. "We should be sleeping. But we're not. So let's get out there and catch a human monster."

The discovery of the crypt deep in a known—but seldom traversed—close was, apparently, huge in archeological circles. Once they were on the Royal Mile, they could see the amount of people flocking just near the area along with the many news stations, papers, online reporters, vloggers and more.

"Let's avoid that, shall we?" Mason suggested, urging Della past the area.

"Hmm. Well, we could move toward the station, staying on this side, in Old Town. I don't believe that he'd be in New Town, just because he's all about the vampire legend, and though vampires were different and known but not huge until Bram Stoker, I think he likes the old."

"Even though new may be old," Mason teased.

"Even though new may be old," Della agreed. She paused. "Mason! The church graveyards. There are several. St. Giles, Canongate, Old St. Paul's... I don't know how many more. Apparently, St. Giles is especially known for being haunted, but—"

"He's not going to choose a place where people like to go ghost-hunting, and I'm not sure any of our helpful ghosts want to hang around such places, either. But you're right. We need an old place. Off the Royal Mile, but not far. Either abandoned, or with a small group of parishioners, and maybe..."

"Like the close where we found the crypt far below... a place where time and rising populations might have outgrown the building or...where religious upheaval over the years might have caused problems. Now it's all just fairly open, but you did have the Reformation here, and..."

Mason was studying his phone and she realized that he had opened the screen to one of the maps that Lachlan had supplied for them.

"Look, look—this side of the train station, a little more toward the castle. Near where the Nor Loch had to be filled in because man-made defense that it might have been, it had just grown to become disgusting in the extreme. Deep earth near there, and the church doesn't sit on the park, but not far from it…here. It's a small place, reading up…there's a Reverend Woods. I'm not seeing any deacons listed…church, rectory, and—" he looked over at Della "—graveyard and crypt!"

"Let's try it," she said.

"Walk this way," Mason said.

"Walk the way you walk?" she asked. "Hmm."

He let out a sigh, rolling his eyes. "Walk the way you walk, just— Della!"

Off the Royal Mile, they followed a close that led to another close and then out to a small street. Crossing the street, they saw a plaque on the old church that told them that it had been consecrated in the late 1300s, and that it had later become Presbyterian after the Reformation. It was small, but beautiful, with double doors beneath a stunning archway adorned with angels. The door was closed and locked but they hadn't expected to get in. They walked around the equally small parking lot to come to the graveyard.

The graveyard was bigger than the church, though a sign on an old brick wall in the center advised them that the graves in the northern portion of the graveyard had been reinterred due to city expansion.

What was there was exquisite. The last burials had evidently been in the early part of the nineteenth century and the funerary art spoke of hundreds of years of human expression. There were aboveground tombs, many family vaults and family sections as well, fenced-in areas with obelisks noting the name, date of birth and date of death of many a family member.

"Where do we start?" Della murmured.

"At the beginning, I guess," Mason said. "Methodically? Left to right, front to back?"

"Methodically it is," she said.

Methodically was the only way to do it, Mason thought. There were areas where tombstones sat separately, areas where several were together, with most of those offering some kind of beautiful little statue, perhaps that of an angel or a saint or a cherub. Many were crumbling; Mason doubted that the budget to keep the cemetery in good maintenance was very large.

At the first vault, he stared at the lock. It was rusting, and it was evident that it hadn't been touched in ages.

"Moving on," Mason murmured.

"Maybe we should just split up and try all the vaults, both ends, working toward the middle," Della said.

Mason paused, looking around. There was no one at the church and, certainly, no one coming to visit their dearly beloveds in the graveyard. And it was an oddly beautiful day for the area—the sky was almost a crystal blue.

"In case he's in any of these—"

"I am armed and you are a scream away," Della said.

"Right. I was just wondering if we should get Lachlan and Edmund over here. I really think that this is a perfect place for Dante."

"It is," Della said. She glanced at him, grimacing. "I hate the fact that I do feel that I know the best, and it isn't a pleasant feeling. But this is his kind of place. Quiet—there must be services on Sundays and even during the week, but if there is something like a rectory, it's nowhere near the church and this graveyard is overgrown and monuments are broken—locks are rusted. It's almost as if it has been forgotten by time."

"Almost, so…"

"I'll go left, you go right."

He nodded, walking over to the far end.

The first vault he approached on his side had a rusted lock that fell apart when he barely touched it. No one had been there for a long, long time, but he opened the creaking doors to look within.

Family members lay along the walls in their shrouds. A few ancient tombs were angled into the small space.

Dust covered everything.

He moved on.

He'd reached the third of the vaults along his way when he noted that his phone was ringing. He saw that the call was François and that it was a conference call.

The Frenchman was so upset at first that he seemed to have forgotten his English or else combined it with his native tongue.

"François, please, calm down, let us know—"

"She's not here. Brianna wasn't sleeping. I went to awaken her, but—she wasn't sleeping. Her bedding was piled up, but the day was getting busy, too much to watch, I went to touch her but it was just bedding. I've called her—I've searched the house. Brianna isn't here and I have no idea where she is!"

"Lachlan, there are police patrols all around that house," Mason said. "Someone must know something…"

"I'll be putting out an emergency summons," Lachlan said. "Please, everyone, I don't know how he could have gotten her—there was no way he got in the house. No friends could have fixed that place, there were too many fail-safes set in motion. She had to have walked out on her own, but I don't know… I'm putting out my call. Team…Brianna is top priority now!"

"Of course," Mason said. "She's one of our own!"

"We need any information we can get—François, can you see if any of the media outlets have gotten anything at all? There may be another clue in it if he's written a poem, something that Della can figure out. We'll be on our way back to the house to coordinate. Della?"

It was a conference call. She should have been on it.

The others were quickly off the line, and he tried to tell himself that Della had merely ended her part of the call, anxious to get back with him and back to the house.

Anxious to find Brianna.

"Della!"

He couldn't see her. Looking across the graveyard, he couldn't see her.

He started running, heading to the first vault she would have tried.

Rusted solid with the stone almost grown into itself.

He hurried to the second. And there, large double doors stood ajar. This was where she had gone in.

Mason stepped inside. There were five standing tombs, two walls of shelving that held dead who had been there so long the shrouds were decaying and blending with bones, and, against the back wall, an altar.

He walked through the vault, looking at the tombs, but none had been tampered with—none opened to a set of stairs or even a stygian pit.

There was nothing in the shelves—except for the long, long dead.

But there were footprints in the dust on the floor and

the amount of dust that should have filled this place wasn't quite what it should have been.

Because someone had been using the tomb.

But there was no clothing here, nothing to indicate that anyone was using it...

He walked up to the altar, came around it and then noted that the ground beneath it seemed scraped, that dust had been swept away.

He took hold of it and shoved.

And he found what he was looking for: stairs that led to darkness, into a cavern beneath the earth.

He started downward.

And he began to find what they were seeking. A pile of clothing. A makeshift desk or very strange dressing table, created from bits of broken coffin.

The trail was leading toward the church, he thought.

And maybe the church, as old as it was, had catacombs, and those might have stretched out to the graveyard, might be attached...

"Della!"

She had probably come through here when she had discovered it, just as he was coming through now.

Except that...

She should have called out to him! She should have told him, should have warned him!

He didn't want to feel the sense of fear that was slowly building in him.

Stephan Dante had definitely been here.

Della had been here.

And now...

She was not. And yet...

He hunched down, seeing something on the floor. It

was one of her rings, he saw, wincing with the agony of knowing that she had left it...

Like a bread crumb. It wasn't an expensive ring, just a citrine, but it had been her grandmother's, something inherited and brought to the States from Norway. He kept his light out and kept walking, following the trail that was, indeed, leading along rows of the dead now toward the church.

He was surprised when his phone rang, deep in the earth as he was, and he answered it anxiously, hoping against hope that it might be Della.

But he wasn't surprised when he heard François's distressed voice.

"It was him, that monster. I dug through Brianna's computer. He managed to get his hands on that girl again, the girl from the pub, Louisa! He told Brianna that the only way that Louisa could live was if she could come and get her. But, of course, he didn't say how or where, just told her to walk to the Royal Mile, and he would take her to Louisa. Apparently, Brianna slipped out while we were still out on the Angus and Rosie reunion, and...she never was in the house. Lachlan found one of the patrolmen who had been watching Eurohouse. She left on her own, smiling, telling him that she was fine, just heading to the store and meeting a friend who was also a cop. He let her go—he knew that they were supposed to guard the house, not stop anyone who wanted to leave it. Lachlan is...not in good shape."

"Neither am I. I'm searching a catacomb Della entered through a vault in the graveyard. I can't find her... I'm afraid that she is missing, too. I'm going to keep following this and determine where it's leading. I think—I think he's demanded her phone, but I also believe that she's purposely shedding objects so that we can follow... Get the others. Tell them where we are. We need to fan out and find him, now!"

He was angry. He was furious. Della had to have opened the vault—and found Dante, waiting for her, expecting her.

And she hadn't cried out for him. She hadn't shot the son of a bitch. She had just disappeared with him...

Of course, there was only one reason for that.

Now, of course...

Brianna. Della would always try to trade her life for that of someone else, especially someone who had become a friend so quickly.

But how...?

Impossible to wonder. Della was the one who could read Dante's signs, follow his cryptic taunts and leads.

And now Della was with him.

All he could do was...

Follow her bread crumbs. And pray they would be enough.

Certainly, this was the worst déjà vu ever. And was she an idiot? Well, she knew something about Stephan Dante and, sadly, he knew something about her.

He would kill Brianna. She had to find a way to save her because, of course, he'd taken Brianna especially because he'd known that Della couldn't let her die.

"Where are we going?" Della demanded, irritated as she brushed another spiderweb from her face. "It doesn't matter. Don't you understand yet? Any stupid thing you do, my team will find you."

He paused in the dark chamber of the crypt, turning to look at her with amusement. "They'll follow me? You know, I admit that I was not pleased that you ruined my favorite place in the world for me! Archeologists! It's so annoying...they'll be dragging the bodies out, inspecting them, trying to date everything...don't you think that the dead should rest in peace?"

"Oh, so you don't even pretend with me that they might rise and have immortal life?"

"Why would I bother with you? But, come on, seriously, who leaves people quite so beautiful? I mean, in a way, they are immortal when I'm done. So beautiful as I lay them out!"

"Psycho," she said.

He shrugged. "Brilliant, a genius, and since you all run around after me like idiots, I think that I've proved it."

"They will get you!" she said.

He laughed again. "And if they do, so what? They'll put me back in jail, they'll hem and haw and they won't have a trial and I'll just get out again, so?"

"Maybe not," she murmured.

But she was almost willing to admit that he was criminally brilliant. He had been prepared to disappear if it had been someone else who had entered the vault.

But she had been intrigued by the altar, determined to find his location. She had found him down the steps and he hadn't blinked when she'd drawn her gun. Shrugging, he had told her that he had Brianna and Brianna was already being bled...if they didn't reach her, she would die. And, of course, only he knew where she was, only he could get to her before she did bleed to death.

"Shoot me, she dies. Call out for your boy toy and

she dies. If you do anything at all other than hand over your Glock and that little gun you keep at your ankle and your phone and follow me, she dies."

"How do I know she's not already dead?" she demanded.

He paused, shining a light on a cell phone—one she was certain he'd purchased the day before. He probably had a cache of throwaways.

"Live-feed connected," he'd told her.

And she could see. Brianna tied to a chair, a needle in her, blood dripping into a bag rather than being transfused into her.

It was dark. Another basement such as they had found the night before.

And he was telling the truth on that. Brianna was still alive.

For how long…?

"How far is this? She won't leave if we don't get there!" Della said.

"Not far."

He stopped and turned again. She flinched as he reached out to touch her.

"No earbuds today. Awe, what a pity. That brilliant team of yours won't be right behind you!"

"Get me to Brianna. And your promise is that you let her go—and take me. Because if you kill us both, I promise you—"

"They'll lock me up twice? Oh, or lethal injection, is it, if I were back in Louisiana. Honey, death only works once!"

"Right! All that load about wanting me as queen."

"You could have been a queen, reigning with me."

"But now…"

"Now I just want to kill you slowly, oh, so slowly…"

"Hmm. The slower you go, the more time you'll give my team to find you."

"That's all right. I want to kill him, too."

"Your hand still not working quite right? Oh, and it's your right hand that's not right, *right*?" she asked pleasantly.

He turned to glare at her and she prayed that her knowledge of his mangled hand might eventually mean something.

A way to wrest a gun from him?

He had taken her phone; he hadn't smashed it into a million pieces. François and tech members of Police Scotland might well be following a trail off a ping on the phone—if it all reached deep into the earth.

Mason would come behind her. She knew that. But there were twists and turns down here…long, long rows of corpses, but like the catacombs in Rome.

She needed to leave a trail…

What else, what else? She was wearing a jacket. Buttons. Small, but Mason was a detail person and he wouldn't be trailing them alone.

Subtly, subtly, she ripped off the bottom button of her jacket.

It fell to the ground in the dark.

A navy-colored button against the dark earth in the dark catacomb.

And yet, it had to be enough.

Mason had to follow. While she was desperate to save Brianna…

He might very well manage to kill them both.

Fifteen

Amazing.

Mason's cell phone continued to work.

He played his light over the walls and the floors, certain that Dante was there, leading Della onward, but even following what should have been an easy path was proving to be a guessing game.

Hundreds of years ago, this place had become sanctified ground. Brianna or Lachlan might know the history of the place. It had been built before the Reformation and perhaps there had been a time when a Catholic congregation had chosen to bury their dead deeply here, lest those who were easily discovered be cast out. But then again, maybe people had just been dying during all those centuries, and out of room in the church and maybe even in the graveyard itself, so for those without family tombs or plots, the catacombs had become necessary.

One thing was certain.

They had been dug deeply, twisting and turning to create more and more hallways with graves for the dead.

Dante couldn't be this insane. He had to know that Mason had been in the graveyard with Della.

Had to know he would follow.

And yet...

He was following and following and...

He paused, stooping down, playing his light over the floor. A button. A navy button. One off the jacket Della had been wearing that day.

He fought down panic, determined to keep himself in control. They had been this route before. Once, it had been aboveground, in the wetlands of the Louisiana bayou country. But they'd been in contact then.

They'd arranged the trap.

This time...

Dante knew how to play them. He hadn't cared a fig that they had gotten any of his accomplices; they were all expendable. In Dante's world, nothing mattered but Dante, and the life of any human being other than himself was about as important as that of a fly.

Except...

He'd had his thing with Della.

She was certainly playing on that.

His phone vibrated and he brought it quickly from his pocket. He had it on silent as he just might be close at some point, and if so, he didn't want Dante knowing how close.

He came to a halt, speaking quietly as he realized that François was on the other end.

"Lachlan has gotten the church open. They are completely aware of the catacombs and we've been given a map... They begin at the church and stretch out to several family vaults. The burial ground has at least twenty thousand legitimate graves, most of which are in the catacombs. But Lachlan is leading a team in from the church. Edmund is with him—Jon and Jeanne are keeping watch aboveground lest he figure a way out through one of the other tombs." François hesitated. "Dante can't get away. Lachlan has almost every man and woman in the department working on this and… he can't get away."

Mason thanked him for the information and ended the call, glad to hear that troops would be flooding through the catacombs.

But if there were exits in several of the tombs…

He was good with directions and he knew that they had been heading toward the church—not deeper into the cemetery.

"Della, where, where…?" he murmured silently to himself.

It was then that he realized he wasn't alone.

Not that he'd ever been alone with thousands of bodies nearby, but…

"Mason!"

He turned to see the spirit of their warrior friend, Boyd Breck.

"He has Brianna and Della, Boyd," he said simply.

"I know. I saw… He has not hurt Della—she is following of her free will, lad. But if ye didna see, she's been dropping buttons and I have friends…"

He lifted his arms and Mason turned around. There were several of the long-dead there, watching him gravely, most appearing in white, as if the shrouds they had worn to their last resting sites had come to engulf them. It was…a sea of ghostly white and grave faces.

He was glad he had not seen such a sight as a boy. He would have been too terrified to accept his gift...

The gift that could now help him save lives.

"They will help!" Boyd told him. "They will spread out, see where these may lead, but, lad, ye must take care, extreme care. Many areas here are caving in, the weight of the modern world atop all that is far too old. Move cautiously, I beg you."

Mason smiled at him. "Thank you! I'm heading this way, due to her last button. I need to warn Lachlan as well—others are coming in and that much motion might cause a cave-in as well."

"Not to worry, Hamish Douglas has seen the arrival of the police—they will find Lachlan."

"Thank you, then!" Mason said, turning to forge forward.

Dante couldn't simply have gone to another area of the catacombs; he would know that Della would be followed.

He was too much of a narcissist to be suicidal. Where had he gone?

He stopped again; there was another button on the floor. And this time, when he bent down and lifted his head, his field of vision was level with a corpse on a ledge. But the wall behind the corpse wasn't just dark because of age-old grime and the earth.

It was dark because it wasn't there.

Della had strategically placed that button. She had done so when Dante had forced her to crawl over the corpse—and into the space behind it.

With Boyd's ghost accompanying him, he crawled on through himself.

* * *

"We had better get to Brianna quick," Della said. "We've been walking down here way too long. I mean, the threat is that she'll die if we don't get to her, right?"

"Doesn't matter much now," Dante said. "I have the Glock and the Baby Browning, a scalpel—couldn't part with that and if you fly with a doctor's credentials, go figure, no one notices such a thing in your luggage."

"How many other lackeys do you have in the city, Dante?" she asked. She inched down a hair; the passage they were traveling was narrow and low. She brushed by the edge of the wall, shivering slightly as dirt and grime came falling down around her.

"Lackeys?" he asked.

"Right. Bad term. Angus wasn't a lackey—you threatened him with his sister."

"You know, I hand it to you on that. My clues weren't that great. I was going to send you one on this, but…to my surprise, I saw you heading right to my cemetery. But, all in all, makes my plan the best because you can't be trusted. You need to have that army behind you. Tough-girl agent!"

"Want to arm-wrestle?" she asked him.

"I may just shoot you," he told her. "Ah, but almost there," he said, before stopping, leaning against the wall and pushing her forward. They entered into another underground room, this one like a cavern, uneven ceiling, uneven wall—but well equipped. Dante had dragged chairs down somehow from somewhere, and he had several medical bags in the center of the room.

And he had Brianna…and another girl. Louisa, the poor young girl who had been so terrified.

How the hell had he gotten his hands on her? Or…

"Brianna!"

She'd been slumped in one of the chairs, tied to it, just like the girl Louisa. But when Della and Dante entered, Brianna lifted her head.

The other girl did not.

There was a gag in her mouth, but the look Brianna gave Della was heartsick, a look that showed the fact that she had prayed that Della wouldn't have been as trusting as she had been—believing that Dante would let any of them go.

But as Brianna looked at her, heartsick, Della noted that she was looking beyond her.

Turning, Della saw that Hamish and Margaret Douglas had found them. "Ah, lass, fear not—this madman has now played his game too far, they are but a few twists and turns away!" Hamish said.

She nodded and said, "Thank you."

"You're talking to the dead?" Dante asked, bored.

"Sometimes, they're preferable to conversing with the living," she assured him.

"Always a wise-ass, Special Agent Della Hamilton," Dante said, stopping by the girl from the night before—Louisa.

"You see…ah, this lovely lass! She believed in me… Oh, I fear you're going to find one of Edinburgh's finest in a gutter," he said. "I always do especially enjoy dressing up as law enforcement. People are so very gullible…even the other lad on duty accepted a new man, and I just had to wait and bide my time…and I do carry an arsenal of drugs." He started to laugh. "This one…she was so easy! A trip back to the station would do so much good in helping to apprehend the bad guy. She came right at my bidding and looked stunned when I hit her with a needle in the arm. Look at that, will you? She's giving me a lovely supply of blood. Oh, I do drink the stuff!"

"Watch out. You're going to wind up with one hell of a disease one day," Della told him.

He shrugged, reaching into one of his bags for a pair of plastic cuffs.

"I do spend so much time behind bars—and outside of them—studying technology. All I had to do with your dear friend here was assure her that this young lady's death would be all her fault, and…well. I know that it works with you."

Della shook her head. "You're crazy. They are here, you know, running around the graveyard—and they've certainly found the entrance behind the altar. They'll be here, and no matter who is or isn't dead, they'll take you back—"

"And I'll escape again. And, yes, I'm set with people and supplies for years to come! Now, cuff yourself. It's time to get started on you."

"No."

"I have the Glock and your Baby Browning or whatever it is."

"I'm not cuffing myself until you let them go!" Della insisted.

Dante sighed wearily and walked over to the girl, Louisa. He pulled the gag from her mouth; her head still lolled. He jerked the needle from her arm and blood spurted out, causing Della to run to her side, knocking an irate Dante out of the way. But Della ripped at the cotton shirt she was wearing beneath her jacket, using a stretch of it to tie a tight bond around the young woman's arm.

She still slumped down. Without help, soon, she'd be dead.

Dante was furious, promising he was going to shoot her in the kneecap.

"Now Brianna!" Della said angrily. "You said that if I came with you—"

"I said that if you didn't come, she would die. I didn't say that if you came, she would live."

"Let her go and I will cuff myself," Della said to Dante.

"Don't do it, lass!" Margaret begged.

"I have to—he has to let her go," Della told her. "Where's Hamish?"

"Both are near, the police under Lachlan, and your American mate, Mason. They are on their way," Margaret assured her.

"Isn't it a pity your dead people can't help you?" Dante asked. "I still say that if they lock me up, you should be locked up as well. Ah, well, you won't make it. If, and when, they reach me…well, I will have the life of you within me."

"You keep saying that! Words, you're nothing but words!"

He started to laugh. "You think the two of us are staying here? Oh, no, no…we're going to be heading out in a direction that's not from the church—or from the tomb. Fine! I'll undo your friend Brianna. Maybe they'll find these two in time. Who they won't find is going to be you!"

* * *

Mason had to be coming closer—he was almost certain that he could hear the soft rumble of voices.

He found another button. Della was leading the way.

A minute later, he saw that Hamish was coming toward him once more. Help again!

"It's just that bastard, but he has three women there, one poor lass all but gone unless there is help in minutes. Come—come quickly. He's also talking about taking Della elsewhere—he is going to let the others go because he believes they'll die no matter what."

"I'm coming, I'm calling..."

He didn't hear Lachlan's phone ring; but when the man answered the phone, he thought that he could hear his voice through the many walls as well.

"We're going to need emergency personnel, ambulances, the second we can find the women. I think that Louisa is...near death. But according to Hamish, he's taking Della on somewhere else and I've got to get in there and find out where," Mason said.

"We're near, just tons of the dead between us," Lachlan said. "We've got our team at the exits—they'll get EMTs there as soon as they arrive. But...they are alive?"

Mason looked at Hamish. "They live now," he whispered.

Mason suddenly heard a huge rumbling and dust—and corpse remnants—went flying into the air.

"The structure down here is crumbling!" Lachlan said. "Edmund—"

"Here!"

Hamish beckoned Mason and he moved just as a

chunk of the ceiling came down. He nodded to Hamish and they ran along the path, turning again, and again.

Then they burst into a room.

Brianna was on the floor, but the area where a needle had been stuck into her was wrapped in a makeshift bandage. Her breathing was weak but steady. The other woman, Louisa, also had a bandage on her arm—Della's doing, he was certain. Mason was on the ground as Edmund broke through, looking at the two women and then at Mason.

"They're alive!" Mason assured him.

"Jeanne is heading here… I'll bring him to get Louisa to the top and to the EMTS, and Lachlan is behind me, rallying his men around a bunch of fallen rock. I'll get Brianna up there and… She's going to make it, right?" he asked anxiously.

Mason nodded. If these women had been left…

Why was Della still with Dante?

Because he had her gun, of course, and Della would play it out to the very end, determined that her chance would come.

And it would.

It had to.

Edmund lifted Brianna. She protested, eyes barely open as she tried to wave an arm around.

"Brianna, no, don't start bleeding again!" Edmund begged.

"She's trying to say something, trying to point out a way," Mason said.

And she was. Brianna was pointing toward the far wall. Mason hurried to it and discovered what they had the night before.

What looked like a solid wall wasn't. There was a narrow opening, so narrow that he could barely squeeze through...

But he did. And as he emerged into another pathway, one that offered ancient stairs that seemed to head up to one more level, he saw something else.

A button.

Della was still leading the way.

They were going to find Brianna and Louisa, Della believed, and she could only pray that it was going to be on time. And for the moment...

She had to watch. And she was doing so carefully.

Stephan Dante was having trouble with his hand. She'd seen it when she had so desperately tried to stop the blood from squirting out of the site where the pump had been sucking blood from Louisa's arm.

He had kept a grip on the Glock, though she had no idea what he had done with her Baby Browning.

Still...

She had cuffed herself as he had freed Brianna, laughing. He hadn't minded doing it because he believed that it was too late for either woman to live. He hadn't gotten to create one of his beautiful fairy-tale displays with either of them, but he thought that they would die.

Della had to believe that they would live. She winced, hearing more rumbling from the catacombs.

"Too many people," Dante said, amused. "The catacombs themselves might outdo me! Those idiots will all die, crushed to death—with the dead."

"We're not out of the catacombs," Della said. "You may find yourself crushed to death—with the dead."

"Where are your dead friends?" he asked dryly. "Seriously, you are far crazier than I am."

"I'm pretty sure my dead friends are showing everyone where to go."

"Into the afterlife—after the ceiling gets them! My dear Special Agent Della Hamilton! You've ruined my crypt for me, and another down in piles of bones and debris and shrouds…it's nothing."

"So where we're going now isn't a crypt?" she asked.

"Oh, it's part of the crypts. But you'll be the first of the dead. It's an old room where church leaders went when all the stuff with the Reformation was going on. You see, I use history to my benefit. I use friends, of course—"

"Friends that you threaten—like Angus?"

"Ah, well, your FBI has your profilers, or your behavioral science people or whatever you want to call them. But I am a true connoisseur of people! Some are gleeful at the thought of taking life, some can be talked into believing anything, and some… Well, it's good to know the ones with money—especially those locked away forever who would be happy their money was used in a crime—to get to the ones who see money as their main goal in life. I know who is who."

"No, you don't."

"Obviously, I do."

"You thought that because I was an agent, I would happily be your bride and kill with you."

"Now, see, there you go. You could have had all the power in the world. Because you are quite the beauty, you know, and I hear that you excelled in all your classes, especially on the shooting range. That you don't shoot when you should…well, your loss. Because you will die. You will be like all those dearly departed friends you saw tonight…crumbling away to nothing but dust and bits of bone. They will forget your name in a few years. And I will live forever," he said.

"You don't believe that."

"I will go down in history as the king of the vampires."

"You will go down in your own mind as the king of the vampires," she said wearily. "Where is this room we're going to?" she demanded.

"You're so anxious to die?"

"I like to know where I'm going."

"Right, tough girl. You're not going to be in charge, you're going to do what I tell you to do."

"Why would I, if you're just going to kill me anyway?" Della asked.

"I get what I'm after. That girl Louisa…she should have been mine. But I saw you people going into the pub and I figured it had to be trouble. You have been pains—well, on the one hand. Then a challenging game on the other, like a jigsaw puzzle. The thing is, I get what I want. And they keep cops watching them for a while—but I will get Angus and his pretty little sister. I kept her alive just to torture him. See? I rest my point. I could have gotten that man to stab himself in the eye if it meant saving her."

"Like Karen stabbed herself in the heart."

"She thought she was doing it for me! For immortal grace. Now, really, is that such a bad way to go? Here's what I'm doing with you—draining you. Slowly, so slowly. I'm going to watch you believe for the longest time that help will come for you. Then I'll watch that hope wither in your eyes. Then, well, I'll probably prick you or stick you with my scalpel because I really don't want you going out peacefully in any way. Oh! Didn't you love my presentation at the play? Now, that was truly a moment of the artist at his most amazing! A beauty, an audience and a prince waiting to deliver love's true kiss—but screaming in horror instead!"

Della didn't respond. They had gone up steps, and now they were going down them. Underground, it was dark; only his light showed the way now.

But she had cuffed herself. She'd done it in a way that made it appear she was truly cuffed. But she could slip her hands free when the opportunity came.

And it had to come, except...

She suddenly heard a soft whisper in her ear.

"He's close—they've taken the women. They are alive, dear lass, they are alive. Keep strength—keep courage!"

She smiled. The whisperer this time was Boyd Breck. A man who truly loved his native land, and hated any evil within it.

"If anyone knows, it's you!" she said softly.

"Indeed, in a way...I was a blessed man. I fought and lost many battles but, in the end, lived to see the crowning of my king. Now, dear, you will live to see this fellow vanquished."

She smiled. Her ghost was giving her a pep talk. But she imagined that upon a field of battle, the commanders for any army had given speeches, because belief and morale could do so much.

He took one last turn, and pushed a brick—and here,

a loud sound seemed to reverberate through the cata-combs. Here, there was a secret door, and pushing the stone caused it to slide on ancient mechanisms, provid-ing entry to the room beyond. She winced inwardly; she hadn't counted on Dante being able to close the two of them off so completely.

But Boyd, Hamish, Margaret…and maybe more were with them.

Boyd would find Mason.

Entering the room, Dante turned back, grabbing her by the arm to pull her in. He then pushed another stone.

The terrible groaning sound seemed to shake every-thing again. The wall slid back into place.

She could imagine the room during the days of re-ligious strife, so many who would lead the confused, the passionate…

The room had an altar. An old wooden stool was in front of it.

One of Dante's medical bags with needles and tools was by it.

"I've planned for this!" he told her.

"I don't see an exit. When you leave, they'll get you."

"No, they won't."

"Where's the exit?"

"I guess it doesn't matter if I tell you," he said. He pointed to the altar and stepped behind it to where a cross had been painted on the old brick there. The paint was faded and peeling, but Dante touched the right ex-tension and the place groaned and shook again, but the wall behind the altar slid away, showing steps that led…

Somewhere.

Out of the catacombs, perhaps into a close or wynd above.

"Now sit!"

He waved the gun at her.

"I really don't want to sit."

"I will shoot you in the knee," he promised. "In fact…"

"Maybe I'd like to sit," she murmured, walking across the room to the chair.

She had one chance. When he came to put the needle in her arm. And she had to be careful; his hand might be damaged but he was a big man—a strong man. She had to judge the way to throw her weight, how she might get the gun…

She sat.

She looked up at him, waiting.

He laughed, truly savoring every second of having her there. "Blood! Blood! Blood! It is so very delicious."

"Well, I do give it away all the time."

"You?" he queried.

"Something hereditary," she said. "It coagulates well."

"You gave it? You didn't sell it."

"My dad taught me that it would be wrong. Blood gives life. If we're blessed with it and it can save the life of another, you give it when it's needed."

"Oh, how noble! How sickeningly noble!" he said. "Well, then, I expect this special blood of yours will be especially delicious!"

He reached for the case at her side with his left hand; he was holding her Glock in the right.

As she had expected—and hoped—he had some

trouble maneuvering his hold on the Glock, given his determination to get the things he needed from his bag.

"You know what?" she asked him.

"What?"

"My dad is a really cool guy. You know what else he taught me?" she asked.

"I guess you're going to tell me!"

He had the bag open; he was still struggling to gather what he needed one-handed.

"He told me that life could be tough. That when we could, we helped others out. And he also told me that I should never expect to be helped out just because I was a girl. He taught me that sometimes, everyone just had to help themselves." She studied him as she spoke. He was such a detail-oriented person, but this time, he'd forgotten a very important detail.

He needed two hands to insert his needle, to start his pump. And she knew that it was then—or possibly never—and she jerked her hands free from the cuffs.

Startled, he fixed his grip on the Glock, but his hand shook with the effort and she threw her weight at him, causing him to fall...

Causing the Glock to slide across the floor.

He slammed her head with a blow that sent her mind reeling, but she was still on top of him, the gun was still a distance from either of them...

The secret door made its groaning sound. Dante's arms were longer and he had nearly reached the Glock when...

An explosion of gunfire filled the room.

She knew that Mason, who hated killing, had still longed to shoot Dante.

But he hadn't. He'd fired at the gun, causing it to leap away. But then…

A curious sound filled the room. A rumbling that was horrific as it grew and grew…

Mason was in the room, catching her hand, pulling her to her feet above Dante. She started to go for her gun, but he shrieked, *"No,"* pulling her back, swiftly dragging her toward the door.

He whisked her through it as the mechanism shuddered; the wall seemed to tremble and then the ceiling in the little room came crashing down in massive, heavy chunks…

Burying Stephan Dante beneath them.

Della was alive and well. Of course she was. She was an incredible fighter. But she was also frozen for a second, staring in stunned surprise. They were just outside the door—everything within it was covered with huge chunks of what had been the roof above. Bits and pieces of bones…of skulls…rested in the mix.

And something was still rumbling.

"This way! Back toward the graveyard, quickly!"

It was the ghost of Boyd Breck; Hamish and Margaret were just ahead, leading them along a narrow alley that suddenly began to move upward.

The rumbling continued.

Mason prayed Lachlan had gotten his men out. It sounded as if the entire structure was going, perhaps causing cave-ins elsewhere near the secret room and the catacombs.

"There, there, can ye boost the lass up, she'll cast a ladder down!" Boyd said.

Mason saw the opening. He seized Della by the waist, hoisting her up. She caught hold of the rim of an opening, hiked herself the rest of the way and disappeared briefly. She was quickly back, sending an old ladder down for Mason.

An old ladder...

He couldn't count on it long so he took the rungs as quickly as he could, thrusting himself toward the opening and catching the rim just before the ladder seemed to disintegrate into a thousand pieces.

He hiked himself up and rolled to discover that he was lying next to a jumble of bones clothed in a torn shroud that was disintegrating as badly as the ladder.

Boyd was there, apologizing. "Ah, ye made it, lad! Thank the good Lord above! I'd forgotten the weight of the living."

The light in the tomb they'd come up in was almost nonexistent—and yet some was creeping in through a small window at the back of the tomb.

He looked at Della. She, of course, had rolled across the corpse, too, to leave the tunnels and catacombs below. He had to smile.

She looked as if she had dressed for Halloween as a witch doctor.

He couldn't help it. He smiled, really smiled.

"You may need more than a shower," he told her. "Um..."

"You may need total detoxification!" she said. But he rose quickly, drawing her into his arms. And as the moments passed, he just held her.

He turned to Boyd then. "Thank you!" he said.

Boyd shook his head. "Thank you. Thank you, eternally. Thank you for allowing me to be a part of this, of ridding the land of monsters!"

Della smiled at him and glanced anxiously from Boyd to Mason. "He—he is gone, right? No one could have survived…"

Mason lifted her chin, meeting her eyes. "Della, he is gone. Now we need to find Lachlan and his officers and pray they made it out!"

He started to head for the door to the vault and prayed he could just slam it open, that this vault had a lock that had long ago rusted.

But Della cried, "Wait!"

He turned.

She pulled a bone fragment out of her hair and tried to straighten out the skeleton that had rested where the secret passage came through.

He walked over to help her.

She looked up at him. "Sorry, I just…"

"No, I understand. Good call. Now…"

He threw his weight against the old door to the vault. Maybe too much weight. He stumbled out into what remained of a beautiful day in Scotland.

The sun would set soon. But now, the sky was blue; the sun was beautiful, about to cast off its last rays before evening was upon them.

He glanced at Della, taking her hand. François was there, hurrying across the graveyard, dodging broken stones, to reach them. He nodded an acknowledgment to Boyd and told them, "Lachlan and every one of his men made it out safely. Louisa and Brianna have been rushed to the hospital, but both had pulses and…you're alive, too!"

François hugged them both effusively and then kissed them on both cheeks.

Mason smiled. He was a Frenchman! And a dear and valued friend and colleague.

"Paperwork?" Mason asked dully.

"Lachlan is seeing that people come to the house. I know you want to get to the hospital, but the doctors and nurses need a bit of time and I don't mean to be rude, but perhaps..."

"Showers and detox?" Mason asked him.

"Something like that," François said. He looked at Mason worriedly. "And Stephan Dante?"

"It will be a long time before they dig him out," Mason said.

"Did—did you shoot him?"

"I didn't have to. Maybe there is such a thing as divine intervention," Mason said quietly. "Anyway...let's get to the end of this thing."

"Right away," François said. He was on his phone, letting Lachlan know that he'd found the two of them and that Stephan Dante was beneath the rubble.

A police car quickly brought them back to Euro-house.

They were such a mess that a shower didn't seem like all that much fun so Della gathered her things and used Brianna's shower while Mason used theirs.

When they were done, an officer was waiting below.

François, Jon Wilhelm and Edmund were there by then as well, along with Jeanne, who had left the hospital last.

Brianna was doing very well; Lachlan was staying in the hopes that the transfusions she was receiving would allow her to come back to the house that night.

Louisa would be in the hospital a few days but her family and friends had been informed and she would make it.

The paperwork lasted a long time with each member of their team describing what had happened. Their words were all honest.

"At the last, I'm a bit confused," the interviewing officer said. "Neither of you shot the man?"

"When he was trying to get his needle out to get it in me, I took my chance, freed my hands and jumped at him, trying to wrest my Glock from him. I didn't get it—it went flying," Della told her.

"When I had a chance, I shot for the hand he was reaching for the gun with," Mason continued. He hesitated. "The place had been rumbling ever since I started walking through it. I admit, I was afraid that there was about to be a cave-in. And shooting in that situation was not the smartest thing in the world, but Dante is a strong man and—"

"Anything might have set that off after all these years," the officer said, writing away. "I believe that they will attempt to dig him out, but the engineers will have to come out and let everyone know that it's safe. But you know that he's dead."

"I know that he's dead. He wasn't a vampire and he wasn't superhuman. Hundreds of pounds fell on his body—he was crushed."

"And me, too, nearly—if you hadn't been so fast!" Della said.

"Oh, I know you. You would have moved in time," he told her.

The officer smiled, rose and was about to leave, but Lachlan arrived—with Brianna.

Brianna was obviously still weak. She was clinging to Lachlan's arm.

But when she saw Della, she released him and hurried across the room, taking her into a massive hug.

"Thank you, thank you, thank you!" she cried, pulling away to stare at Della. "Thank you, I can't believe that you…that you…"

Della laughed. "Brianna! You tricked us all and disappeared—to save Louisa. Thank you! You truly are a beautiful human being."

"Stupid, but a beautiful human being," Lachlan agreed.

The two of them spoke with the young woman taking all the statements. François, Jeanne, Jon Wilhelm and Edmund had already done so. They made tea and coffee.

They'd called for pizza—something people did even in Scotland, Lachlan assured Mason dryly.

The night went on, filled with commotion. Then just their group was in the house and they sat together in the parlor, all still a little disbelieving that they were all all right—and that it was over.

"Question," Lachlan said to Mason. "Would you have shot him?"

"If I had to. I don't like to kill—I do when it's necessary—"

Lachlan shook his head. "We're a country without a death penalty—for the very good reason that you can't go back and bring an innocent man to life if he's been executed. And still, I wonder about myself. I wondered today what it was going to be like if we confronted him…if I could just arrest him again, knowing he had killed when he escaped."

Mason leaned back, smiled and let out a long sigh.

"Honestly? I don't know. I don't know what would have happened…but now I don't have to worry or question my own decision. I'm going to leave it at divine intervention—and, of course, thank God that everyone got out all right! And now…"

"Oh, yeah, we never did sleep last night!" Lachlan said.

Laughing wearily, they all trailed up to bed.

In their room, Della turned into his arms, just holding him tight for the longest minute.

"We already took showers," she said with a sigh.

"Half the battle!" he teased.

He swept her up into his arms, holding her, kissing her…

And through the night, he cherished her.

Life was good.

Life *with* Della was amazing.

Epilogue

"In honor of our achievements, many of the city's police and government have asked for our presence at a ceilidh!" Lachlan told them.

"Party, right?" Della asked. "That's lovely."

She was at the breakfast table with Lachlan and Brianna. Mason was on the phone, catching Adam and Jackson up on everything that had happened. Della had headed downstairs, feeling a little restless now, and truly anxious to do some of the things she loved in the the city. They'd get a break, she knew. But they'd also be called home soon enough.

"A lovely party! Dancing, bagpipes, delicious food and drink—and no crazed maniac making our every movement torture. The presenting of the haggis…quite a deal at such an event, but you'll see!" Brianna said.

Lachlan looked at her, concerned. "You're sure you're all right, luv? They wanted you longer at the hospital."

"I'm best here with you, with friends. And as for Monsieur François Bisset, he is incredible. He cracked my codes as easily as if he were reciting the alphabet, he's a wonderful liaison, terrific with the press, with news conferences…we need him!" Brianna said.

"In truth," Mason said, entering the kitchen, "we need you. And Lachlan."

The two of them frowned, looking at them.

"You're going to receive official invitations—Adam has already spoken with your superiors. They don't want to lose you, but… You have time to think about it. You're officially being asked to join Blackbird."

Walking in behind, Edmund said, "We'll have covered much of the British Isles. We started with an Englishman, of course, but we'll have each other to torture over being Irish, Scottish or English, and maybe somewhere along the line, we'll find a good Welshman— or woman."

"We could use someone German or perhaps Swiss," Jeanne said, amused as he filed in behind Edmund.

"Nothing wrong with my friends from Denmark!" Jon Wilhelm added, joining them in the kitchen.

"This is—real?" Lachlan said, looking at them, amazed.

"Real, and no one is expecting you to answer right away. Blackbird is…a responsibility and a great deal of travel. But…I always have a feeling that Jackson and Adam always know exactly what they're doing, finding people. Even when happenstance is involved, they seem to have a knack," Mason said. He smiled at Della. "He chooses amazing people," he said quietly.

"He does!" she agreed.

"So no more discussion on this right now. There's a party tonight," Mason said.

"You already know?" Della asked him.

"I do. Lachlan told me about it last night while you lovely ladies—hmm, tough law enforcement chicks—were being checked out at the hospital."

"I don't like the 'chicks' part," Brianna said, wrinkling her nose and looking at Della. "And I wasn't very tough. But I would love to take classes and become capable of taking care of myself, at least in some situations!"

"Well," Della said, glancing at Mason, "if you become part of Blackbird, I believe that you might still have to go through classes here, there…or…anyway, they'll be offered!"

"That they will," Mason said.

Lachlan looked at Brianna, taking her hand. "It's a big decision. I'll not go without you."

"Take your time," Mason said quietly. "For now…"

François chose that moment to walk in and join them. "Day of touristry is set! We shall begin at the beginning. The castle, and then onward! To Camera Obscura and World of Illusions, and the two will probably take us until the evening and the soiree, and tomorrow, onward! St. Giles, Holyrood, palace, park and—"

"No graveyards!" Della said.

"No graveyards," François promised.

They began the day. They didn't discuss their time in the catacombs, and they didn't discuss the ending of Dante's reign on earth—what mattered that day was that the world was safer, that they had all come through, and it was an awesome time in which they could just love the wonder and beauty that man could create.

Edinburgh Castle was incredible; Camera Obscura

and World of Illusions was fascinating and fun and, naturally, filled with children.

None of them minded acting like kids, too, zipping through the various attractions.

They headed home to prepare for the party, held on the Royal Mile, and while it was solemn as their team was thanked for all their help, it was also filled with music and dancing.

Pipers.

Dancers dancing to the pipers...

And everyone dancing to anything.

There was, of course, as Lachlan had warned, the presentation of the haggis.

As it went by, Della and Mason politely abstained, and Della was quite surprised when she saw that Lachlan abstained as well.

"But it's your country's dish!" Della reminded him.

"And I'll tell you what my father told me," Lachlan said. "I work for a living. I can actually afford a decent piece of meat, and I'll take one, thank you!" He grinned. "Hey, shepherd's pie, pizza, all kinds of ethnic or country meals—they are what was left for the people once they'd sold off the good stuff for survival. Anyway! Tonight, I'll not argue with good Scotch whiskey!"

They laughed, and then Della was surprised when the commissioner made an announcement, bringing Lachlan and Mason up before the others.

A bagpiper wearing his kilt came and took her hand, leading her up as another led Brianna up as well, by her side.

They were brought to stand next to Mason and Lachlan.

The pipes played.

Then, to Della's amazement, both men spun in moves that would have done a professional dancer proud and went down on their knees.

She didn't know what happened anywhere else at that moment. Because Mason produced a diamond from his pocket and said, "Will you marry me? Is this any better? I've never done this proposal thing before!"

She laughed, drawing him to his feet, and the room was filled with thunderous applause as the two couples kissed.

There had been yeses in both places, most obviously.

The night went on. And, as if it hadn't been enough fun, Lachlan and Brianna told them that yes, they would be happy being a part of Blackbird.

In their room for their last night in Edinburgh, Mason asked her, "Was that all right? I mean, some people would say that I should have found a romantic restaurant, had rosé champagne. That we should have been alone, that it shouldn't have been a double thing at an event…"

She laughed, pulling him to her. "Married or not, I will love you all my life. And I think it can go either way these days! Maybe I should have done something far more romantic and asked you!"

They had both laughed and he'd pulled her to him.

He had been the one to suggest a shower. Showers were fun.

They could be made to be incredibly romantic. And he would show her just how…

He did. And she decided that she could be equally romantic in turn.

Two weeks later, they were in Miami on vacation—

they'd been given a few weeks while Lachlan and Brianna made their move and settled into their new positions.

Della's parents had wanted a small family get-together. And that was good. Naturally, Mason was at his best and her parents were happy.

But there was something equally important to Della. She brought Mason to the cemetery where so much had begun for her, where she had once been attacked by a serial killer, and the ghost of a dear high school friend had taught her about her own strengths and abilities.

Jose Garcia, killed in a truly freak accident when they had been young, had been the first of the ghosts, or soul survivors, as some liked to call themselves, to appear for Della. They had been the best of friends. Jose had also encouraged her to use her talent—to use it for law enforcement.

Naturally, he and Mason also hit it off splendidly. And she didn't care that they might have looked like full-blown crazy people, sitting by a tree in a bench at the cemetery, talking and talking until the light faded, and it was time to go.

They spent time at the beach, time with family and, most of all, time together.

Because this kind of time was precious and they knew it.

And Blackbird was growing, destined to soar again.

* * * * *

New York Times *bestselling author Heather Graham
kicks off yet another thrilling case with a pit of bodies
in a cave beneath the Colorado Desert!*

Read on for a sneak peek at
Shadow of Death

A Stygian Darkness

And when he had opened the third seal,
I heard the third beast say,
Come and see.
And I beheld
And lo, a black horse,
And he that sat on him had a pair
Of balances in his hand.
And I heard a voice in the midst of the four beasts say,
A measure of wheat for a penny,
And three measures of barley for a penny;
And see thou hurt not the oil and the wine.

Prologue

Caves

Carey Allen paused, looked around, and breathed in deeply. She loved this area of Colorado just outside of the bustling city of Denver. The sky on a day like today was amazing. Blue just touched with delicate white puffs of clouds here and there. And the air! It was fresh, clean, delicious, and the scent of nature was wonderful.

Of course, she shouldn't have been where she was without permission and a guide, but she was an experienced hiker. She had climbed all manner of mountains, and she had received her diver's certificate at Lake Mead and gone on to cave dive! Hey, it was America. She was an adult, she knew what she was doing, and she had every right to be here.

She closed her eyes for a minute, listening to the sound of the nearby waterfall. Then she dove into the freshwater lake, shuddered slightly at the chill that seized her, then let it fall off. Surfacing, she looked back to the shore.

Don Blake was watching her with admiration, she hoped. She'd had a crush on the man for the longest time, and she'd enticed him out by telling him she knew the caves here and had explored them on her own before. He waved to her.

"Come on in! The water is great!" she told him.

"Freezing!" he countered.

"Wimp!"

He laughed. Don was anything but a wimp. He'd served two tours in the Middle East and was still in the reserve. Tall, not dark but redheaded, and very handsome. Working with him at Barrington Advertising, she'd fallen a bit in love the minute they had met—something, she hoped, she'd kept to herself. She had tried very hard to always be casual, fun, and flirty, not like a puppy with a wildly wagging tail.

But when they had talked about the caves, he'd shown a real interest in her.

"Wimp?" he returned and, as she knew he would, shed his hiking boots and socks, dropped his backpack and dove into the water.

Carey swam toward the waterfalls and the entry to the caves she knew she would find behind them. She hadn't slipped in here in months, but nature had created the phenomena of the falls and the caves over hundreds of thousands of years. They couldn't have changed much in a few months.

She crawled up the rocks that rose behind the falls and waited for Don. He arrived shortly, dripping as he joined her on the rocks. They'd both worn tank tops that would dry quickly, but the hiking pants would take longer. In the crisp air Carey had loved so much, it was cold.

"Follow me!" she said.

There was a winding path that led into a slew of caves, some deeper than others. And, of course, as they progressed, it grew darker within.

She stopped, turning to Don and smiling. "Well, I guess this is as far as we go—"

He was frowning. "What's that light?" he asked.

She turned. He was right. There was a strange glow coming from deeper within the earth.

"I don't know," she said. "Shall we?"

"Well, of course!"

They headed in the direction of the light. Nearing it, Carey suddenly felt the earth slipping beneath her feet. She'd hit an odd angle in the earth and it...

Led to nothing.

She fell and fell, landed hard, hurt everywhere, and wondered if she had broken bones.

She tried to move and cried out to Don. "Careful! There's a slope and...nothing."

He didn't answer her. The dim light they had seen was pale here, barely alleviating the darkness. She turned, trying to see if her limbs would work and to assess her position.

That's when she saw him. The dead man.

His face was skeletal. His eyes were open. No. He didn't have eyes. He just had eye sockets. But they seemed to be...

Staring. Staring into her eyes.

She screamed. She forgot her pain as she tried to

inch away. And as she did, she saw the dead man wasn't alone. There were other bodies there and all of them…

Down to bone. Not all were completely decomposed, just…

Down to nothing but *mostly* bone. Flesh remained on some limbs. Decaying fabric clung to other forms. Some of them had eyes that were still partially there and remained open, just catching the glint of pale light that seeped into the deep hole.

The scent of death rose around her, so she used her hands to push back. As she did so, she touched something small and hard, dark and plastic. She barely registered she had touched something as she started to scream and scream as she cried out for Don.

There was no answer. Her cries grew hoarse. She managed to drag herself to her feet to seek a way out…

There was nothing but dirt; no holds, nothing. No way out of the deep hole in the earth into which she had fallen.

She looked at the thing in her hand and then she looked around at the starved and rotting corpses around her. There were no children, she thought thankfully, not that she could see. She was losing her mind; she could die here, too. She didn't know what had happened to Don. He wasn't answering her, so he must have also fallen…

Into a pile of dead.

No, no, no, no, he had to be okay. He had to be out there…going for help, she thought. And then she looked at the thing in her hand at last.

She held…

A horse. A tiny little black plastic horse.

Confused, breathing in death, she felt terror sweeping into her like something liquid and icy cold.

And she started to scream again.

One

The sun was just rising. Amy Larson emerged from the water, dripping, feeling the rays of brilliant heat fall on her. The day was beautiful, perfect and warm. It was wonderful. There were few places on earth she loved as much as she loved the Florida Keys and Key West. In all honesty, the best beaches could be found on the state's west coast but to her, the Keys were a little bit of heaven. Key Largo was an escape from the massive metropolises of Miami-Dade and Broward Counties. And moving southward, the smaller islands were a taste of a purer time. Marathon offered the incredible Dolphin Research Center, and on down to Key West one could look out for the tiny Key deer. Then at the tail end, Key West itself is the island of rich history, bizarre stories, music, and water sports.

It had been good to come here. Hunter had needed to be here after taking a bullet; even with a vest on, he'd needed a bit of convalescence. Yet, while trying to shake off the last two cases they'd worked along with the salt water, memories still plagued them of the murders in the Everglades that had begun the bizarre Four Horsemen case and those that had followed when she'd received the little red plastic horse in the mail.

Because it wasn't over. Someone wanted to play God, and they were using the Four Horsemen of the Apocalypse and Revelations to do it.

She smiled and slid down on a towel next to Hunter Forrest. He turned to her and ran a finger along her cheek. "This is the life," he said softly. "I almost feel guilty. Days in the sun, diving this afternoon, nights with the sunset and the music. I could do this forever."

"No, you couldn't," she said, amused. "You became an FBI agent because you were a child stuck in a horrible cult, and an FBI agent saved you and your parents. You need to be out there. You saw how your mom and dad got suckered into it. They saw people needed help, and those with a lot of money liked to keep it and weren't always generous. Some people—some rich people—are great. But what your mom saw made her want a better way, and she thought she had found it. You saw evil could masquerade in many forms." Her smile faded slightly. "You grew up and became an FBI agent because you're determined to slay the evil that man does to his fellow man."

"Sure. Right. Well, you know, second choice. Wrong era to be a knight in shining armor. And you've met my folks. They just wanted the best, and they were young and naive and looking for a better way. Anyway, we are what we are. But Clint Bullard is playing tonight. We'll have some dinner, listen to him sing and play... maybe one of us will join him on a country music hit.

We won't stay too late, because we have a great room with those windows that open to the sunrise."

"Sounds good, especially since we only have a few days left before vacation and leave time are up," Amy said. She sat up pensively. It had been weeks since the showdown that had left Hunter injured, and his bones had healed. And while they worked for two separate agencies—he was FBI and she was Florida Department of Law Enforcement—she was now on loan to the FBI because of the Four Horsemen case. And although they'd taken down some of the players in the deadly enterprise afoot, they knew another shoe would drop.

Someone out there wanted the Apocalypse. Or they were in it for power or money or both and made use of the easily beguiled they could use in their quest. People who believed they would be the chosen when the world came to an end. And if murder was asked of someone, it was simply a means to an end.

"What are you thinking?" Hunter asked, studying her face.

She loved Hunter. Everything about him. Tall, dark, blue-eyed and fit not just because of his chosen vocation, but because he loved doing things. He loved the water, boats, and watching college and pro football games, along with basketball, baseball, and hockey. If he didn't know about something, that was okay, he was eager to find out.

And he cared about people.

"I can't help it. I mean, I have relaxed, I swear. But I was thinking of my old partner John Schultz and the first cases. I will miss him, but he will enjoy his retirement. I think back to the first case with the white horse, and finding the woman crucified in the Everglades. I think about putting away a bad guy, and then receiving the little red horse when we were vacationing before. And I think about the crazy lady we put away after that, and how she's still convinced she's a warrior and the lives she took don't matter because she'll be lifted up at the end. And I think—"

"Hold on," Hunter said quietly. He had reached for his phone; she hadn't heard it ring. He'd kept it on vibrate.

She watched his expression change as he listened. "All right. What time did you say? Thanks. Yep, we can do it."

When he hung up, she knew.

"The black horse?" she asked.

He nodded, still studying her face.

"We have a plane to catch," he said.

"Okay," she said slowly. "First out of Key West. And then where?"

"Denver. Via Miami. There has been a rash of disappearances, apparently."

"But why would that indicate anything to do with the Horsemen cases?"

"A little black plastic horse. This time, it was received by a colleague of mine, a guy I worked with years ago. Andy Mason, Assistant Field Director out there. He has no idea where it came from. It wasn't mailed to him—it was on his doorstep when he went home last night. The entire agency has been briefed on what did happen with the previous Horsemen cases and to be aware we've been warned it isn't over. Andy talked to the brass, and we're to join him and see if the horse and the missing people do align. Andy is a good guy and a good agent. He didn't miss the little horse, and he's the one with the theory the missing people may have something to do with the horse."

"No luck on getting our crazy incarcerated 'red horse' to talk, right?" Amy asked.

"She has an attorney who has advised her to keep her mouth shut. Poor attorney. Our 'red horse' is so proud of herself for being in her position, she doesn't seem to appreciate the fact she shouldn't be saying she orchestrated life and death. I think she really is a true believer."

"She wanted to go into politics. That's what I can't wrap my head around," Amy said lightly.

"And God help us all. She had it together until the end. Imagine if she had started in office in state government and moved on to *national* prominence."

"Terrifying. Anyway—"

"Hey, vacation was ending. And they have a nice place for us in a hotel on the outskirts of Denver. I mean, it won't be hot, and our days won't be filled with diving and our nights with music and heat—"

"Hey!" Amy teased. "Mr. G-man, it will be hot wherever you are."

"Thanks—I'll take it," Hunter said. "So our plane out of here is in just three hours—"

He paused, stopping to look at his phone before answering it again. He sat silent for a moment before saying, "Um, sure, thanks."

He hung up, grinning.

"Never mind. Our plane is in two hours, direct to Denver."

"And we're going to get to the airport and through security and—"

"Private plane," he told her. "The brass is sending us off right. We won't even have to worry about lunch."

"Cool. Okay, so…"

They still had to hurry. They had to forgo the tour of Fort Zachary Taylor they had planned for later. They had to make good time—it was a six-hour flight at best. With the time change, they'd get a few hours back, but now that they were going…

Amy wanted to move.

Within two hours, they were in the air. It was one nice plane—Amy had to thank the powers that be who had provided for them.

Amy looked out the window. She really did love Key West.

Hunter was at her side. "I know. I'm sorry. Watching sun and sea and a bit of nirvana disappear into a tiny speck."

She turned to him. "I was thinking it was darned nice to be partnered with an FBI agent who draws this kind of attention from the bigwigs."

He smiled. "Depends on the case."

"Hunter, will this end?" she murmured. "There could be copycats out there. There were so many people involved, people who lost loved ones. This horse left on your Agent Mason's doorstep…maybe it's someone playing games. This is big and it could be endless—"

"Well, yes, I figure the Apocalypse can be big," he said, and she loved the way he spoke, half teasing, half respecting her words. "It will not be endless. And there will not be an apocalypse. Because these people aren't believers—not in any true religion."

He was right. "But what is the endgame?" she murmured.

"Now, on that," he said, "as of now, well. Hmm. I don't know. But Denver is great."

"Yeah, it's a great city," she agreed.

And it was nice traveling on the private jet. But as they flew, she found herself bringing up the Book of Revelations and going through its various stanzas.

"'And he that sat on him held a pair of balances in his hand,'" she quoted aloud.

"'And I heard a voice in the midst of the four beasts say, A measure of wheat for a penny, and three measures of barley for a penny; and see thee hurt not the oil and the wine,'" Hunter finished.

"And from what I'm reading, biblical scholars say it refers to hunger, to famine, and to disease," Amy said.

"Well, we didn't need a criminal mastermind for the disease part," Hunter said. "But it's also true there are many diseases that have been controlled—but can still be cast out on the public with purpose. But you'd need access to a lab and… Hunger. Famine. And 'hurt not the oil and the wine'—from what I've read that refers to the wealthy. I don't know what we're dealing with here or even if the missing persons cases are part of this, but we'll land on the answers soon."

Amy nodded and looked out the window. She was taken by the scenery beneath her. They'd left behind the eternal blues and greens of the Everglades, the ocean, the flat land, and now traveled over miles of dusty colors, land that rolled and curved, and crossed hills and mountains in all kinds of colors. She smiled, loving the beauty of the country. She had always known she would be with the Florida Department of Law Enforcement, but she realized she loved the diversity of the ground itself, the expanse that was the country; she felt a passionate swell of determination.

They would find the black horse.

The captain's voice came over the speaker warning them to buckle in.

They did so. Amy watched as they came down to earth in the city of Denver.

Andy Mason was at the airport to meet them, sweeping up one of their bags, smiling and nodding as Hunter introduced Amy to him. He was a big man, maybe in his late forties, dark-haired, but with one streak of solid white heading back from his forehead as if the coloring was that of a backward skunk.

"Of course, we've all been on alert across the country. But I didn't come across a body—and God knows with some of the media that's gone out, some kid who knows what I do for a living might have thought it was funny to leave a plastic horse on my porch. But we've gotten calls lately from police stations between here and Boulder. People have been disappearing at an alarming rate. Now, those disappearing are adults, and adults are legally allowed to disappear if they choose. But from the people I have managed to get to interview, their loved ones don't sound like the kind to disappear. And just yesterday, we got a new one. So, if you're good with it, we'll leave your baggage in the trunk and I'll take you to speak with a woman who is insistent something had to have happened to her friend. I've checked you into the hotel already," he added, handing Hunter an envelope with hotel key cards.

"Thanks. And fine with us," Amy assured him.

"Amy likes to hit the ground running," Hunter told him and grinned at her as they both climbed into Andy's SUV.

She tried to smile in return. But while she'd honestly relaxed and enjoyed the time they'd had together just playing in Key West, the knowledge that nothing had really ended kept haunting her.

"The woman I interviewed about her report is Hayden Harper. She's midforties, and an advertising exec at the Barrington agency," Andy Mason told them as he drove. "She reported her friend Carey Allen missing when she didn't show up for a lunch they had planned. She was told, of course, that someone wasn't considered missing just because they didn't show up for lunch. Hayden was persistent. When Carey didn't show up for work the next day, she hounded the police again. And with all that has gone on, the police informed us. I came out to see her, and she sounds legit and may give us real help. She doesn't live far from Red Rocks. Amy, have you ever been to a performance of any kind at Red Rocks?"

"I have not," Amy told him.

"An incredible place. A natural amphitheater. But there is so much incredible here. We're going to have to show her around the place, huh, Hunter?"

"I spent some time here four years ago, I think," Hunter said. "Yes, Andy, Colorado is amazing. The natural wonders are phenomenal."

"I mean, you're from Florida," Andy said.

"Hey!" Amy protested.

"I mean, it's just flat, right?" Andy said.

She laughed. "We have a few hills in the Ocala region. We also have the only continental reef in the country, alligators *and* crocodiles—"

"I'd head straight down for that," Andy teased.

"Freshwater springs, diving in sea and in freshwater, the Everglades—"

"Great place to hide bodies, I understand," Andy said.

"Where there's a will, there's a way," Hunter said. "I've seen bodies hidden in just about every possible geographical location. Yes, Florida is a great state. Colorado is a great state—"

"She just has to see some of our beauty," Andy insisted.

"I'm sure I will," Amy said.

Andy was pulling into a driveway. The house they were visiting was two-story, built to resemble an old colonial. The yard was well maintained, and she knew it didn't matter what state they were in, the owner was making an upper-middle-class income.

"She's nice—you're going to like her," Andy said.

"Great," Amy murmured.

Hayden Harper *was* nice—and anxious. She opened her front door before they reached it and quickly asked them in. They had barely stepped across the threshold and already she was eagerly asking if they'd be more comfortable in the dining room or the parlor. Andy told her they were happy wherever. She wanted to get them coffee, tea, or—though she wasn't sure if it was allowed—something stronger.

"Ms. Harper, we're fine, thank you so much," Amy told her. She wished she could alleviate some of the woman's anxiety, but she knew it could be terrifying to wonder what had happened to friends or loved ones. She thought the woman was usually composed and at ease. She was closer to fifty than forty, an attractive woman some might call "completely together" with her casual but perfect linen pantsuit, impeccable makeup, and beautifully coifed silver hair. "Please," Amy added, "if you'd like something, feel free. We're here to listen to you."

The woman nodded, then led them into her dining room and indicated the chairs. "I'm fine. Maybe I'll get coffee. Maybe I've had too much coffee."

Maybe she had, but Amy said gently, "You need to do what works for you right now."

The woman smiled. Maybe she had grasped for some of her executive training because she managed to calm down.

"I'm fine. Too much coffee. So. I'll tell you about Carey. She's one of the finest little artists I've ever met. She can do sketches at a meeting with a client that blow your mind. We became friends soon after she joined the agency. She's a health nut. A vegan. And she runs and hikes and you name it. The kid is in perfect shape. And that's what I've been trying to tell the cops. She was going hiking. She told me she was super excited. She had enticed a boy she'd had her eye on to come with her on an adventure. Here's the thing. We have caves and waterfalls you're only supposed to visit with licensed guides. And I'm pretty sure Carey intended to go *adventuring* where she shouldn't go," Hayden said. "I talked to her on Saturday just before she started out. She was supposed to meet me for lunch on Sunday. She didn't show, and I couldn't make the cops understand Carey didn't do things like that. If she couldn't make something, she'd call you. She's that kind of courteous. Then her phone started going straight to voice mail. It's Tuesday now, and I know something has happened, and something worse could happen if she isn't found soon!"

Hayden was passionate.

"Do you know who she was meeting? Or taking on her adventure?" Hunter asked.

Hayden shook her head. "She wouldn't tell me because she didn't want to jinx it."

"Is anyone else from your office missing?" Amy asked.

Hayden frowned. "Um, I don't think so. But that's hard to say because our account execs have to travel out of town to see their clients, so... I don't think so. But I don't know who is supposed to be here now and who isn't. Of course, I can do a roundup of our secretaries and get some schedules, if you think that will help." She frowned. "What makes you think the man she's interested in works at the agency, too?"

"We meet people at work," Andy said, glancing dryly at Amy and Hunter. "Sometimes, especially at the executive level, we spend all our time at work and, well, there you go."

Hayden nodded. "I will find out. But time is—"

"Where do you think she went?" Amy asked. "And we will start looking while you start trying to get us more information."

"You got a map?" Hayden asked.

"We all have phones with great GPS," Amy assured her.

"Of course." She looked at Amy skeptically for a minute.

"Special Agent Mason said you were in from Florida."

"That's right. I'm the one from Florida, though," Amy said. "Hunter has worked all over," she added, hoping to assure the woman.

"And I'm here," Andy said. "Colorado born and bred."

"Of course. Okay, here," Hayden said. "This area has the most gorgeous caves and waterfalls, not far from the Arkansas River. Worst comes to worst, you'll see some spectacular scenery. But the area can be dangerous, too. There are areas people see with a guide from one of the companies, and areas the ranger service controls. But Carey has done just about every hike and walk—and swim—possible in the state. And if she were going to impress someone, I think she mentioned this little bit of land right here. The rangers' office police part of it, and part of it is policed by the county."

"We'll get hiking," Amy said, rising.

"You'll have a couple of hours of daylight left at best!" Hayden whined.

"We'll use those hours," Hunter said. "Andy, can you get us a ranger?"

"Of course," Andy said. He looked as if he were about to grin at Amy and realized Hayden Harper was far too anxious for any kind of levity. "This isn't flat land, you know. You up to it okay, Amy?"

"I think I'll be okay," she told him. "Thankfully, our things are still in the trunk."

"And you can change here and move quickly!" Hayden said.

"We can do that," Amy said.

They did, and fast. In minutes, they were both ready in khakis and hiking boots. They headed out with Andy, who was—more or less—the same size as Hunter and had borrowed clothing from him so they could all drive out. He'd also talked to the park services, and they were set to meet with Ranger Sam Harrison at the site.

"Well," Andy said as they drove out, "I did want you to get to see the scenery."

"And it's beautiful," Amy assured him.

It was.

As they left the suburbs behind, the earth became dramatic with rises and falls, colors and spectacular flowers that grew despite the crisp, dry air. Then before her, Amy saw the rise of cliffs with areas where water cascaded down, catching what remained of the sunlight.

"Beautiful," Amy whispered. "Outstanding."

"I told you," Andy said.

There was a park service car before them, and a ranger leaned against the driver's seat already waiting for them.

"How do you do? Ranger Sam Harrison," he called to them. He looked to be in his midthirties, wore his hat high on his head, and sported a mustache and neatly trimmed beard. They introduced themselves in return and listened as he told them, "We do have wildlife talks out here—and on occasion, we bring people by boat under the falls and into the caves. I was behind the falls just yesterday, though, and didn't see a thing."

"Were you in the caves?"

"No, just in the boats." He grimaced. "We use some stolen jokes. Disney's *Jungle Cruise*. We show people the backside of water."

"Okay, I'm sure people love the tours. But how do you reach the caves?" Hunter asked him.

"Oh, we use the same small boats," Harrison said. "It's just a different tour. If you want to get over there and into the caves, I'll get some boats for tomorrow. The only other way is to swim—"

Amy glanced at Hunter and he nodded, knowing she meant to get there now. She was already removing her sweatshirt, determined she'd best keep her boots, even if heavy in water, for whatever flooring they might find in the caves. Her Glock was waterproof, though she was sorry to wet the nice new belt and holster she'd just purchased. But they would dry.

"Oh, she's going to swim," Harrison said, his face twisting with surprise and confusion.

"Time may be everything. We'll get there now," Hunter told him.

Amy smiled, then turned back to see him already doffing his sweatshirt, too, and heading toward the crystal water. It really was spectacular, the falls appearing to create bursts of crystal in the air as the water poured from them.

Cold water! Very, very cold water!

Maybe that was good. Amy moved quickly. Hunter reached the rocks behind the falls as she did, hopped up and reached for her hand. She took his and murmured, "We aren't going to have much light, but I do have my little penlight."

"And I've got mine. These lights are small but powerful. We're going to be okay. And tomorrow, if we need to keep searching, we *can* take boats."

"Hah, hah," Amy laughed dryly. "Sorry. I believed that—"

"We needed to move. Me, too. That was—refreshing."

"You mean freezing."

"I do," Hunter said. "But be careful. Caves here can lead to more caves."

"Okay, so… Hunter, she had to have come here. From everything we heard and learned, she's the super sports girl who would do something like this."

They were following an opening that led to the cave on the right. Then it split. Hunter indicated he'd take the left.

Amy kept going.

Beneath her feet, she felt as if the ground changed. It had been rocky and solid. Now slippery dirt seemed to be covering it, and the ground itself seemed to be headed on a downward slope. She moved more slowly, then—only wincing slightly at the concept of the mud— she went down like a snake to slither forward.

And she was glad. The earth would have given way beneath her feet.

Amy threw the slim but powerful light she held down into the hole.

She'd seen so much.

And still…

She'd seldom seen a sight quite so horrible.

"Hunter!" she called. "Hunter, careful, it's slick, it's almost a trap—maybe it is a trap. Come, quickly, please!"

As she called him, she realized she'd inched closer to see better; the slick mud was taking her down. She didn't fall. She just slid down to lie next to a body.

Her gag reflex went into motion, and she couldn't believe she hadn't been warned earlier by the smell of death. Running her light over the muddy hole in the middle of the cave, she could see bodies were in different stages of decomposition.

Some of the dead lay with their eyes, or what remained of them, open in horror.

Some no longer had eyes. Cavernous sockets seemed to stare out at her.

Hunter was there, somewhere near her. "Hey!" she called. "We need a team, Hunter. I can't even count. I don't know how many people are here."

"Lord!" he exclaimed, and she could see he remained by the ledge, looking down at her. "Calling for help. I'll be right with you," he told her.

She was trying desperately not to breathe through her nose. She almost dropped her light; when she did so, she saw there was a woman near her. She didn't appear to be decomposed. Amy reached over to touch her.

She was cold. For a moment, Amy thought there was no hope since the woman's limbs were so cold.

Still, she sought a pulse at the woman's throat.

And it was…there. Faint, but there.

"Hunter! We have a living person!" she shouted. "I think it's Carey Allen!"

He was back with her in seconds, sliding down the strange embankment, rolling next to her, then making it to his feet and drawing her up to hers.

"She doesn't appear to be injured, just…"

"Finding herself here, it's amazing she didn't have a heart attack," Hunter said, looking around.

"This is…really crazy. How are all these people here? They don't appear to have been shot or stabbed, though it's hard to tell," Amy murmured. "The black horse," she added thoughtfully.

"Trapped—and starved. Hunger and famine," Hunter said.

"Starved. Oh, my God, you mean they were purposely trapped here and left to starve to death?"

He nodded. "You can tell," he said quietly.

"Okay…"

"Amy, look at that man. Look at his leg."

She did. Again, she fought her gag reflexes. The man's pant leg was frayed and mostly gone. So was his flesh.

He'd been gnawed.

"Rats," she murmured hopefully, looking at Hunter. "It's a cave, and if not rats, Colorado is known for its wildlife. Creatures chewing on these poor people."

"Desperation in human beings—not creatures," Hunter said quietly. "Down here, if a park ranger wasn't right above, you could scream forever—and no one would hear you to help."

"Then, you think…"

"Yeah, cannibalism. I believe we'll discover the creatures chewing on them were human. Human beings starving to death, losing their minds, and becoming both insane and desperate."

He hunkered down by Amy where she had knelt by

the living woman, the young woman she believed to be Carey Allen. He frowned and reached for her hand to uncurl her fingers.

And produced a child's little toy.

"The black horse didn't just arrive—he's been here!"

Don't miss
Shadow of Death
from New York Times *bestselling author*
Heather Graham,
available wherever
MIRA books are sold!